A SENSE OF THINGS BEYOND

RENÉE BELLIVEAU

Vagrant PRESS

For Keegan

Vagrant Press is an imprint of
Nimbus Publishing Limited
3660 Strawberry Hill Street, Halifax, NS, B3K 5A9
(902) 455-4286 nimbus.ca

Nimbus Publishing is based in Kjipuktuk, Mi'kma'ki, the traditional territory of the Mi'kmaq People.

Printed and bound in Canada
NB1765

Editor: Stephanie Domet
Editor for the press: Whitney Moran
Cover & Interior Design: Bee Stanton
Cover artwork: *On the North Sea* by Olga Wisinger-Florian (1844–1926)

Library and Archives Canada Cataloguing in Publication
Title: A sense of things beyond : a novel / Renée Belliveau.
Names: Belliveau, Renée, 1995- author
Identifiers: Canadiana (print) 20250246732 | Canadiana (ebook) 20250246740 | ISBN 9781774714522 (softcover) | ISBN 9781774714539 (EPUB)
Subjects: LCGFT: Novels. | LCGFT: Historical fiction.
Classification: LCC PS8603.E4687 S46 2025 | DDC C813/.6—dc23

Canada Council for the Arts Conseil des arts du Canada

Nimbus Publishing acknowledges the financial support for its publishing activities from the Government of Canada, the Canada Council for the Arts, and from the Province of Nova Scotia. We are pleased to work in partnership with the Province of Nova Scotia to develop and promote our creative industries for the benefit of all Nova Scotians.

CHAPTER 1

The world is just beginning to stir as Rose sets off home, the air still cool against her cheeks. It has rained all night, the sun now breaking through the grey mist that obscures the tops of buildings on Bay Street, the wet streets dampening the hem of her skirt. A cab pulled by a glistening black horse slows as it nears but Rose shakes her head, half lifting the umbrella clutched in her hand, and the carriage speeds off down the quiet street.

It is early. Earlier than she would have normally returned home, but her patient passed at the veil of first light and Rose decided to give the family some time alone before the doctor returned to fetch the body. She had spent most of the night checking vitals and brewing tea, trying to make them all as comfortable as possible with the inevitability of death, and although she is bone tired, there is solace in a quiet passing of an elderly man surrounded by his family. A tender testament to a life well lived, a serene surrender to the natural rhythm of time. Still, she had been at Mr. Humphrey's side for close to five months, and even natural death came with a grief she knew would thread the fabric of her life for weeks to come.

Sometimes she wished she could stay past this point, to assist the family with the next stage of life. To nurse hearts as well as bodies. To hold Mrs. Humphrey's hand when she should unexpectedly weep after finding a button waiting with a needle and thread next to a shirt her husband would no longer need, or to sift flour while his daughter and granddaughter prepared the ingredients for a tart on the day that would have marked his seventy-sixth birthday. But

Father Thomas had already strongly implied that hers was a duty to the body, not the soul. She was only to care for the living as they approached death, not stay beyond it.

She turns onto College Street and follows the veering path towards Queen's Park. Here is her refuge. The route she must take to shed the weight of the hours she has spent as Nurse Avery and find herself again as Rose. It is the path she takes on those days when the hours feel heaviest, and knowing she will have to tell Anna and her father that Mr. Humphrey has passed, she lingers under the canopy of linden trees, taking in the crisp smell of a wet summer morning. The trees have shed their seeds in the rain, and she is watching birds pecking at the ground when she sees a foot—a scuffed black leather boot with a gaping sole and a hole forming over the toes. Carefully, she moves around the tree to find a man lying on the ground, shivering in sleep. She instinctively bends to reach him, her hand outstretched, and he wakes, startled.

"Are you all right, sir?" she asks, pulling her hand back.

His eyes are wild and it takes him a moment to register her presence. Rose's gaze lingers over his soldier's uniform. Only the jacket—drenched, tattered, and stained, but recognizable even in the worst conditions. She feels the urge to turn away but remains. "Are you all right?" she repeats.

He finally nods, keeping his eyes averted as he struggles to sit up. She offers her hand to help, but he does not acknowledge it.

She has seen veterans here before. Men hiding in the shadows of trees or lying out in the open on the wooden benches by the path. They never stayed long. The police officers walking through the park made sure of that. Even when these men wanted to be seen, wanted to be acknowledged, visitors to the park would only turn away and pull their children closer, unwilling to listen to their stories.

Rose remembers attending Peace Day celebrations in this same park only three years ago, in 1919. She had somehow convinced her sister Anna to leave the house, a significant feat in those early days of grief when even sunshine coming through the windows of the living room seemed an affront to their endless well of sorrow. But Anna had agreed to come, dressed in black despite the sweltering heat, and they had joined the thousands of people gathered to celebrate the end of the war. Other parts of the country had organized parades, sporting competitions, speeches, and fireworks, but the crowd in Queen's Park had assembled only to sing peaceful hymns and patriotic songs. Even then, the tone of these events had felt unsuitable to Rose, but seeing Anna quietly move her lips to the songs, wiping silent tears, she could only feel relief. Relief at being home, relief at finally being able to put the war behind her and move on. Relief at the coming of a new dawn. Until the following morning, when she had read in the newspaper that elsewhere in the city, a mob had thrown bricks at a Jewish peddler on the street, setting his wares ablaze, while rioters had vandalized streetcars and restaurants, including one owned by a Chinese family—aliens, they said, who had been warned to close for the holiday, lest they profit from the deaths of thousands. The restaurant had been closed. The owner had simply forgotten to turn off the lights. But that mattered little to the angry crowd. Was it really peace they were celebrating? Rose wondered. Or had peace itself been drawn along the same bitter lines as war? It certainly made no allowances for those whose experiences disrupted the narrative of victory. Even those veterans who had been welcomed back with booming cheers and waving flags were swiftly cast aside when they failed to meet the public's expectations of a hero, and the ones who returned haunted lost even the right to their pension.

Rose dips a hand into her pocket and pulls out two coins.

"Here," she says. Mrs. Humphrey had been too bereaved to pay her the rest of her wages that morning, and Rose had no immediate need for it. But now she wishes she had more to give.

The man finally looks up, eyes hazy, and she can tell he has been drinking. After a moment, he accepts the coins with a nod.

Rose glances at the branches above, the leaves still shedding droplets of water. It offers a comfortable awning, but she knows he will be pushed out of here when the policemen begin their morning rounds. She picks up the umbrella she placed on the ground. "Please take this as well." She would have rather given him a blanket, or a hot meal, but the umbrella might at least shield him from the rain and the sun that would beat down in a few hours.

The man's eyes lift again but do not meet hers. "Thank you," he says softly.

She rises to her feet. "Take care," she says before returning to the path.

Once home, Rose slips off her shoes and begins to unpin her hat. "Hello?" she calls into the hallway. Her voice is swallowed by silence, and she feels a quiet relief.

The house is cool, the curtains drawn. Rose steps inside the sitting room to let in some light and finds a piece of paper propped up by its fold on the table by the window, her name inscribed on it. *Gone to the fish market* in Anna's familiar scrawl. She would not be long, then. Rose moves to toss the note into the dormant fireplace, averting her gaze from the frames lining the mantelpiece. It is easier not to look. Not to let the flood of memories sneak up on her. But as she brushes past, something catches her eye—a new photograph, larger than the rest, of Leo standing proudly in his military uniform, badges gleaming. She steps closer, her breath caught in her throat. She has seen this one before. Leo had mailed her a postcard copy once, all the way to France. She had gotten it framed at a small studio near the hospital and kept it by her bedside next to the oil lamp that was her only source of light in that canvas tent she called home, Leo's smiling face often bathed in flickering shadows.

There had been no photographs left on the walls when she returned home after the war. The ones that had hung in the upstairs hallway showing all their stern and happy faces at various stages of life were gone, put away, chains hanging limply from the brass picture rail, dark squares and circles on the wallpaper where the frames had once hung. Only in the last year had Anna started filling those gaps again, pulling the photographs from storage and framing more, building a sort of altar for her son above the fireplace where she liked to sit and read. But all those photographs had been from a time before the war.

Rose picks up the frame, resisting the urge to turn it to face the wall. His uniform looks crisp and clean, nothing like the dusty, rumpled khaki Rose had last seen him wearing on the platform in Boulogne. She remembers the pride she had felt upon first receiving the postcard, tinged with worry at knowing better than he did the reality that lay ahead, and how ill-prepared he was—how ill-prepared they all were, those bright young men, facing the war with a vigour that would extinguish almost as soon as they saw the muddy fields of Europe. With her thumb, she caresses the short blond curls peeking out from beneath his cap. She can hear his voice in the back of her head, that easy laugh that used to fill up a room.

"Doesn't he look handsome?"

Rose turns to find Anna standing in the doorway, dressed in a silk pleated black blouse and skirt, a single white rose wilting from the side of her broad-brimmed hat. Her cheeks are flushed, wisps of dark, greying hair curling around her face. She is smiling in that way she has learned to smile in recent years, her joy not quite reaching her eyes.

"You startled me," Rose says, the frame suddenly much too heavy in her hands. "I didn't hear you come in."

Anna sets the woven basket down at her feet, a faint briny smell escaping from its cloth covering. "That was the last time I saw him, you know," she says. "The morning before he went overseas. I accompanied him to the photography studio." She steps forward, gently taking the photograph from Rose's hands and replacing it on the mantelpiece. "This is where I kept it. I was so glad to have it during those long years he was away. Those years when I heard little from him." She turns to Rose. "Little from either of you," she adds, her tone light, but Rose still feels a stab of guilt.

"We were busy," she says quietly.

Anna sighs. "I know. So was I, I suppose."

Rose also had her portrait taken before she left, in those whirlwind weeks she had spent in Montreal. As soon as she received her cornflower blue uniform, she had darted to the photography studio on rue Sainte-Catherine, the starched veil still foreign on her head while later she wouldn't feel it at all. She had tried to look serene as the bulb flashed, but she imagined her face must have reflected some of the excitement she felt at the time. Scheduled to depart for England the following day, Rose had given the man her address in Toronto, hoping the photo might entice Anna to finally respond to her letters. It occurs to her now that she has never seen the portrait, but she is not certain she wants to.

Rose has learned to avoid these moments, to steer around the conversations Anna tries to pull from her, but for once she makes an effort. "It must have been a comfort to see him looking so proud," she says. For he did look proud: shoulders squared, head tall. A boy pretending to be a man. Rose can at least find solace in the fact that this is the last image Anna has of her son, and not the one Rose herself carries in her mind.

"Yes," Anna says in that same tone of voice she uses whenever Leo comes up in conversation: a quiet admiration drowning in a sea of grief. Then she gives a weak smile, her eyes searching Rose's face. "You seem tired. Long night?"

Rose instinctively runs a hand through her hair, pushing wayward strands behind her ear. "Yes. I cabled to say I wouldn't be home. Did you receive it?"

"I did. How is Mr. Humphrey?"

"He passed this morning."

"Oh," Anna says. "Poor Mrs. Humphrey."

"Yes. She seemed quite calm, until the end."

"How old are her daughters?"

"I'm not sure. They have children of their own now."

"The house will be so quiet."

Rose knows the same weighs on Anna—silence in a house once so crowded and overflowing with chatter. She shifts the conversation. "Is Father home?"

"I don't think he came home last night either," Anna says.

This was not unusual for their father, who often stayed at the hospital for days at a time. During the war, he had closed his practice to assist with the labour shortage at the hospital as more and more men took their leave, and had since started teaching at the university to make up for the fact that most of them had never come back. "We need more men," he often complained, as though they could somehow materialize out of thin air.

"He might have had an early surgery this morning," Rose says. She looks at her watch and yawns. "I'm famished," she adds, thinking back to the meagre slice of bread she had inhaled at some point in the middle of the night.

"There's some porridge on the stove. I could heat it up for you."

"No need," Rose says, already turning towards the door. "I'll go." She can still feel the weight of Leo's gaze from the mantel.

Anna follows her into the kitchen a moment later. She removes the fish from the basket to place in the icebox. "What will you do now?"

"Now?"

"Now that the Humphreys no longer need you."

Rose stirs the porridge, buying herself time. "I'm not sure."

"You could always come to work with me. We're always looking for nurses."

For a year now, Anna had been volunteering at the Christie Street Veterans Hospital, reading to recovering soldiers. She had invited Rose to join her on several occasions, but each time, Rose had refused.

She had been uncertain whether she wanted to continue nursing after the war. She had been sent home to recover before the final guns had sounded as she was *not in a state to carry out her nursing duties with the required care and attention.* While the mere thought of stepping foot inside a tent to operate under heavy shelling or to listen to the faulting heartbeat of dying young men amidst booming artillery had sent her reeling, she had felt compelled to contribute as the influenza epidemic began to spread.

In the calm and quiet of houses and local hospitals, she knew she could rely on her old nursing skills. There was no blood, no severed limbs, no fear of gangrene. No man-made horror. Only the 'flu. However, when it came—when it really came—it was almost as horrific as war. For months, she visited three hospitals a day, helping where she could, and every night reading the newspaper lists of the dead—all so young, and so many soldiers. All those lives she had fought to save during the war, swept in an instant by the 'flu. Rose had never seen illness like it. It seemed to tear through the world with a vengeance, seeking retribution for the atrocities witnessed on the battlefields—a brutal reminder that men could not play God. That God was still more powerful, could still strike them down in one fell swoop.

She had sworn off hospitals after that, settling on private nursing, only to discover that most patients seeking nurses were returning soldiers in need of long-term care. She could not bear the thought of it. During the war, her only focus had been their survival: the quickest, most efficient way to stop the bleeding, to remove the shrapnel, to suture the swelling wounds. She did not think she would ever be able to face the permanent damage that followed.

Rose shakes her head. "I don't think so."

"I know how you feel about hospitals," Anna presses. "But this is not like most hospitals. It's a sanctuary. Those young men gave up so much for us."

"I can't," she says sharply, and Anna falls quiet.

The porridge is steaming, the ice box stocked. Rose takes out a bowl, her appetite gone. Anna continues to flurry around the kitchen nervously, putting things away. At some point she sits down and takes out her knitting. Rose wishes she would leave, let her be, even knowing Anna only wants her company.

Her bowl emptied and clean, Rose turns towards the door. "I'm going to bed," she says.

Anna looks up from her grey stocking. "Should I wake you for dinner?"

The thought of sitting down for a meal with her seems impossible. Rose shakes her head. "I'll be out again. I have errands to run."

As she passes by the study, movement draws her eye. "Father?"

He looks up over his square spectacles, his hair slightly mussed, his collar loose. "Good morning. Or should I say good evening?"

"I was going to try to sleep. When did you get home?"

"I only came in a moment ago to pick up a few things. I have a surgery scheduled for this morning." His jacket is hanging on the back of the chair, his briefcase dropped by the door. He shuffles paper on his desk, then looks up again. "Is Anna home as well?"

"Yes, she only just returned from the market. Will you be home for dinner?"

Rufus peers at his pocket watch. "It depends on how well the surgery goes."

Rose wonders when they had all settled into their isolated routines. "Mr. Humphrey passed away last night," she says, trying to keep him a moment longer.

"I'm sorry to hear that. I know how difficult it is to lose a patient." He gives her a sympathetic look and half-rises from his seat. "I should go, or I'll be late."

"Did you see the new photograph?" she rushes to say.

"Which photograph?"

"The one of Leo. On the mantel." Then, "in his uniform."

Her father glances up, his expression unreadable. "Yes, I did see it," he says, still sliding papers into his briefcase.

She hesitates, watching him. He does not look at her, his movements slow and deliberate, as though her words have drifted past him. She curls her fingers against the palm of her hand. "She seems to be sorting through more of his things lately."

"It's part of the process," Rufus says cautiously. "Her way of coping."

Rose's throat tightens, but she pushes forward. "Can she truly cope without knowing the truth?"

Her father straightens, hands on the desk. There is a large painting on the wall behind him, and when he stands, he almost looks to be part of it, one of the men standing cliffside, two herons taking flight overhead. "Rose," he says wearily. Once, he might have tried to rationalize with her, to calm her fears, but since Leo he always seems to be on the verge of saying something he cannot speak. After a moment, he closes his briefcase and picks up his coat. "I'm sorry, but I really must go."

She steps aside to let him pass. He pauses at the front door, hat in hand. "I nearly forgot," he adds. "There's a letter for you." He gestures towards the study and within seconds is out the door.

Rose peers inside. A single blue envelope sits in the mail tray on the desk. She enters the room, immediately comforted by the smell of echinacea and ink, books and medicinal tinctures lining the shelves on the wall. She spent most of her childhood in this room, waiting for her father to come home by reading through his collection of medical journals. Even now she wants to pick one off the shelves and read it while hiding under the desk. Instead, she reaches for the envelope and tears it open, sitting down in her father's leather armchair. She can tell by the stamp that it is from her sister Jeanne.

The note is brief—a word of thanks for the chocolates Rose sent for the children, an exaltation of the weather on the coast, and at the very end, an invitation to visit her in Nova Scotia. The words settle over her with promise. Every summer Jeanne invited her and every year Rose claimed to be too busy with work. But now there were no patients waiting for her, nothing to fill the emptiness of her days. She folds the letter with care and slips it back into the envelope. For a moment, she lets herself imagine it: the salt air, the quiet mornings, the break in the pattern of things. Perhaps that is exactly what she needs. A place where she might finally be able to breathe.

CHAPTER 2

The headlines could hardly scream louder. NONE TOO SEVERE A PENALTY IMPOSED ON THE HUNS. Splashed on the front page, or tucked in the small print of subsequent pages, the bias is clear. Even now, in 1922, Frederick would be hard pressed to find evidence of impartiality in this newspaper. He flips from page to page, hoping for some semblance of objectivity, but only finds more of the same: journalists revelling in the penalizing of German goods, the failure of the economic conference in Genoa, the endangerment of the Treaty of Versailles. No mention of the people dying as a cause. No word to the suffering, the burden, the economic strain. Nothing on compromise or aid. Frederick folds the paper and throws it in the wastebasket by his desk.

His brother leans against the doorframe of his office, eyebrows raised. "Careful, or there might be more news in your trash than in the paper."

Frederick smiles in spite of himself. "Do we need to be in the shipping business? Maybe we should buy a paper."

"Now there's an idea." Silas sweeps one hand across the air, delineating a headline: "Munro Shipping: The Standard for Excellence."

"I was thinking something a bit more political."

"I'll leave the politics to you," Silas says, straightening. "How was the Stewart meeting this morning?"

"It went well."

"Did they sign?"

Frederick shakes his head. "I outlined all your changes, but they said they needed more time to review the contract."

Silas purses his lips. "Very well. I'll leave that with you. But can you take another meeting for me next week?"

"Certainly. When?" Frederick reaches for his calendar.

"The sixth of July, I believe. Jeanne's sister is coming for a visit, and I said I would meet her at the station." Silas looks up. "You remember Rose."

Frederick brightens. "Of course."

He had first met Rose at Silas's wedding nearly ten years ago. Silas had seemed unusually nervous that morning, sweating in his dark woollen suit despite Frederick's words of reassurance. Then Rose had appeared, serene as a quiet breeze, and laid a steadying hand on Silas's arm.

"My sister looks beautiful," she said. "You're a very lucky man."

Silas let out a nervous laugh but immediately relaxed. "Yes. I know. I am."

They shared a knowing smile before Rose turned, eyes bright. "You must be Frederick."

She wore a light blue dress adorned with delicate white embroidery cascading down the front, her hair pinned back to reveal the fine angles of her face. Frederick was struck by her beauty. He searched for something charming to say but only managed a soft-spoken "Yes."

There had been little time for conversation in the flurry of the day, Frederick stealing glances at her throughout the ceremony as they stood dutifully by their siblings. From afar, he had observed Rose charming his mother, fixing her dress, offering help, their lips exchanging morsels of French throughout the afternoon as relatives crowded the happy couple in the garden of the family home, the heady aroma of lilacs permeating the air. His mother, who laughed easily in company but whose demeanour was usually one of politeness, seemed unable to contain the crinkle in her eyes that occurred with every whispered word from Rose.

Frederick spent most of the afternoon answering questions from relatives who wanted to know how he was faring in Germany, where he had been studying for the last three years. His visit home to Nova Scotia that summer had been the last before war broke out and he found himself detained in Germany. Had he known the wedding would mark his final taste of home, he might have tried harder to engage Rose in conversation. Instead, he simply bowed his head in thanks as she passed him a glass of champagne during the toast and waved her farewell at the end of the night.

"It looks like Mother gained two daughters today," he told his father as they watched Rose escorting his mother back to the house.

His father had thrown him a slightly intoxicated smile. "She deserves it after all the grief her two sons gave her."

In the years that followed, Frederick learned little more about Rose, save for the occasional comments from his mother. *Rose has completed her nursing studies. Rose has been posted to a hospital in France.* At some point during the war, Rose had sent him a care package, writing that she knew how worried his mother was about his health. Unable to respond directly, Frederick had asked his brother to thank her on his behalf. *Tell her that I will repay her when this dreaded war is over,* he had written in his tight pencil script. Perhaps the chance had finally arrived.

"How long is she staying?" he asks Silas.

"A few weeks, I presume. Jeanne didn't say. But you'll be fine to take the Fleming meeting on your own? I could always reschedule—"

Frederick gives a faint smile. "No, that's fine. I'll take it."

They had been bequeathed equal shares in the business when their father passed a few years earlier, but despite Frederick's new role as vice-president, it would always be Silas's company. Though Frederick was the eldest, their father had never pushed him to take over the business, perhaps recognizing that he was not suited to it.

It was true Frederick's business acumen had never been strong. He had always preferred languages, learning English from his father, French from his mother, and German at school. In university, he tried Latin, Italian, and dabbled in Spanish, basking comfortably in all of them. After graduation, when he might have joined his father, he had instead decided to pursue a master's degree at Cambridge. Silas was still at university then but had already begun his venture into the family business, taking a position Frederick had always assumed would be his own by default, though he was not sure he wanted it. What he wanted was to see the world, so at the end of his second semester at Cambridge, Frederick had packed his bag and left England for France. For three weeks, he wandered along the coastline, sending postcards to his mother. *Perhaps this is where our ancestors came from,* he wrote on the back, entirely unsure about the Acadians' migration roots. From there, he ventured to Paris, beautiful Paris, then Belgium, eventually making his way to Germany. He had been sitting at a restaurant in Freiburg, soaking up the din of conversations around him, when it struck him, quite suddenly, that perhaps Germany was where he had meant to be all along. That realization stayed with him as he continued through Russia, then Turkey and Egypt, journeying through Greece to Albania, Croatia, before finally arriving in Italy. He spent the remaining summer months there, refining his Italian. Yet, the pull towards Germany did not abate, and by January of the following year, after completing his studies at Cambridge, he had relocated to Berlin without so much as a plan.

For a time, he taught English and French to businessmen recommended by his father, then to families with children, until finally he crossed paths with a professor at a small gathering. After speaking for two hours, Herr Kaplan asked Frederick to join him in the linguistics department at the university. "I could use someone with your diverse language skills," he said, the pad of his index finger drumming against his bottom lip.

It was as if a door Frederick had never imagined had quietly opened, and at that moment, he decided once and for all that his place was not at the helm of the family business but out there, in the world. Once he began his doctorate at the Friedrich-Wilhelms-Universität in Berlin, everyone seemed to be in agreement. Silas would succeed their father as president of the company, leaving Frederick to pursue his own interests.

But then Frederick's degree was interrupted by the war, after which any career in German linguistics seemed impractical. When Frederick returned home, there seemed no other choice but to accept the position offered to him by his brother as vice-president. It was a title in name only, but he felt he had been here long enough to know how to play the game, to court the clients.

"Besides," he continues, hoping to ease Silas's concerns. "I'll hardly be alone, will I? Adams will be here."

Silas chuckles. "Yes. Yes, he will be." He taps his hand against the doorframe. "Adams?" he calls out. "Frederick will take the Fleming meeting on his own. Help him prepare, will you?"

From the reception desk, the secretary looks up. "Yes, of course, Mr. Munro." He turns his gaze to Frederick, his fingers paused on the keys of his typewriter. "Anything you need, Mr. Munro."

CHAPTER 3

Rose pulls open the doors of the wardrobe once more, as though something new might have appeared in the few moments since she last peered inside. Everything looks drab, none of it suitable for the sunshine and glittering sea she imagines waiting for her on the coast. Drab, though not old, most of it purchased after her return from France. After years of wearing the same uniform, Rose had come home to find that nothing from her previous life fit her. She had lost so much weight that the fabric pooled around her like drapes, and to appease Anna, she had purchased most of her new wardrobe in black. But while Anna still donned her mourning dress, Rose does not want to bring these tainted clothes with her. This visit was meant to be a break from all this heaviness.

She turns back to the suitcase sprawled open on the bed and removes one of the black blouses she has packed and repacked countless times, replacing it with one of her older white ones. Its vibrancy is dulled, the cuffs faintly stained, but it is better than wrapping herself in the weight of grief. Perhaps Jeanne would be able to restore it—perhaps they could even go shopping.

Rose steps back to consider the packed clothes. The suitcase is only half full, none of it appealing. She feels the urge to abandon it, to bring nothing at all, but turns instead to the trunk of clothes by the window. The lid sticks for a moment before it gives way, releasing the faint scent of cedar. She pulls out a red knit cardigan, holding it up to the light to find it dotted with moth holes, then a skirt, creased with disuse. It used to be her favourite, though she doubts it will fit her now. Even so, she takes it, shaking dust from the soft brown wool.

A folded piece of paper slips out, drifting silently to the floor.

Rose pauses. Her eyes follow it, an odd, weightless feeling settling over her. The paper lies there, yellowed and worn. She kneels to pick it up, her fingers brushing the soft creases. Something stirs faintly in her, a memory not yet formed.

She carries the telegram to the bed along with the skirt. The paper feels thin. She smooths it open, careful not to tear the fold. The typed words appear in faint, uneven ink. ROSE AVERY STOP YOU HAVE BEEN SELECTED—

The room seems to hold its breath. Rose stares at the words, her chest tightening as the memory sharpens into focus. It pulls at her, drawing her back, back to the day it arrived—

YOU HAVE BEEN SELECTED AS A NURSING SISTER FOR SERVICE ABROAD.

That was all she had time to read in the front hallway before Anna called for her from the other room enquiring about the post. Folding it quickly, Rose had slipped the telegram into the pocket of her skirt, allowing herself only a small smile before stepping into the sitting room.

Anna barely looked up when she entered. "Is there a letter for Jarvis?" she asked, her knitting needles clicking continuously over the cream-coloured wool that pooled in her lap. "He was waiting for word from a colleague."

"Three." Rose flipped through the envelopes. "And two for you."

Anna extended her hand to receive them, the needles temporarily silenced.

Rose sat down at the desk by the window and broke the seal from one of the letters addressed to her. The paper unfolded in her hands and out slipped a crumbly pincushion flower, its lavender hue impressed on the page, covering Margot's familiar purple ink. Her sister had gone to New York for the summer, visiting relatives and friends from college. Rose scanned the page. *The weather is divine,* she wrote in her sloped scrawl. *You should have seen—*

"Have you heard from Ellen?" asked Anna. Paper bristled, and the clicking resumed.

"No, only Margot. Did she write to you?"

Anna's voice rose an octave. "It seems she has decided to enlist with the Canadian Army Medical Corps."

"Did she?" Rose's mind flashed to the telegram hidden in the depths of her skirt, her heart quickening.

Anna was silent for a moment. "I cannot imagine where she would have picked up such an idea. And at her age! It's unseemly for a woman of her years to be so reckless."

Rose tried to think of something to say. They were nearly a year into a war that showed no sign of slowing down. They needed more men. They needed more women.

"It's preposterous," Anna continued. "Don't you think?" She huffed and her voice turned. "And what if she encourages Leo to do the same?"

Rose set Margot's letter down on the desk. She should have known Anna's concern was for her son rather than their eldest sister. She moved to join her. "Anna," she said softly, crouching by the chair. She placed a hand on her shoulder. "Leo is home. He's safe."

Anna's eyes were slick. "Yes, but for how long?"

Leo had only recently completed his second year of university and had shown no prior interest in enlisting.

"For as long as he chooses to stay here," Rose said. "There's nothing you can do to stop him if he chooses otherwise."

Anna looked away as tears spilled over. This was unusual for her, normally so stoic. She reached for Rose's hand and gripped it tightly. "Promise me you won't encourage him. Promise you'll help me keep him safe."

The telegram burned in her pocket. *You can't keep us safe forever,* Rose wanted to say, but the words would not leave her. How could she convince Anna, who had spent most of her life protecting them? Anna, who'd barely had time to settle into her marriage before their mother had died from consumption, leaving behind three young daughters. Rose had been three years old at the time, Margot, five, and Jeanne, the youngest, barely two. Ellen, the eldest, had still been in nursing school, so Anna, at nineteen, had convinced her new husband, Jarvis, to move out of the house he had secured for them near his workplace to take up residence in the family home, where she would be better able to help care for her sisters. "You were much too young still to be on your own," she had told them once. "Father proposed to hire a nursemaid, but I couldn't bear the thought of strangers raising you." When Anna gave birth to Leo a year later, the youngest sisters had welcomed him as a brother rather than a nephew. It was only natural that Anna ask Rose to share in this burden.

"You have nothing to worry about," Rose assured her, though she could not be certain. Nothing felt certain these days.

Anna drew a handkerchief from her pocket and wiped her tears. "You're right. I'm being silly. It's only that little Geordie from down the street has already left for France, and now Ellen."

Rose reached for the letter. "Did Ellen say she was leaving, or only that she intended to apply?"

"What difference does it make?" asked Anna.

Quite a difference, Rose thought. There was no guarantee the CAMC would accept Ellen even if she did apply. Rose had heard they had been inundated with applications, and though she was experienced, Ellen was also in her mid-forties. Likely not the kind of candidate they were looking to send overseas. Besides, Ellen had worked as a private nurse for close to twenty years, ten of which she had devoted to the same elderly woman, a Mrs. Sutherland who needed company more than she did care. As much as she admired Ellen, Rose could not quite envision her in a field hospital. War required a different kind of nursing—something more in line with hospital nursing, which Rose had been doing since completing her nursing course the previous year.

She had been drawn to hospitals for as long as she could remember, ever since those days when her father brought her along on patient visits as a child. Even then, she had seen the way she could lift their spirits, their eyes brightening when she smiled or spun in her yellow dress, but dimming when her father addressed them in that grave tone all men in crisp white coats seemed to use.

Rose had never wanted to wear one of those coats. She wanted to heal, to improve the health of others, not cut them open like her father did. When she had broken the news to him at age nine that she did not, in fact, intend to become a surgeon, he had only smiled and pinched her nose. "I'm certain you will be astonishing however you decide to spend your time," he said. He might have told her that an Avery daughter ought to marry and never work, but Ellen had fought that battle long ago. Later, when Rose announced that she, too, intended to pursue nursing, her father had given her a pleased look and said, "I think that's a wonderful idea."

Rose was a good nurse, and delighted when people recognized her skills, even when the compliment bore a sense of partiality. She often wondered if her father's position at the hospital coloured people's perceptions, making her accomplishments seem less her own and more a reflection of his influence. "Miss Avery is formidable, just like her father," Matron Wilson, the senior nurse in charge of staff, always said, casting her a look of pride. When war was declared and the call for nurses issued, Rose had seen the opportunity to prove herself on her own merits. With Matron Wilson's recommendation, she had applied to the CAMC and waited for her chance to leave. She was beginning to think she might never receive word of a posting when the telegram had arrived that afternoon.

Despite her assurances to Anna, Leo was the first person Rose wanted to tell. She found him sitting on the edge of his bed later that evening, pulling shoes from his feet.

"Hello," he said. He was still dressed in his football jersey and shorts, specks of mud peppering his bare legs. Without a word, Rose handed him the folded slip of paper.

"What's this?" he asked.

Rose bit the inside of her cheek as Leo read the message.

He arched an eyebrow and grinned. "Well, well. When did this happen?"

"The telegram arrived this afternoon."

"When did you apply?"

"Last September."

He chuckled. "Does your father know?"

Rose shook her head. "No one does. Not yet."

Leo read the telegram again. "When are you leaving?"

"Any day, I suppose." She waved her hand and brought it to her lips, concealing her smile. "I have to confirm my acceptance by tomorrow."

"We have to tell them," Leo said in an excited whisper. "You have to announce it."

"I know." She reached for the telegram. "Your mother will be furious."

But it was shock more than fury that awaited her the next morning when she shared her news. Pursing her smile, Rose cast her eyes around the breakfast table. Leo raised his arms in celebration. Anna dropped a spoon in her teacup. Jarvis barely looked up from his newspaper. Rufus simply tapped the side of his egg with a butter knife and dropped the top onto his plate.

"I beg your pardon?" Anna finally said. She raised a shaking hand to pick up her spoon, only to drop it again.

"I must report to Montreal as soon as possible," Rose said. "I purchased tickets for the Sunday evening train. That should give me enough time to get my affairs in order."

"You've accepted?" Anna asked brusquely. She shifted her gaze from her sister to her father, waiting for him to intervene.

"Of course, I have." Rose gave a shrug. At twenty-three she was at liberty to set her own course.

Anna looked to Rufus again. "Father?"

Rufus sipped his tea and smiled. "We're terribly proud of you," he said, muting Anna's protests.

A door closes down the hall. The yellowed telegram still in hand, Rose drops it in the suitcase, quickly pulling the skirt to cover it.

Anna appears in the doorway a moment later, dressed in a black dress, black slippers, and black shawl. "Are you all packed?"

"Almost," Rose says.

Anna enters the room, box in hand. "I wanted to give you this."

"What is it?"

Anna lifts the cover, revealing a fan. "It belonged to Mother." Carefully, she extracts it from the box and flicks it open. It is a vibrant blue with spills of yellow and green. "I thought you might like to have it, or perhaps you could give it to Millicent. I know she's young, but it would be nice to pass something on to the next generation."

Rose feels a twinge in her heart as Anna places it in her hands.

"I'm sure Jeanne would like that. Thank you."

Anna sits on the bed, careful not to disturb the piles of clothes. "Jeanne must be looking forward to your visit."

"I think so, yes."

"It will be a nice time for it. With the children out of school."

Rose forces a smile, pulling at a shawl. "Oliver wrote a list of planned activities on the back of his mother's last letter."

"That's nice." Anna runs her hand across the shawl Rose has just placed inside the suitcase, straightening the folds. "Do you know how long you'll stay?"

"I haven't decided."

"I wish I could go with you," Anna says. "I would love to see them all. It's been so long."

Rose only nods. Anna has twice told her that she would love to accompany her but could not possibly leave *her boys*—the veterans—on such short notice. Who would read to them? Who would sit with them?

"I was thinking perhaps..." Anna begins slowly. "That perhaps we could take a trip. Just the two of us."

"A trip?"

"Yes," Anna says. "To visit Margot in France."

Rose tenses, but Anna seems not to notice, hand still pressing at the folds.

"We could do a tour. Mrs. Stanley from church was just telling me about them. She went recently, on one of those organized tours of the battlefields." Her voice quiets. "I think I might like to see what Leo saw. I think I might like to visit his final resting place."

Rose turns back towards the wardrobe. She tries to hide her shaking hands but cannot conceal the quiver in her voice. "You want me to go to France with you?"

"No, not right away. Perhaps next spring, when the flowers are in bloom. It would be so lovely." Anna pauses, lost in her fancy. "You had the chance to go. I never did."

It is the lightness in Anna's voice, the blithe ignorance of what her words might mean to Rose, that strikes hardest.

Rose had enjoyed France's spring blooms once. But the mud and the blood had drained them of any beauty.

Had Anna seen nothing of her pain these last few years? Was it possible that, in her grief, Anna had lost the ability to hear her? To see her? For most of Rose's life, Anna had acted more like a mother than a sister. The sixteen years between them had ensured this, though Rose had pushed against this dynamic when she reached adulthood, trying to cultivate a sisterly bond rather than continue to live under the scrutiny of Anna's parental gaze. And yet, after the war, after everything, this was precisely what she had desired most. A mother. A parent. Someone to chase away the monsters, the misery, the hurt. To comfort her. To support her. Rose could forgive the fact that Anna, having lost her only child, might have initially been too bereaved to see any of it. She knew they had both failed to provide for one another what they could not even source for themselves during those lost months following the end of war. But Anna's suggestion to visit France shows more than an inability to see her pain. It is a deliberate refusal to do so.

"No," Rose says. "I will not go back there." The look of surprise on Anna's face is more than she can handle. She closes the suitcase, still half empty, and reaches for her coat. "You'll give Father my best?"

"What are you doing?" Anna asks.

"I'm leaving."

"Your train doesn't leave for hours. Jarvis was going to drive you. He'll be home any minute—"

"I'll take the tram." Rose is boiling. A small part of her knows she should not leave like this. Knows she should embrace Anna, who now seems so frail sitting on the edge of the bed, shoulders slumped. That she should let them accompany her to the station and dutifully wave farewell as the train pulls away. But she knows even this will remind her of Leo. Even leaving will remind her of war.

She lifts the suitcase. "I'll write when I get there," she says, and without a final glance Rose walks into the hallway, down the stairs, and out of the house.

Rose reaches the train station with time to spare and settles on a bench by the platform. Now that she has thought of it, she cannot unsee it. Leo on the platform. Leo at the window, waving goodbye as the train pulled away towards safety, towards England. Rose, left behind in France. She breathes in deeply, the air tinged with the smell of coal.

The telegram has unsettled her, but being here stirs something deeper. To her left is the clock under which she awaited her train to Montreal in 1915. To her right the same kiosk where she had purchased a newspaper to shorten the journey. Had it really been seven years? That time seemed to have slipped through her fingers like water, though much of it had at times felt interminable. All of it, still so clear, and yet splintered—travelling to Montreal, to Halifax, then England. The endless days at sea, each wave folding the horizon further onto itself. Rose looks at her watch, trying to anchor herself in the present, but her mind reels back to the rattling of the rails beneath her, the sweep of the ocean.

Three weeks she had stayed on the ship, three long weeks Rose had mostly spent with her head in a pail, absorbing the motion of the waves in her limbs, in her stomach, in her ears. In her cabin below deck, she had clenched the bed sheets, grasping for any semblance of stability while her bunkmate, Mae, fussed over her on unsteady feet. *It's a good thing I've been so quick to make a friend*, she wrote to Jeanne from her bed, closing her eyes to keep the page from spinning.

She was especially glad to have Mae by her side once they reached England. Rose had assumed, given how rushed their training had been, that they would immediately be sent to France. Instead, they were escorted to a hotel and told to wait. For weeks, they wandered the streets of London, playing tourist. They walked to Bond Street, to Regent Street, to Oxford Street. They got lost on their way to Buckingham Palace, only to land at Queen Victoria's memorial. They visited Westminster Abbey, took lunch at Charring Cross, then bussed to the Tower of London.

The city teemed with life, but reminders of the war were everywhere: men in khaki weaving through crowds, recruitment posters plastered on walls. They had landed at the Royal Exchange building just as recruitment speeches were starting one afternoon. A tall man in a tailored suit stood at the top of the steps addressing the crowd below. "Unless more men volunteer, this nation will need to resort to conscription," he shouted. "And how will you be treated by men who voluntarily accepted the call to arms, when you are forced to come to their aid?" He paused, his eyes scanning the crowd of women, children, and men already in uniform. Rose listened, uneasy. *It rather makes one feel ashamed,* she had jotted down in a letter to Leo. *It seems people from the dominions are keener than the English. Shouldn't we all do our part?*

Rose was delighted to finally be here, within reach of war, and delighted in having someone share in her enthusiasm. While many of the nurses who had accompanied them across the ocean would have happily stayed in England, Rose wanted to venture farther, as close to the Front as they would allow her. Mae felt the same. They hummed with anticipation, checking in with Matron daily, until finally it came—a posting to France. Both of them together, just as Rose had hoped.

They arrived by steamer, the passage wet, wind slicing through their thin coats. In Boulogne, a steady stream of ambulance wagons navigated the steep incline of Grande Rue, avoiding the flocks of soldiers traipsing the streets near the harbour. The French fishing boats that still dotted the marina looked oddly out of place on a pier crowded with lorries, cavalry horses, guns, and an armoured train cloaked in dull browns and leafy greens. They seemed like ghosts of a past life bobbing on the water. All around came the noise of hooves, wheels, of marching feet, the din of Australian, Canadian, British, and Indian accents.

"I wonder how far we are from the firing line," Mae said as the ambulance took six of them to the hospital, luggage tucked at their feet.

"Thirty-seven miles, Sister," the driver yelled from the front.

They rode through the hills and villages, the road stretching south before them. Rose took her surroundings in silence, admiring the landscape dotted by cathedrals.

When they finally reached No. 1 Canadian General Hospital, they found a sea of tents and huts pitched in fields of daisies and buttercups, their fragrance subdued by the breeze blowing from the Channel. A nurse came out from one of the huts to greet them, raising one hand to shield her eyes from the sun, revealing a streak of red on her apron. "You've arrived at an optimal time," she told the group as they toured the compound. "Only a few months ago, this was all but an assortment of tents. The men are coming quite steadily now."

Rose opened her eyes to the light filtering through the flap of her tent the next morning, Mae snoring softly in the cot next to hers. From her cot, Rose could see the sun rising over the water, ascending like a paper lantern in the sky. The larks were whistling their morning song, the delicate notes drowning in the distant sounds of the guns. *At last*, she thought. She was here at last.

A sudden hush on the platform pulls her back. A door slams somewhere behind her, a muffled voice calling out instructions. Rose looks down at her hands, still clutching the handle of her suitcase, the leather warm from her grip.

The train pulls into the station, its whistle sharp and commanding. She rises to her feet, eager to leave this place and its past behind. Once aboard, she claims an empty compartment and sits by the window, placing her suitcase on the seat beside her to discourage anyone from joining her.

Her nerves finally settle as the train begins to pull forward, shoulders easing, fingers unknotting. She is glad to be moving eastward, towards the sea.

CHAPTER 4

A crowd has gathered on the front lawn of the Munro residence, joyful chatter filling the air. As soon as Frederick arrives, he spots his nephew Oliver darting between clusters of people, another boy on his heels. He raises a hand in a half-wave but decides not to interrupt. Instead, he scans the crowd, searching for a familiar face, but these guests are strangers to him. On the veranda, he pauses at the door, not knowing whether he should knock. This had once been his house, too. He pushes it open and steps inside, making his way through to the back door.

A table has been set up in the garden, its checkered blue linen cloth covered with cakes and sandwiches, devilled eggs baking in the heat of the afternoon. More guests mill about, the grass flattened where they gather. He spots Rose standing near the bed of irises, bent in conversation with his mother, Émilie. He is struck by how different Rose looks, though just as beautiful. He does not think the ten years since they last saw each other have been quite as kind to him. Rose leans forward to listen more closely as his mother explains something, one hand gesturing wildly in front of her. Both women suddenly burst apart, laughing. Her mouth wide, eyes squinting, Rose finally catches sight of Frederick standing on the patio, and smiles. His mother turns and waves him over.

"Good afternoon," he says when he reaches them, bending down to press a kiss on his mother's cheek.

"Frederick, dear. You remember Rose, don't you?"

"I do." He nods, feeling suddenly shy. "How are you?"

"I'm well, thank you." Rose's eyes are bright, cheeks flushed.

"How was your trip?"

"Quite pleasant."

"When did you arrive?" He already knows the answer to this question but can think of nothing else to say.

"Early Thursday morning."

"And she's already made herself useful," Émilie says. "Did you know Rose could prepare herbal medicines? I woke with a frightful headache yesterday and she cured it, with just a few ingredients she found in our garden."

"Well, the garden is a testament to your capable hands," Rose says.

Émilie waves a hand. "That was all Michael, I'm afraid. A hobby botanist, if you will. Never met a plant he did not try to propagate."

Frederick looks down at the mention of his father, but Rose changes the subject. "Your mother was just telling me about the time Silas leapt from the roof of the shed with branches tied to his arms."

Laughter stirs in Frederick's throat. He eyes his mother, who returns Rose's smile before bringing her teacup to her lips. That story was as much about his own engineering of the branch wings as it was Silas's blind trust of him. A mistake which had resulted in a broken arm but thankfully had not prevented Silas from trusting him again. He feels a hand strike his back before he has the chance to say anything.

"My ears are burning," Silas says. "Have you nothing better to discuss than our childhood antics, Mother?"

"I can only say, dear, that you're lucky you only have one son to contend with," Émilie says.

As if on cue, Oliver comes running around the side of the house, now with two boys in tow. All three of them hunch low, arms extended at their sides. Oliver spots his uncle and swerves quickly, narrowly avoiding a pair of women admiring the rosebush, who raise their hands to their chests in surprise.

"Uncle Freddy!" Oliver exclaims, launching himself at Frederick's leg, disregarding his grandmother's admonishments. "Are you staying for the party?"

Frederick chuckles, patting Oliver's head, which already feels hot from the sun. "Yes, I am."

"Good. Mama made a strudel. Your favourite, I remembered!"

"Millicent's favourite too. Where are your sisters?"

Oliver shrugs. "With Mama."

Silas seizes his son's shoulders. "Why don't you take your friends to play on the swing?" he says, guiding him in that direction. Oliver finds the two boys waiting idly nearby, and off they go again, slicing through the crowd.

"See what I mean?" Émilie says.

"The girls aren't a picnic either," Silas says. "Speaking of which, Jeanne sent me to fetch you. Something about an accident."

"Oh dear. I better go check on them." Émilie excuses herself, and Silas follows, leaving Rose and Frederick alone together.

"I must say," Rose says, raising a hand to block the sun from her eyes, "although Jeanne boasted in her letters about the fine summer weather, I had not expected such heat."

"It has been unusually warm," Frederick agrees, the weight of his eager expectations at their meeting again leaving him lost for words. He tries again. "But it won't be long before the rain returns."

Rose raises an eyebrow. "No, I suppose not." She peers around the garden before turning to him once more. "I could use a drink. Care to join me?"

"Yes," Frederick says. "Please."

Lemonade in hand, they find a shaded spot beneath the willow tree where Oliver had been instructed to bring his friends, the swing still tethered to the trunk. Without waiting for Frederick to offer, Rose unfurls it and settles onto the weathered wooden seat his father had carved all those years ago. The rope had been replaced over time, but the seat endured, with ample room for two. Frederick leans against the tree instead, taking a sip of his lemonade.

"So, tell me about these friends of yours," Rose says.

From their spot beneath the canopy of branches, they can observe most of the people gathered in the garden. The crowd seems only to have swelled since Frederick arrived, and he cannot help but wonder at all these people who apparently know his family. "To be honest, I know very few of them."

"Our siblings must be more popular than we are."

"That has long been the case between Silas and me."

"Any family members I should be wary of?"

"Plenty." Frederick smiles at the sound of her laughter, delighting in having evoked it. He gestures vaguely with his glass, ever mindful of pointing, his mother's voice ringing in his head. *Ne pointe pas!* "The elderly lady in the canary yellow hat is our aunt, my father's sister, Charlotte. He always referred to her as Lottie. And the woman standing beside her is Suzanne, her daughter-in-law."

"That explains the coordinated attire."

"Indeed, it does."

"And what about the gentleman sporting the top hat?"

Frederick had failed to notice him until now. "That would be Uncle Robert, my father's uncle, if you can believe it."

"He looks sprightly."

"Likely fitter than most of us."

"Do you only know the older crowd?" Rose asks, now gently swinging, her feet grazing the ground.

"I have met a few of Silas and Jeanne's friends. The Winters are standing by the refreshment table. They're the ones surrounded by children. Twins, around Millicent's age, and three more after that. Speaking with Jeanne is Eliza Campbell and her husband, whose name escapes me now. And then," his eyes are searching. "George and Mildred Brown. George works with us at the company. Has been there longer than either of us."

"Silas said business was good?"

Frederick nods. "It has been, recently. For a few years, I think. I suppose everyone has shipping needs. Perhaps now more than ever."

Rose swings forward, more daring now that her glass is emptied. "The last time we met, you were studying in Germany."

"I was."

"Were you there for work?"

Frederick shakes his head. "No. Not at all. I was in the middle of a doctorate in linguistics. Nearing the end, in fact."

"Your passion is languages, then?"

"In a sense."

"But you're working in business."

"I was grateful for the opportunity when Silas offered it."

"After the war," she says.

"Yes. After the war." He considers thanking her for the care package but is not certain she would remember. It was unlikely to have meant as much to her as it did to him. And despite the mention of war, he does not want to bring up Ruhleben. Not here.

"Are you still working as a nurse?" he asks instead.

Her eyes dart towards the guests. "I was. As a private nurse, before I left." She does not offer more, and he does not ask for it.

"How long will you be staying?"

"I haven't decided yet."

"Have you made any plans for your time here?"

"A few outings, but not many. I have a friend in New Brunswick I'd like to visit. And, of course, spending time with my sister and the children."

"You must not have seen them in some time."

"It has been a while. I barely recognized Millicent when I arrived, though she's the spitting image of her mother at that age." The corners of her lips wind into a smile.

Frederick can appreciate this feeling. He had received photographs of his nieces and nephew over the years, but by the time he had met any of them, Millicent, the eldest, was nearly five, with dark, untrusting eyes. Oliver had been more open, eager for a new companion, but it was only Amelia whom Frederick had known since the beginning. Since before she was even born—a bright new hope on the gloom of the world. "Amelia looks more like you," he offers.

"Do you think?"

He nods. He had not noticed it before, but watching her now, he sees the resemblance. The honeyed locks, the dark blue eyes that bring to mind the depths of the sea. "Yes."

Rose smiles, locking eyes with him. "That must mean she looks like my mother."

Later, Frederick slips into the house and makes his way to the kitchen for a glass of water. He feels parched despite the lemonade, his tongue heavy in his mouth. Though he desperately wants to take his jacket off, he knows he would find spots of dampness on his shirt. Instead, he takes large gulps of water, swallowing hard, then eats three olives in a row. Gazing around the room, he considers the small ways Jeanne has made her presence known in the kitchen that used to be his mother's domain. The newly published cookbooks lining the shelf by the window, the glass jar filled with cookie cutters in a wide array of shapes and sizes, the new electric toaster. All signs of a younger family having made this place their own.

Frederick found the house changed upon his return from Germany. It had been five years since his last visit, and longer since he had left home. Perhaps naively, he had expected to find everything from his former life the same. But after his father's death, it had only seemed logical for Silas and Jeanne to move in with their growing family to assist Émilie.

The watercolour paintings his mother had once scattered around the sitting room upstairs had vanished, replaced by children's books and toys. His father's pipe, which had always occupied a corner of the desk in the upstairs study, had been replaced by a silver desktop calendar, and the neatly stacked sheets of letter paper had given way to a typewriter. Even the things Frederick had expected to find waiting for him in his childhood bedroom—the books, the clothes, the mementos—were packed away, his room now occupied by Millicent. It was a jarring change.

For years, when he envisioned coming home, he had imagined this home, only to find it occupied by a new family. Still his family, in a way, though not quite. Frederick was an outsider to their unit, and he could not help but feel a stitch of resentment that his younger brother had gotten it all—the wife, the children, the house. The gulf between them seemed wider than it had ever been, leaving Frederick to feel like he had no place left to truly call home.

This realization had prompted him to purchase a plot of land nearby, where he had built a small cottage by the sea. That had been the beginning of his attempt at a normal life. Once the cottage was completed, Frederick had returned to retrieve everything still stored in the house to bring to his new home. "You don't have to take everything with you," Silas insisted, standing at the top of the attic stairs, the air stuffy and warm, flies buzzing against the dusty windows. "We can store things in one of the guest bedrooms if you prefer." Frederick knew what Silas was trying to say. That this was still as much Frederick's home as it was his. But Frederick shook his head. "I said it would only be until I was settled," he huffed as he carried one of the trunks down the rickety stairs. "Well, now I'm settled." He had taken everything, even childhood mementos, and crammed it all in the small attic of his cottage.

Now, Frederick looks up as a man strolls into the kitchen, stumbling a little. The man pats his jacket pockets, then the top of his head. He startles when he sees Frederick standing there, then smiles. "I'm sorry. I seem to have lost my glasses."

Frederick swallows another mouthful and looks around the room. "Do you know when you had them last?"

"In the motor car, I believe. Though it might have been in the study." He hiccups.

"It might very well have been in the study," Frederick agrees, smelling the sharp scent of liquor on him. Prohibition was still in effect, but Silas had connections. "Why don't you follow me, sir?"

He leads the man up the stairs and into his father's old study, which still smells of whisky and cigars, despite the changes to the rest of the house. Frederick sometimes wonders if Silas did not light cigars and refresh the decanter only to keep this piece of the house intact. If so, he appreciates the effort. His eyes roaming the room, he spots a pair of glasses perched precariously on the edge of the desk. "Might these be yours?" He hands them over.

The man squints, his forehead creasing, and slides them on. "Why, yes, they must be!" His eyes brighten, his face focused. He looks at Frederick gratefully. "Thank you."

"My pleasure."

The man studies him more closely. "You must be Michael's son."

Frederick returns his smile. "I am."

He thrusts a hand forward. "Mr. Geoffrey Doyle."

"Frederick Munro," he says, shaking the man's hand.

"I was terribly sorry to hear about your father. A good man, he was. But I heard you have taken your place at the helm of the company at last."

Frederick wavers. "That would be Silas. But I am working at the company."

"Silas, yes. The youngest boy, isn't he?"

"That's correct."

"Well, there's no shame in that."

"None at all." Frederick tries to smile.

"You're the one who went to war. Good lad."

Frederick opens his mouth to correct him, but hesitates. How to explain to this stranger that he had been to war, yes, but not quite in the way of those *good lads*? He had quickly realized upon his return home how little people had thought of him during his internment. A *civilian* prisoner of war. He had spent four years imagining in detail the outrage, the sense of injustice that his countrymen must have felt on his behalf, at his being interned so unjustly, only to realize that most had given him no thought at all—had never even heard of Ruhleben.

Given his age, people often assumed he had served at the Front, and he had learned not to correct them, lest they turn on him and call him a shirker. This had been a surprise as well: the vitriol with which the public seemed to view those young men who had not served, even for reasons beyond their control. He did not want to risk being at the end of it, and yet, letting them believe he had served felt dishonest. Even knowing he had been part of the war, Frederick could not shake the feeling that he had somehow missed out on it. That even in this, he was an outsider.

Now reunited with his glasses, the man seems uninterested in the details. He stumbles towards the decanter, reaching for one of the three used drinking glasses abandoned on the desk.

"Your wife must be looking for you," Frederick ventures. He does not even know if Mr. Doyle has a wife, but the snort that comes as a response suggests he does.

"She sent me to get her more cheddar," Mr. Doyle says, turning too quickly.

Frederick reaches for his arm to keep the man from falling. "You don't want to keep her waiting, do you?" he says, steering him away. "Let's get some food."

CHAPTER 5

The weather turns suddenly, the sunny haze of morning giving way to a rainstorm. Frederick runs back to the cottage, a soaked towel draped around his neck as thunder claps overhead, dark clouds pressing down. He had gone for his daily swim as usual, but within minutes the sea had shifted, the gentle waves whipped into a fury as they tossed him around the Minas Basin. Grateful now for the shelter of the awning, he turns to watch the rain come down in a torrent and cannot help but laugh. He had promised Rose rain, after all.

Once inside, he puts the kettle on and rummages through the ice box. Finding a piece of lamb, he takes out the butter and retrieves potatoes from the pantry. He is never without food, though he has had to learn how to cook for one. Taking out a knife, he begins peeling two small potatoes, slicing them over the cutting board he carved from the same maple as his cabinets.

Frederick painstakingly built this cottage himself. Cut every beam and joist, nailed every board. He had never intended it as a permanent home—he only wanted, after years of uncertainty, a place to call his own. Even this simple wooden lodge was an infinite improvement on the horse stall he had shared with five other men in Ruhleben. The solitude had been a blessing, at first.

Even though he had yearned for the comfort of his childhood home, he needed time and space to return to his old self, to slowly unravel the habits he had picked up in camp. The swearing, the wolfing down of food. Sleep, too, had become a fractured thing, and even laughter had felt strange—short, brittle, cautious—as though he had forgotten the sound. Only recently had he begun to feel like his old self. But while the cottage had at first provided sanctuary, now it was starting to feel stifling. Too quiet.

Looking around the kitchen, he tries to imagine sharing it with another person. A wife hanging red flowered curtains from the window above the counter, or frying eggs, her feet bare despite the dirt that accumulates in the cracks of the untreated pine floors. A wife stretching on the stool by the back window, gazing out at the Fundy cliffs, a blank canvas waiting before her. The more he tries to imagine it, the more the figure begins to take a familiar shape.

The lamb sizzles in the pan, and he adds more butter.

By the time he has eaten and changed into dry clothes, the rain has stopped. Dusk is falling, peepers chirping loudly. Frederick lights the oil lamps, carefully trimming the wicks to a fine point, and makes his way to the small desk by the front door. There is an envelope waiting for him. It has been sitting there for three days, but he has refused to open it, knowing what it contains. He can always tell by the weight. With the small brass letter opener, he slices the top and pulls out the pages.

After careful consideration, we regret to inform you that we will not be able to publish your piece— The rejection letter has been typed on official letterhead, affixed to his article by a paper clip. He flips through the pages. At least it is not heavily marked this time. He turns back to the letter. *We do not believe the content of your piece is aligned with the editorial stance and sensibilities of our readership.* More polite than most of the rejections he has received in recent months. One said, *Our readers are unlikely to appreciate, let alone tolerate, a narrative that seeks to exonerate those responsible for such widespread devastation and loss.* Frederick would hardly have called it exonerating. It was not Imperialist Germany he was defending, but its people—the German public, now paying the price of their blind faith.

A few months after his return to Canada, Frederick received a series of letters from a friend from Ruhleben who had remained in

London after their release. As a journalist, Ira had wanted to remain close to the pulse of events, to capture the end of the war as he had its beginning. But it had come as a surprise to Frederick that only months after their release, Ira had willingly returned to Germany to document the revolution and the aftermath of war, hopeful the new democratic government would be able to right the wrongs of the war. What he had found instead was widespread poverty and starvation. *This is a different Berlin altogether*, he had written to Frederick. *Different even from when we left.* Even then, Frederick had found it changed—dismal and desolate.

Thousands of soldiers are now returning, unemployed and unsupported, Ira wrote. *They crowd the streets, begging for food, trading stolen goods. They feel betrayed. Humiliated. No one dares to address them, though they are a nuisance to everyone, because we all know they have hidden rifles and ammunitions in the cellars of the city. Everyone fears igniting the powder keg of social unrest.*

Frederick could sense Ira's helplessness in those early letters, but it had only grown worse. *Nearly everything I brought with me, gone,* he wrote months later. *All the food, clothing, supplies. I have given it all away. How could I not? Starvation plagues the city. The few shops left untouched by either war or revolution are struggling to stock their shelves, and when they do, prices have increased tenfold. It reminds me of those miserable early days in camp, only worse. Children are dying, Frederick. Children are dying because their malnourished mothers are unable to suckle them. Last week, I saw a horse die in the street and within minutes, it had been reduced to carcass—skin and flesh ripped from bone by hungry hands. People are desperate. I'm not sure they will survive. I'm not sure I will survive.*

Lost for words, Frederick had sent a similar reply to every letter. *What can I do*? he asked. *How can I help?* He offered to send food, but Ira refused, saying it was unlikely to reach him. *Use your voice,* he had asked instead. So, that was precisely what Frederick had tried to do, writing a dozen articles for the press, trying to promote the idea of sending aid to the German public. Only one had been published, a letter to the editor denouncing the biased reporting he had grown tired of encountering daily in the papers, which had received an onslaught of vile responses in turn.

He wanted to help, because Ira had asked him to, and had it not been for Ira, Frederick might never have survived Ruhleben. But it went beyond his desire to help a friend. He wanted to help Germany.

It was from Germany that Frederick first had witnessed the war's earliest days.

He was in his flat the morning the newspapers reported the assassination of the Austrian Crown Prince in June 1914. "This might make for a change of pace," he told his flatmate, turning the newspaper for him to see.

Christopher rolled his eyes. "Balkan disputes are so commonplace," he said, already bored by the news.

It was true that none of their friends at first seemed to believe anything significant would arise from the situation, not for them at least. But within a month, Christopher had decided to leave Germany for good, abandoning his research at the university for the security of his father's house in England.

"Surely it's not as dire as that," Frederick chuckled, watching him pack up his half of the apartment. For Balkan disputes *were* common—this was the third one in as many years.

"Father's orders, I'm afraid," Christopher said, sliding notebook after notebook into his leather briefcase. "He even sent for our grandmother in France."

After Christopher's departure, Frederick paid closer attention to the newspapers, to the story taking shape. The prevailing sentiment seemed to be that Germany's progress was stalled by other nations, and they needed to defend themselves in order to claim their place on the world stage. Among his university friends, most of whom were German, there was only excitement at the prospect of this growing political tension erupting into war. Would Russia support Serbia? Would Germany retreat from its obligation to support Austria-Hungary? Would Britain enter the conflict? It all seemed possible, and their eagerness was contagious. When Germany invaded Luxembourg and declared war on Russia, Frederick joined the jubilant crowds gathering under the shade of linden trees on the balmy city streets, celebrating Germany's march to war.

That had been three days before Britain, to Frederick's utter surprise, joined the fight and cast him aside. Letters from Britain and its colonies were stopped and censored. Those who tried to leave Germany were arrested and detained. *Civilians are safe*, he assured his family. *I am certain I will be shipped home once mobilization is complete.* But did he want to leave? Six years he had lived here. He had built a life in Berlin—a career, a reputation. It was his home. Besides, he was on the verge of completing his studies. Leaving would mean renouncing his doctorate. His most pressing concern was not finding a way out of Germany, but rather finding a way to stay.

"We will make sure of it," Herr Kaplan said when Frederick shared his concerns. He suggested Frederick apply for permission to remain in Germany. "We could use someone with your diverse language skills," he told him. The same thing he had said on their first meeting, though this time the comment seemed to imply something different. *We,* meaning the Germans, surely.

Frederick felt uneasy at the thought, but he complied, making his way to the polizeipräsidium the next morning to request a domicile permit. With unsteady hands, he gave the officer a letter of support from Herr Kaplan, vouching that he was a doctoral student and had been living in Germany for many years. Kaplan even claimed that Frederick was engaged to his daughter, though in truth, Frederick had only been seeing Klara for a few months and they had never discussed marriage. "He only wants to help," Klara had assured him. Initially nettled by her nonchalance, Frederick had later begun to worry that the officer would make his impending marriage to a German a condition of his permission to stay.

The man scanned his papers carefully, a scowl permanently etched on his face, before reluctantly filling out the permit. Frederick could remain in his flat but was prohibited from leaving the city and had to report to the station every three days. "Do not miss your appointment," the officer warned, glaring down from his raised chin. "Or your next visit might not be voluntary."

Frederick was then, quite simply, an enemy alien.

Despite the new restrictions, Frederick continued to enjoy relative freedom, dining in restaurants, attending operas, and watching the city rise in celebration. The streets flooded with pamphlets, books, and songs of triumph. Children wearing paper helmets and wielding wooden swords played soldiers in the street, looking hardly younger than the actual soldiers parading in uniform. Berlin pulsed with a patriotism that gave the impression of swift and certain victory, and even now they were at war, Frederick found it difficult to muster a sense of allegiance towards either the Germans or the English. In those early days of war, he did not feel like he belonged to either country. Not really. What was he but a citizen of the world?

But as the newspapers grew more critical of the British, they gradually shaped his allegiance for him. The story was shifting. Britain was painted as duplicitous, driven solely by imperialistic greed, its involvement in the war cast as a calculated move to destabilize Europe for its own gain. Germany had been betrayed. Words of treason—*Verrat*—and hypocrisy—*Heuchler*—saturated every page. Threatened by Germany's rising independence, Britain sought only to preserve their global empire. They were *Barbaren*—barbarians—*Kulturlose*—uncultured. An oppressive force, out of place in European affairs. For Germany, this war was a defense of all that was pure, a righteous struggle against a deceitful, morally inferior empire.

The authorities already knew Frederick was an *Ausländer*, so there was no way for him to hide. But as the propaganda machine turned its gaze on him, so did those around him. His university friends distanced themselves, only one of them reaching out to explain their sudden coldness. "I am sure you understand how it looks," he said, raising his hands in a gesture that begged forgiveness but offered none. The other tenants of his building glared at Frederick with a hatred once reserved for their Russian neighbour. Even the Kaplans, who had come to act like family, shut him out. When he visited, Frederick saw the curtains move while the door stayed firmly shut, and in the department halls, Herr Kaplan seemed always to vanish into his office each time Frederick passed. When the café he had frequented for years refused him service, Frederick ceased speaking or writing in English altogether, retreating into German, wearing the language like a cloak.

Meeting the same narrative now from the other side of war troubled him. Frederick could never separate reading from his training as a linguist, and what he saw when he opened the newspaper was a mirroring of the language he had once encountered in German papers. Words such as *Hun* and *barbarian* were used as weapons—each a small, sharp tool, carving out the boundaries of belonging. In every slur and slight, Frederick heard the echoes of a society clinging to its wounds, defining itself by what it was not. They, the civilized. The other, uncivilized. From both sides, the war had always been cast as a struggle between those two opposites, and in all of it, Frederick saw only a futile attempt at righteousness.

Frederick folds the rejection letter and tucks it alongside the others in the top drawer of his desk. Though he had abandoned his linguistics degree, he still believed his words could matter—that they could bridge understanding. But how could they, when no one would publish him?

CHAPTER 6

A week after the garden party, Silas invites Frederick to join them for dinner. "Only a small group," he says. "We invited Chester and Sarah Winter as well. We thought Rose might like to meet a few more people." He gives him a pointed look. "You could also use a few more friends."

"I have friends," Frederick protests, but can think of no one Silas would know. The names that come to mind seem to be from lives past, in Cambridge and Berlin. "What time?"

"Six."

The Winters arrive at seven. Jeanne greets them at the door, her lipstick already faded.

"Munro!" Mr. Winter greets Frederick like an old friend, though they've only met once or twice. "How have you been?"

"Keeping busy, I suppose." The man is tall and broad, and Frederick has to tilt his head to look him in the eye.

"Silas working you too hard?"

"Only trying to keep the business running."

Mr. Winter laughs boisterously and slaps him on the back. Frederick nearly spills his drink.

Jeanne ushers them towards the dining room, pointing for Frederick to take the seat next to Rose. Dishes have been placed at the centre of the table, emanating a rich scent that reaches them even before Jeanne lifts the lids. Oysters, steaming roast beef with Yorkshire pudding, and a colourful array of roasted root vegetables, pieces of carrots tumbling over parsnips. Frederick reaches for the oysters first, offering the plate to Rose. She examines them closely before lifting one onto her plate and passes him the vegetables.

The conversation drifts from food to the weather. Mrs. Winter asks after the children, who have been sent for an evening walk with their grandmother, then Mr. Winter enquires about Rose's travels, taking the opportunity to expound on his knowledge of Toronto, listing the restaurants he prefers and the hotels he knows best. Rose listens, offering polite smiles and the occasional nod, taking small, measured bites of her food.

They hardly have time to finish their plates when the children return. Frederick watches with amusement as his mother tries to wrangle them upstairs without interrupting dinner, but the children are too impetuous, too certain of their right to be anywhere. He never would have been allowed anywhere near the dining room when guests were over, and he takes a small pleasure in seeing his mother unable to exert the same control she used to. Jeanne accepts Amelia's outstretched arms, chiding Oliver as he reaches for a piece of carrot with his fingers. Frederick turns to find Millicent standing quietly by the door. She throws him a look of exasperation almost identical to the one his mother is wearing.

"Children!" Émilie tries, to no avail.

Silas rises to his feet and hoists Oliver up by the underarms, directing him towards the hallway. "Off to bed!" he orders.

Oliver follows Millicent morosely up the stairs, but Amelia refuses to leave the comfort of her mother's arms.

"I'll be right back," Jeanne excuses herself.

Mrs. Winter smiles. "Ours are the same," she says indulgently.

"Yes," her husband adds. "No sense of respect. Children used to know how to mind their manners."

"It's no trouble, really," Mrs. Winter assures Silas, who smiles tightly.

Mrs. Winter looks at Rose, on the verge of saying something, when her husband turns to Silas. "Have you given more thought to what we discussed last week?" he asks.

Silas raises an eyebrow and shakes his head slowly, still chewing. "No, I can't say that I have."

Mr. Winter leans forward. "I would not normally bring this up at the dinner table," he says, gesturing to Rose and his wife, "but Rankin and I feel strongly about this."

Frederick shifts his gaze from Mr. Winter to Silas, but his brother ignores him. Mr. Rankin, he knows, is one of the senior members of the board, installed by their father thirty years ago. He wonders for a moment what Mr. Winter could possibly have to say about their business, when Silas answers his question.

"I have given both you and your father-in-law my thoughts on the matter," Silas says. "Now, we don't want to bore the others with—"

"Silas," Mr. Winter says with a chuckle. "Surely you see how short-sighted it is for you to continue working with them."

"I am only trying to honour my father's wishes," Silas says.

"Rankin tried to convince your father on numerous occasions. It was unwise for him to continue doing business with the Germans during the war, but now it's only foolish."

Frederick looks up from his plate. Silas had once explained to him how their father had managed to continue trading with a few German associates during the war by using an intermediary in the Netherlands. There were laws prohibiting trade with enemy nations, but Michael had never been one to play by the rules. Once, it would have wounded Frederick to know his father had kept working with them, but now he respected Silas for not abandoning them, as so much of the world had.

"My father had long-standing partnerships in Germany," Silas says, his voice measured but firm. "It would be unwise of us to sever those ties now, especially when they need it most."

"Need it?" Mr. Winter repeats. "These people slaughtered thousands of our men without a second thought. Every penny you earn from those *partners* is stained with their blood."

Frederick opens his mouth, but Silas shoots him a warning glance. "It is not about the money, Chester," he says.

Mr. Winter sits back in his chair, shaking his head. "It should not take this much convincing, Silas. The world agrees. No one should consider doing business with them, not for twenty years at least.

Better yet, until they've paid their reparations in full."

"I'm sorry," Frederick cuts in. His neck flushes with heat, his voice tight. "Are you suggesting that we worsen an already crumbling economy in order to force payment?" He thinks of Ira's letters—the dying, the dead, the starving.

"This crumbling economy, as you call it, is a problem of their own doing."

Frederick shakes his head, unsure of what to say. He is not interested in the blame game. He knows the world has laid it all at Germany's feet, their culpability written into the Treaty of Versailles. But he remembers things differently. In those tense weeks after the assassination that had sparked it all, there had only been uncertainty as everyone tried to calculate how far a Balkan dispute might reach into Europe's complex web of alliances. It had not been evident to him then, but Frederick now knew that the peace preceding the war had been tenuous at best. Tensions had been simmering for years, alliances born out of fear and desperation rather than trust, and all of it predicated on stories—stories crafted from pride, humiliation, and wounds both fresh and old. Every world power believed itself entitled to its empire, and every story they told affirmed that right. That was not to say that Germany was innocent. Far from it. They were as guilty as any other for kindling the fire, each country preparing for war as though it were the only logical outcome. They had all shed blood. They had all, in one way or another, dragged themselves and their men into the abyss. But what had been won in the end was only a victory of narrative, with Germany paying the steepest price.

"These demands for reparations have already placed an unbearable burden on the German people," Frederick finally says. "If we continue to push them into a corner, economically and socially, we risk creating a desperate situation—one which can only lead to resentment, and perhaps even future conflicts."

"Future conflicts?" Mr. Winter's voice rises. He looks to Silas for support, but then settles cold eyes on Frederick. "Without these reparations, we might as well give them the chance to do it all over again. They are not to be trusted. They are deceitful by nature and deserve every hardship. You will not convince me otherwise."

Frederick's face screws up with disdain. Though he daily

encountered this kind of speech in the papers, it was a different matter to hear it in person. But before he can respond, Rose jumps in.

"Mr. Winter, you are an accountant, are you not?"

"I am."

"Then, as an accountant, you must see how economic stability could in fact lead to political stability." Her tone is calm, composed. "Should we not give Germany a chance to rebuild?"

That had been one of the main points of contention at the Genoa conference that spring, but evidently Mr. Winter has not been paying attention, or else does not believe Rose has, because he only scoffs.

"We cannot punish every good, hardworking German for the actions of—" Frederick begins, but Mr. Winter cuts him off.

"Good?" he sneers. "If memory serves me right, those *good* Huns kept you prisoner for four years, did they not?"

Frederick swallows, all eyes on him. "Yes."

"And tell me, how did they treat you?"

Frederick purses his lips, unwilling to admit the truth.

Mr. Winter narrows his eyes. "I paid a visit to one of the camps here—the ones where they kept the Germans and the Austrians. A sorry lot, all of them, and not half as miserable as they ought to have been. If you ask me, they were treated far too kindly. I wouldn't be the least bit surprised if some of them preferred it—lazing about behind barbed wire rather than facing the trenches and shells back home. While our men were knee-deep in misery, those bastards were fed, sheltered, and spared the worst of it. We should have sent them home the minute the first guns sounded."

"They were home."

Frederick turns around to see his mother standing in the doorway, face resolute.

It takes Mr. Winter a moment to register her presence. "I beg your pardon?"

Émilie keeps her eyes, sharp and discerning, fixed on Mr. Winter. "Those men you speak of. They were home."

Mr. Winter seems taken aback for a moment but then smiles indulgently. "Mrs. Munro, I meant no disrespect. I am sure—"

Émilie takes three steps into the room, placing a hand on the back of Frederick's chair. He can sense her displeasure, her tone of voice only too familiar. "Many had lived here for years, in fact," she continues, as though Mr. Winter hadn't spoken. "Built lives, farms, businesses. This was as much their home as it was ours."

The smile falls from Mr. Winter's face. "They were a threat to our country," he says. "Every last one of them."

"You seem to forget, Mr. Winter, that we invited them here. This country was meant to be a new start for them."

"And they brought nothing but trouble. I won't apologize for wanting to protect what's ours."

"Ours? Pray, tell me, how do you define what is ours? The way I see it, this country was built by all of us—everyone who came here, worked this land, and called it home. Who are you to decide who belongs and who doesn't?"

For a long moment, Mr. Winter says nothing, just stares at Émilie with a mixture of anger and something else—something darker, more stubborn. Silence hangs in the air, heavy and suffocating. Finally, he turns to Silas. "Well, it is clear I am not welcomed in your mother's home," he says pointedly. "Sarah?" He barely looks at his wife before pushing his chair back and stalking out of the room.

Mrs. Winter watches him go, her face pale and drawn. "I'm sorry," she says when she finally looks up. "He's had a hard week."

"That is a poor excuse for hate," Émilie says coldly.

CHAPTER 7

By the time Jeanne returns, Émilie has already retreated to her room, and the Winters are pulling on their coats. "Going so soon?" she asks in surprise. "I made cobbler for dessert."

"We really should get going," Mrs. Winter urges, an anxious smile plastered on her face. "The children," she adds by way of explanation, letting the words hang in the air.

Stunned, Jeanne only nods and accompanies them to the door.

"Well," Silas says, looking from Frederick to Rose before rising to his feet. "I'll fetch the bottle."

Rose looks at Frederick, seeing the weight of the evening in the set of his shoulders. "Are you all right?"

"Yes," he answers too quickly, blinking twice. Then he turns to look at her. "Thank you," he says more softly.

"What for?"

"For seeing my point." He frowns, searching for his words. "For—supporting it."

"You're welcome." She has noticed his eyes are a peculiar shade of grey, and for an instant they resemble storm clouds.

"Mr. Winter is not the only one who thinks that way," Frederick says after a moment. "Most people do. Sometimes, I wonder if they're right. I wonder if I should hate them. If it would be easier."

"Hate is never easy, Frederick."

"And yet, for people like Mr. Winter, it is."

"They fail to see the complexity. Or refuse to see it."

Frederick's eyes flicker with something—recognition, perhaps. "I'm sure you can understand why I would defend the Germans," he says. "But why would you?"

Rose tilts her head. "In truth, it's not so clear to me why you would be so quick to defend them. Based on how you were treated."

Frederick smiles weakly, peering down at his hands. "It was not quick. For years, I focused only on what they took away from me. What I lost. And I wanted them to suffer for it."

"What changed?"

He hesitates, pressing his lips together. "I'm not sure how to explain it, other than to say that now I think they have suffered for it. A great deal happened during those four years. And since coming home, I have learned things that have shifted my perspective even further."

Rose wants to ask him to elaborate but does not want to press him. Instead, she asks, "How long did you live in Germany?"

"Ten years in all, but six before the war. Longer than I've lived anywhere else, save home." He gestures vaguely to the room, then shakes his head. "Odd to think of it, isn't it? It feels like another life now, but those years shaped me. It was where I discovered who I was. It was where I found community. When I think of Germans now, those are the people who come to mind. Friends with whom I laughed, or shared a glass of wine. Friends with whom I sat around tables laden with food, arguing over art and literature until the small morning hours. No matter what happened during those last four years—how I was banished, left to rot—I can't think of Germany without remembering first the joy and beauty I found there before the war. I can't think of the *Germans* without remembering the people who made my life there remarkably better."

Rose searches his face. He has always seemed so withdrawn, and yet when he speaks of Germany, he becomes animated. "You found a home there," she says.

"Yes."

"And yet you did not want to fight for them."

"No." He shakes his head. "I would not have wanted to fight for anyone."

The way he says this, with so much confidence, gives her pause.

Rose had not questioned the war when she had enlisted. Not for a moment. She had devoted herself to the cause, believing, as so many did, that they were fighting for something worthwhile.

Shouldn't we all do our part? she had written to Leo. But it did not take long for those ideals to crumble. Only a few weeks, in fact.

Even now, she could almost hear the persistent hum of the motor ambulances grinding through the mud past her hut that had pulled her from sleep one night shortly after her arrival to No. 1 CGH. One after the other, a steady cavalcade of wounded. Still unable to sleep after nearly an hour, she had climbed out of bed, groping for her uniform in the dark, and stepped out into the heavy rain.

The ground was slick, the mud pulling at her boots as she walked along the twisting boardwalk in the dark, her lantern forgotten. When she reached her ward, she watched as a man was unloaded from one of the ambulances, his face a blur of mangled flesh in the dim light, his eyes and nose undistinguishable. She fell in step with the two orderlies carrying the stretcher, leading the way to an empty bed. The night nurses barely glanced up, too busy with other patients. Rose peeled back the blankets, and on the count of three, the orderlies lifted the patient from the stretcher and placed him on the bed. The man groaned, his eyes fluttering towards the ceiling. Rose consulted the paper tag affixed to his bloody jacket as the orderlies left to retrieve another wounded, the ghastly procession ongoing.

The hours extended before them, lamps dimming as the sky grew pale. The Sergeant on duty arrived shortly after Rose to collect the patients' money and valuables, digging into the folds of their soiled uniforms and slipping wedding bands from swollen fingers caked in dirt. The orderlies undressed the men, collecting the blood-stained clothes for the sterilizer and scrubbing their unwashed flesh. Alongside the nurses on duty, Rose checked and redressed the wounds, acquainting herself with the mangled bodies of her new patients. In the quiet recesses of her mind, she began a tally of wounds. Three arms, two feet blown off; one spinal case, paralyzed; twenty pieces of shrapnel lodged in a single lacerated chest; two fractured knees, one pelvis broken clean through; four indiscernible faces, skin and cartilage turned to bloody pulps of tissue. All these injuries, and only nine men.

It stopped raining by the time they had finished triaging the new arrivals. Thirty-seven injured soldiers were assigned to her ward, bringing their total to fifty-four.

"Thank you," one of the night nurses said when Rose joined them at the entrance of the hut, the sun just rising over the fields shining with rain.

"I didn't know we were expecting so many," Rose said, the words leaving her in a croak. She had been told on her first day that patients had recently been evacuated to make room for more, a sure sign that an offensive was in the works. But the expected convoy had not come—until now, it seemed.

"Nor did we."

They were silent for a moment, the wind whistling between them, before the other nurse suggested Rose get some sleep. "There's a few hours before your shift begins. You'll need the rest."

Rose nodded, blinking over dry eyes. "I think I will."

She returned to find Mae sleeping soundly in their tent. Quietly removing her sodden shoes and stockings, she changed her uniform for a nightgown and climbed back into bed. The larks had already started warbling, their song piercing the quiet of morning. Rose felt tired. Exhausted. Her feet ached, her limbs were heavy, but every time she closed her eyes, she saw only flashes of injuries she had observed that night. Torn limbs, shattered jaws, features stolen by burns. She had seen fatal injuries before. Single bullet wounds. Limbs minced in machinery accidents. Even murder, flesh slashed in fury. Never, though, had she seen multiple such wounds on one man. Never had she seen so many at once. As she tried to sleep, she could not help but wonder whether she was fighting death or simply prolonging it.

Silas returns with a full bottle of clear liquid, dust coating the glass. "I thought we might need something stronger," he says. He pours them each a glass, and without waiting for Jeanne to return, raises his own in a toast. "To surviving the evening," he says. "And the war," he adds before downing his glass.

Frederick laughs humourlessly. "I'll drink to that."

Silas pours himself and his brother another round and takes a deep breath. "I should go apologize to my wife for letting her evening go astray," he says. He swallows his second drink, then departs once more.

Rose takes a sip of her first glass, trying to hide a grimace.

Fredericks smiles warmly. "Not to your taste?"

She wrinkles her nose. "Even the oysters smelled better." She sets her glass down. "Can I expect this with every meal?"

"The oysters, the liquor, or the quarrel?"

Rose laughs. "All of the above, I suppose."

"I can't make any promises for Silas, but a meal with me is unlikely to feature any of those."

It takes her a moment to understand his meaning. She sits up straight. "Is that an invitation?"

"Would you like to have lunch with me this week?"

Despite the tone of the evening, the corners of her mouth lift into a smile. "That sounds lovely."

CHAPTER 8

Rose slips out of her coral blush dress and rummages through the dresser in search of something more sensible. Frederick had written to advise her to wear shoes that could withstand a little mud but had not said anything about where they might be going. Thankfully, Jeanne has offered her a pair of rubber-soled shoes, but rifling through her new silk blouses and pastel cardigans, Rose doubts she has anything suitable for this outing. Jeanne had insisted on taking her shopping on the first day of her visit, easily convincing her that none of the clothes she had packed would do for summer, but the choices jostled before Rose seem more frivolous now than they had in the shop. Her new summer wardrobe has already lost some of its lustre.

A soft tap on the door. Jeanne enters, closing the door behind her. "Here," she says, handing Rose a pair of sturdy brown leather boots.

"Thank you. Now if I could only decide what to wear."

"Where is he taking you?"

"He didn't say. Only to wear sensible shoes."

Jeanne chuckles, approaching the dresser. "This one," she says, taking out the gabardine skirt. "Pair it with the white blouse. It should keep you cool, at least."

"Thank you," Rose says. Then, a moment later, "I miss having a sister."

They exchange a sad look, Jeanne quickly understanding her meaning. "And how is Anna?"

Rose shrugs. Her shoulders are bare and feel bony, fragile as bird wings. "She's coping."

"She's been through so much," Jeanne says, her voice soft. "I cannot imagine losing a child. And in a war, of all things. It's hard enough to bear the losses of strangers, but your own son..."

Rose does not immediately respond, feeling the weight of Jeanne's gaze on her, the unspoken question hanging in the air between them. She is not ready to discuss this. Not with Jeanne, who has always been perceptive, quick to see through the cracks in the facade Rose so carefully constructs.

"And Papa?"

"He has improved, I think," Rose says. "He keeps busy. Rarely at home these days."

"It must be quiet in there."

Rose pulls the skirt to her waist and begins fastening the hooks. "It was."

"And how are you?"

Rose forces herself to meet Jeanne's gaze. "I'm better now that I'm here."

Jeanne smiles warmly, then crosses the room to the vanity. She lifts the top of the jewelry box Rose packed in her suitcase, sifting through the few items contained within. With careful fingers, she lifts a rose-engraved locket hanging from a chain. "Where did this come from?"

Rose catches a glimpse of it in the mirror and turns, watching it dangle from Jeanne's long fingers. She hesitates. "From France."

"From France?" Jeanne smiles coyly.

"From Leo. It was a birthday present."

"Oh," Jeanne says. "I thought it might have been from someone else."

"What do you mean?"

"I mean—you wrote to me about someone. While you were in France."

"I did?"

"Yes," Jeanne says, eyes wide.

Rose racks her brain, wondering which of her patients she might have included in her letters home.

"That boy from down the street," Jeanne says, exasperated. "John."

Rose's mouth goes dry. "James."

Jeanne considers this for a moment. "Right. James. You said you met him again in France."

"I did."

Jeanne looks at her expectantly, but when Rose adds nothing, she laughs. "I thought perhaps—" She shakes her head. "I don't know what I thought. What a small world."

The world had felt anything but small at the start of the war. Traversing an ocean had made it seem vast, as though she was travelling to another world entirely, but it kept shrinking, year by year, as more people Rose knew became embroiled in the war. James was the first person from home she had met in France. During her first few days, she had tried to familiarize herself with her patients' charts, quickly looking over their age, rank, and names before delving into the details of their injuries and course of treatment. Most cases were mild. A broken collarbone, surface burns, or bullet wounds. Injuries that would not need more than a few days or weeks to heal. So, she allowed herself the time to settle in. She visited each patient, introducing herself before asking for their names. Then she would ask an unusual question. Their mother's favourite flowers, what their last home-cooked meal had been, if they had ever read *The Wonderful Wizard of Oz,* or played Chutes and Ladders.

She never knew what she was going to ask until the words left her mouth, and the question often surprised her as much as it did her patients. It was something she had done as a civilian nurse, generally with children, but she found that its purpose worked even better with soldiers. Her first patient beamed as he explained that his mother preferred lilies over daffodils but liked tulips most of all. The second licked his lips when he described his wife's pot roast. The third inspected her for a moment and then burst into laughter. Other patients looked up, curious about the disruption. By the time she had reached her sixth patient, the atmosphere of the tent had shifted. The men were animated, talking among one another, remembering life before the war.

"Rosie?" she heard one of them say.

She looked up from the chart she had picked up. He looked familiar, but in that instant, she could not recall his name. She had the vague sense that if she had encountered him somewhere else, she would have been able to place him immediately. His pale green eyes, shock of black hair. But here, far from anyone she knew, he was a stranger.

His smile faltered and he lowered his voice. "Rose Avery?"

She glanced at the chart again.

"It's me, James. Leo's friend." A stitch of concern appeared between his brows, his cheeks turning scarlet.

She found the name printed in black, the ink streaked across the form, blurring the words in the next field: *James Cyrus MacLeod.*

Her eyes flashed to his face. Laughter bubbled in her throat. "Jimmy!" She reached for his hand. "How are you? I didn't know you had enlisted."

His face relaxed. "I did."

"When did you ship out?"

"In April. Barely made it across the pond before I landed here." He grimaced.

Rose shook her head. "Leo never said."

James and Leo had been inseparable as children, though Rose had not seen him around the house since Leo had started university a few years earlier.

"Well, we haven't kept in touch much. But I've thought about writing."

"I'm sure he'd like that." She slipped her hand from his. "Now, what landed you here?"

"A shell exploded a bit too close to where I was crouching in the field. Didn't mark me, but the blast sent me flying, and I broke my leg when I landed."

She scanned his chart. A fractured femur. Compound, the bone having pierced the skin. He must have been in agony waiting for rescue. Had the wait been longer, the blood loss would have no doubt sealed his fate. "Well, let's make sure you tell Leo I take good care of my patients," she said. Her tone was steady, pleasant, but her nerves frayed. When she had imagined herself in France, she had not pictured Leo's school friends as patients. She had not pictured Leo.

She lifted the sheet from the bed. His pyjamas had been cut short on one side, the wound swathed in gauze. His leg was in a long splint, suspended from the rail at the foot of the bed, and an iron ring was wrapped around his thigh. Rose had seen splints before, but never so elaborate. "Is it painful?"

He nodded, his features tense. "Yes."

She replaced the sheet and prepared a needle with morphine. "This should help."

His face relaxed with the injection. She poured him a glass of water from the carafe on his bedside table.

James smiled weakly between sips. "You know, I wasn't surprised when I heard you had gone into nursing."

"Why is that?"

"You always took such great care of Leo. Like that time he skinned his knee during track, and you rushed to his aid, completely disregarding the other runners. I think you even outran a few of them."

Rose laughed. "I remember that day. The soles of my shoes were destroyed."

"I don't think my sisters would have cared as much."

"Aunt," Rose corrected.

"What?"

"I'm Leo's aunt."

James nodded, swallowing. "I always did forget you weren't siblings."

"Most people do."

Despite her initial reaction, she enjoyed seeing James's familiar face every morning. In those weeks before the first big convoy, her ward still mostly empty of men, Rose had taken the time to sit with her patients, and always spent the most time with James. When he told her that he enjoyed poetry, she procured a short book of poems for them to read together on those long afternoons when nothing seemed to happen. Tennyson, bound in emerald cloth with a golden lute player embossed on the cover. They took turns performing, beginning each poem in low tones that rose as the tent around them hushed. Rose had seen James writing in a little notebook of his own, pages dusted with dirt, but mostly his writing efforts seemed contained to staring into space with a pained expression on his face.

They talked of home often, though mostly they talked about Leo.

"He plans to enlist, you know," he said one morning.

Rose had been changing the bandage on his leg when her fingers seized, the gauze slipping from her grip. He always blushed at having her hand so close to his groin, his voice growing more strained. Rose could almost feel his temperature rising under her touch. She politely averted her gaze and reached for the ball of gauze. "He wrote to you?" Rose tried to keep the surprise from her voice.

"I'm sorry. Maybe I shouldn't have said anything."

Leo had never once said anything about enlisting—not to her at least. She remembered the pride he had exuded for her when she had announced she was leaving and thought of all the letters she had sent him since her departure. His replies were always so enthusiastic.

Rose shook her head and clipped the end of bandage. "No, that's all right. I won't tell him you told," she said, but later, after the first convoy, it was all she could see—Leo being unloaded from a lorry like a crate of spent shells. Leo laying on the stretcher with a gaping chest wound. Leo howling in pain. Everything she had seen up to that point suddenly took on a different flavour, and she could not escape it.

Even now, those terrible images were never far from her mind. Even as she gazes at her own reflection in the mirror, surrounded by Jeanne's things. Rose is learning to live between two worlds.

She pulls her blouse from the band of her skirt an inch further. "Good?" she says, in this world, to her sister.

Jeanne smiles. "Perfect." She begins folding the clothes strewn across the bed. "And how kind of Frederick to invite you out," she says, her tone light.

"We're friends," Rose says, avoiding Jeanne's suggestive gaze. "You wanted me to make friends."

Jeanne arches an eyebrow, a hint of sarcasm in her voice. "Of course. Frederick *always* invites me on afternoon strolls."

CHAPTER 9

The car rolls along the winding coastal road, the engine humming steadily against the crash of the waves below. The day is warm, the sky above a flawless expanse of blue. Frederick's hands rest on the steering wheel, his grip easy. The wind streams through the open windows, ruffling his hair and bringing with it the scent of salt. He glances at Rose in the passenger's seat. Her face is turned towards the ocean, the wind catching strands of her hair and brushing them across her cheek. There is a peacefulness to her expression, a stillness he has not seen before.

"I could never get tired of this view," Rose says, raising her voice over the noise of the engine.

Frederick nods to let her know he heard her. "Just wait. It gets even better."

They round a bend, then Frederick eases the car onto a narrow shoulder. With practiced hands, he switches off the engine, letting it sputter into silence.

Rose's gaze sweeps across the horizon. Below them, the valley sprawls in patchwork fields, each dotted with a distant farmhouse. Beyond, red cliffs rise against the soft blues of sea and sky.

"You're right," she murmurs. "This is better."

They sit in contemplative silence for a moment longer, Frederick stealing glances at her, savouring the quiet wonder of seeing the world—his world—made new through her eyes.

She catches his gaze, then smiles. "How long have you had the motor car?"

"A few years," Frederick says. "It was one of the first things I purchased when I returned home."

"Why?"

"I suppose it was a way for me to regain my independence. After living in Berlin, I knew I would not take well to the unpredictable train schedules. Trains here were never on time, even before the war—stopping for passengers to collect blueberries or flowers from the fields, or for porters to chase pigs or sheep from the tracks. I wanted more control, more..." He lets the words hang.

"More agency?" Rose offers.

"Exactly."

She looks down at the space between them. "May I ask you a rather personal question?"

"You may."

"What was it like for you to come back? After so many years?"

Frederick considers her question, his gaze drifting back to the sea. If asked by anyone else, he might have found the question intrusive. But even the few words they exchanged after dinner the other night seem to have opened a new avenue for them. "It was strange," he finally says. "Like trying to find my way back to something that had ceased to exist. The world I knew—it was gone."

"And yet so many things remain."

"Yes," Frederick says. "Like the unpredictable train schedules."

They exchange a brief smile, then Rose stares ahead. "I was grateful at first to come back to a place that had been relatively untouched by war," she says. "In France, even in England, people moved cautiously—like the world might suddenly fracture beneath their feet. Here, people moved with confidence. Unafraid. It was as though we had experienced different wars. And I suppose we had."

"Did you write to Jeanne while you were in France?"

"I did. Though perhaps not as much as I should have."

"I was always surprised when I received letters from Silas, detailing the normalcy of their life here," he says. "I couldn't wrap my head around it—how they could travel, attend a wedding, host a party, when all around me the world seemed to be crumbling."

"Jeanne's letters had the same effect on me. I think I might have even written to her less than the others because of it."

"What do you think it was like for your family when you came back?"

Rose blinks in surprise. She opens her mouth, but the words take a moment to come. "I think their relief for me was eclipsed by their grief for Leo," she says after a moment. "My own feelings about being home might have also been lost in the haze."

Frederick gives a slow nod. "I was sorry to hear about your loss. My father died only a few months before my return. I'm sure it was not the same—not at all. And yet, I understand the feeling of coming home to a sombre house."

"I'm sure he would have been glad to see you home."

"Yes. Though he might have found me changed."

"Anna certainly found me changed. And I, her. It didn't quite feel like home anymore."

"But now you're here."

She looks at him, face filled with a thousand tangled emotions. "Now I'm here."

"I'm glad you're here," Frederick says.

"I'm glad we're both here."

Frederick's stomach begins to grumble as they leave the Annapolis Valley. Glancing at his watch, he sees it is almost one o'clock, his breakfast of toast and bacon now a distant memory. "Shall we find a place to picnic?"

A tentative smile spreads across Rose's face. She nods.

Frederick steers the car around a corner, slowing to allow a woman to cross the street. They continue along the winding roads until they find a park. Frederick guides the car to the roadside, wheels crunching on gravel. The park lies mostly deserted, except for a few young mothers pushing prams and an elderly gentleman tossing bread to the birds pecking at his feet. A newly constructed path encircles the park, surrounded by large trees that rustle in the wind. Retrieving a basket from the back of the car, Frederick leads Rose to a shaded spot beneath an elm tree. He spreads a blanket on the grass, motioning for her to sit, before emptying the contents of the basket.

"Did you prepare all of this?" she asks.

"Most of it. Some of it I raided from my mother's cupboard." He holds up the jar of pickles.

"Impressive."

They eat in pleasant silence, lobster sandwiches and potato salad spread out between them.

"I'm glad we decided to do this," Rose says.

Frederick chews slowly. "It's a lovely day to be out."

"You know," Rose says, her gaze drifting to the birds darting and chirping in the branches overhead. "Jeanne and I used to have a parrot."

Frederick raises an eyebrow, smiling into his sandwich. "A parrot?"

"Yes. His name was Mr. Hughes. His feathers were a brilliant green, with a smear of red atop his head."

"Where did you get Mr. Hughes?"

"From a friend."

"A friend?"

"Yes, a ship captain." A wry smile graces Rose's lips.

"Do you mean a pirate?"

She ponders for a moment, eyes gleaming. "Perhaps he was. I don't know what he did when he was out at sea, but when he returned to port, he went by Captain Clark." She takes a bite of her salad.

"Captain Clark," Frederick repeats.

"Yes. We weren't allowed to venture near the docks, but we all did anyway. Captain Clark was always kind to us, asking if there was anything we wanted him to bring back. Usually, we'd ask for treasures, or a whale. But when he set sail for Africa, Margot asked for an ostrich feather and a parrot."

"And he actually brought them back?"

"Yes!" Rose's eyes dance with excitement. "Margot had the ostrich feather fixed to her hat and wore it all the time. It drove Anna wild."

"But the bird didn't?"

"Oh, yes. The parrot too. But Leo grew quite fond of him, so we had no choice but to keep him. Lived with us for fifteen years."

"In the house?"

Rose feigns offence. "Of course, in the house. Mr. Hughes was a member of our family."

Frederick laughs. "From what Jeanne has told me about Anna, I can hardly imagine her with a parrot in the house."

"Well, she used to be different." Rose quiets. "Strict, yes, but never severe. We must have exasperated her, but she loved us dearly." She presses her lips together.

Frederick tries to lighten the mood. "I don't suppose you have photographic evidence of Mr. Hughes?"

"We do!" Rose brightens again. "Margot took him to the photography studio on Queen Street and had her picture taken with him and her ostrich-feathered hat."

Frederick lets out a bark of laughter, feeling lighter than he has in years.

After lunch, Frederick suggests making one more stop, and Rose agrees. As Frederick steers the motor car into a driveway, Rose's gaze lands on a quaint shingled house peeking through the trees. Frederick must sense a shift in her because before she can utter a word, he says, "My cottage. But not why I brought you here." He watches her intently, gauging her reaction. She nods.

He leads her not towards the house but around it, past his garden and shed to a set of stairs leading down the side of the cliff. As they reach the end of the stairs, a fling of sandpipers lifts into the air. The tide is retreating, the waves now mere ripples in the distance, where a large blue heron plods unhurriedly.

Frederick bends down to untie his shoes and roll up the bottom of his pant legs. "You can keep your shoes on if you prefer," he suggests, but Rose follows suit, sliding her stockings down the length of her legs and tucking them into her boots, which she sets by Frederick's brown loafers on the stairs. Stepping onto the mud, she feels her feet sink into the soft earth.

Frederick looks at her expectantly, eyes wide with anticipation.

"What is it?" she asks, unable to contain her own smile.

"Do you know where you're standing?"

She scans her surroundings. "On a beach."

"You're on the ocean floor. A few hours ago, this was covered in water."

She looks to her feet, swallowed by thick, wet mud. It is something she has witnessed before—the push and pull of the tide. It was one of the ways she had marked time on the coast of France. In the whirlwind of her days, the tides were the one thing that remained constant. Predictable. But seeing Frederick's excitement, she cannot bear to tell him, so she lets him explain—how every few hours, the ocean advances, swallowing the mudflats until its waves crash against the walls of the cliffs, before receding, folding onto itself in its retreat.

Frederick starts walking in the direction of the heron, following in its slow movements. "Over time, the tides gradually erode the soil from the cliffs, revealing its concealed relics. I have found fossils here on more than one occasion. The first time was the summer I built the cottage." He looks over his shoulder at her. "I was impatient—could hardly wait for the stairs to be finished, so I climbed down the side of the cliff on a rope. I'm not entirely sure how I did that now," he adds, looking up at the towering cliff. "But evidently no one had visited that particular spot in a while, because I found a handful of gems and fossils."

"What did you do with them?"

"Some are on shelves in the cottage, but the rest I donated to the museum."

"Is there a museum in town?"

"Yes, there is. A recent addition." He turns, his dark hair flapping in the wind. In sunlight, she can tell the colour is tinged with his mother's auburn tone. "I could take you there one day."

"I'd like that."

The sea breeze whistles as it swerves from the cliffs. Rose hums along, feeling settled in a way that surprises her. It is an odd feeling, so far from home, but Toronto has not offered her this kind of comfort in years.

They wander along the sea floor, drawing near and drifting apart. Frederick settles near a boulder, picking rocks and turning them over in his hands. Rose approaches slowly, her skirt bunched in her hand.

"See here?" he says, holding out a slim piece of coppery rock. He dips it in a pool of water, and its colours become more vibrant. Rose leans forward to peer into his hand. "On the corner. Do you see?" At first, she only sees a small, dark indent with thin veins running through it. "It's a fern fossil," he says.

She looks again, noticing the symmetrical curves of the leaf. She reaches out to take the rock in her own hand. "I never knew plants could fossilize," she admits, astonished.

"Most people only look for fish scales or insects, but there's so much more life preserved in these rocks."

"I see that," she says.

They continue searching for fossils, Rose occasionally lifting her head to the sea to check if the tide has started to creep back. At one point, she sees a man approaching, hat raised in greeting.

"Ah, Mr. Cameron," Frederick says when he spots him.

"Afternoon," Mr. Cameron says, replacing his hat on the few strands of hair pasted to the top of his head. "Found any treasures today?"

"Only this one. I think it might be a fern," Frederick says.

Mr. Cameron examines the rock. "Yes, it is."

Frederick turns to Rose and introduces his neighbour. Rose greets him with a smile.

"Yes, right around the bend here," Mr. Cameron says, pointing farther down the beach. "I have to come this way often to make sure Mr. Munro isn't keeping all the best fossils to himself."

The men laugh, and finally Frederick introduces her. "Miss Avery is my sister-in-law," he says, wavering on the words. She supposes they are siblings-in-law, though it feels strange to say.

"It's a pleasure to meet you," says Mr. Cameron.

"You as well," Rose says, clamping her soiled hands in front of her skirt.

They exchange a few more pleasantries before Mr. Cameron says he really must get back, leaving footprints in the mud.

Rose and Frederick continue walking the length of the beach until finally, undeniably, she notices the waves have crept closer, and Frederick suggests they start making their way back. It is with regret that Rose agrees to leave, her eyes searching for the heron on the rich brown horizon, but there is only the approaching sea.

CHAPTER 10

They return home in the early evening to find Millicent and Oliver in a heated debate over a game of chess, Amelia clinging to her mother as she moves through the room, picking up after the others. Oliver breaks away from the board as soon as he sees them, Millicent getting to her feet and crossing her arms over her chest. "Where were you?" she demands as Oliver begins bouncing up and down in front of Frederick.

"We went out for a picnic," Rose says. "And then we went to the beach."

"You promised we'd play this evening. Oliver doesn't know any of the rules."

"I'm sorry," Rose says, pulling off her boots. "I'm here now. Let's set up a new game."

Millicent glares at Frederick as though it is all his fault. He bends down to keep Oliver from jumping as the boy tells him about finding a bird with a wounded wing beneath the tree in the yard that morning. "There was a nest, too, up in the branches, though we couldn't see if it had eggs, but she might have been their mother, so I wanted to pick her up, but Father said no, and he came inside to fetch a towel before lifting her from the ground, and she was scared, I could tell, but I tried to tell her my father would help, and then—"

"That's incredible," Frederick interrupts. "Is your father still at work?" When Frederick took the afternoon off, he had assumed Silas would do the same.

"Yes."

Amelia lets out a piercing wail as Jeanne tries to set her down. "Okay," Jeanne says, looking frantic. "It's okay."

"Where is your grandmother?" Frederick asks.

Oliver shrugs. "I don't know." He turns on his heels, already bored with this conversation, and moves towards Rose.

"In the back garden," Jeanne says, catching Frederick's eye.

Frederick steps out into the garden, the air tinged with a hint of lavender and roses. He finds his mother seated on the wrought iron bench, a small notebook in hand, a discarded pair of gloves on the bench beside her. Her fading red hair is pulled back in a loose bun, her face shielded by a large straw hat.

"Bonsoir Maman," Frederick calls out so as not to startle her.

Émilie looks up, her face breaking into an easy smile. "Frederick! I didn't hear you come in. How was your day?"

"Great," Frederick says, joining her by the lavender bush. "We took a drive to White Oaks Park, then we went to the beach."

"I'm glad to hear it." She pats the bench beside her. "Come, sit."

"What's this?" he asks, picking up the notebook. The early evening sun is spilling through the tall trees around the garden, casting golden light across the meticulously tended beds and neat rows of flowers.

"I like to keep notes. Every year, I track the weather and how the flowers are progressing."

That was not something Frederick recalled her doing when he was younger. It was his father he remembered spending the most time in this garden, on those slow mornings or evenings he was not pulled into work. "And how are they progressing this year?"

"Très bien." Émilie points to the tall, slender stems topped with clusters of white flowers. "The valerian has been doing particularly well. Your father planted that to make tea for his insomnia. Though I'm not sure it helped." She throws him a sad smile, then turns towards him. "I wanted to apologize for my outburst at dinner the other evening."

Frederick shakes his head. "You have no reason to apologize."

"Silas says that too, but has been acting coldly all the same." She sighs. "I should not have interfered. But how could I not? That man has no business speaking to either of you about this."

"He seems to think he does."

Émilie gives a dismissive wave. "He is only doing Rankin's bidding. I never liked that man. But your father insisted on keeping him on, even after all the trouble he caused, trying to turn the board against your father."

"Why didn't Father simply listen to him?"

She looks at him, surprised. "For you, of course."

"What do you mean?"

"You were the reason your father kept those business associates. It was foolish—we all knew it. Even Silas asked him to reconsider. But he insisted. He wanted to make sure he had friends in Germany who could help you if it came to that." Émilie cocks her head. "Did you really not know?"

Frederick lifts his shoulders. "No."

She reaches for his hand. "Darling, he did everything he could to help. Not just in Germany, but everywhere. He wrote to universities across the UK, begging them to give you a job, to find a way to get you out. He even wrote to the federal government. He contacted anyone who might have been able to exert even a sliver of influence."

Frederick is surprised. Some men had managed to leave Ruhleben through political influence, especially in the first few months of their internment. Frederick had asked his father to help, and Michael had told him he would take care of it. But then, nothing seemed to come of it. "He never said."

"You know your father. He did not want you to know he had failed. We felt so helpless. Your father insisted he should have made you come home the moment rumblings of war reached us." Émilie ponders this for a moment, eyes far away. "But none of us knew, did we? None of us could have predicted what happened."

Frederick had often considered the same thing, regretted not leaving when he'd had the chance.

Émilie searches his face. "He felt culpable."

"It wasn't his fault."

"No. But he felt responsible." She pats his hand, then sighs. "One associate did agree to help, so long as we could do the same for his nephew. A young man from Galicia, likely younger than you. He had come here before the war to work. Your father reached out to him, but when his uncle stopped responding to our letters, Michael wanted to cease all communication. I insisted that we continue sending care packages. I did what I would have wanted someone to do for you."

"He was interned?" Frederick asks.

"Yes. He was taken to the Halifax Citadel before being transferred to the camp in Amherst."

"What was his name?"

"Petro Koval." Émilie looks down, her fingers absentmindedly tracing the edge of her notebook. "We sent him food, clothes, and money. But mostly I think he was just glad to have friends."

"What happened to him?"

"I believe he might still be in Canada. He talked about moving to a city, somewhere he could be more anonymous, after the war. I meant to stay in touch, but I didn't want him to feel obligated or indebted to us. I wanted him to find his own way. He sent me a very dear letter, after your father died. Said there was no need for me to help anymore, though I still wanted to."

Frederick is silent for a moment, turning this new information over in his mind. "Do you still have his contact information? I'd like to write to him, if that's possible."

Émilie nods. "I'll get you the last address I had for him."

CHAPTER 11

Back home, Frederick pulls the page from the mouth of the typewriter and reads it over once more. His floor is littered with crumpled half drafts, words crossed out by the drowning blue of his pen. How to address a man he has never met? How to let him know that he wants to speak to him because he, too, was interned, cast out as an enemy alien? What is he hoping to achieve by writing to Petro Koval? Frederick is not sure. Since his return, he has struggled to explain his experiences to anyone. Strangers made assumptions about his time abroad. His family knew, of course, where he had spent those four years. But was knowing the same as understanding? He had considered the same today with Rose. She knew he had been interned, but how could he describe the years lost, the endless days that had blurred together in a haze of hunger and monotony, the cold that had seeped into his bones and never quite left? How could he make her understand what it had been like to be cut off from the world, to be reduced to nothing but a number, a name on a list, a man without a country?

It was morning when they came to arrest him. Frederick had been at the window, drinking a lukewarm cup of tea, his eyes fixed on the courtyard below. The window was cracked open, the brisk October air dispelling the smoke from one of the cigarettes Christopher had left behind. The cigarettes were a new indulgence—Frederick never smoked but he'd been too anxious for breakfast that morning, knowing they would come.

A week earlier, Germany had issued its ultimatum: if Britain refused to release interned Germans, English civilians on German soil would face arrest. At first, Frederick had clung to the hope that Britain would concede, and for the first time, he had welcomed the thought of leaving the country. The university had cancelled his defence without rescheduling it, the letter strongly implying that they were unlikely to ever grant a degree to an enemy alien. Nothing was keeping him in Berlin anymore, isolated and under surveillance. But as the days slipped by and the deadline loomed, hope had curdled into a desperate certainty. Britain would not negotiate. They had abandoned him.

When the sound of boots echoed in the hallway outside, Frederick only set the cigarette down in the ashtray, embers glowing faintly against the cold light of morning, and waited.

They brought him to the local police station first, locking him away in a cell with half a dozen Englishmen, including a London businessman, an Oxford student, two musicians, a professor, and a retired dentist who had been vacationing with his wife and daughter. The dentist sat in the corner, murmuring to himself that he should have stayed in Bristol, that he never should have brought his daughter to a place like this. For hours they waited, the gnawing unease in Frederick's stomach turning painful as his hunger intensified, the taste of tobacco dense in his mouth.

By late afternoon, a guard came to unlock the cell door and ordered them out. Frederick joined the long procession of men filing down the corridor, the shuffle of boots echoing along the stone path. Where would they take them next? Somewhere worse, surely.

Outside, he blinked in the sudden sunlight, startled by the lines of armed policemen, the crowd of men, women, and children gathered on the street behind them. An officer barked an order in German and the men began to line up in fours, some of them stumbling with their luggage and trunks. Frederick clutched his bag and shrank from the crowd, now laughing, jeering, hurtling insults. He flinched as the officers shoved the men into place, using batons, the tips of their rifles. Frederick, terrified, tripped over an abandoned suitcase and a guard pulled him up, shouting in his face. His eyes were dark with rage.

Something had shifted. Something had changed. Over the last few months, Frederick had learned to move through the world unobserved, trying to hide the fact that he was English. For the most part, he'd succeeded. But now they had been marked as a group, and the vitriol grew to scale. He could scarcely believe what the war had wrought. That the horrors unfolding on distant battlefields and in the private offices of military leaders could bleed so seamlessly into the streets of a place he had once considered home. That the same people who had not so long ago met his gaze with a smile, who had kindly retrieved his dropped scarf or borrowed his newspaper, now looked at him as though he were something vile, less than human. How swiftly the veneer of civility had crumbled. How quickly war made enemies out of friends.

The officers ordered the men forward. Heart pounding, legs trembling, Frederick fell in step with the others. Within seconds, a boy darted from the crowd, directly into his path. The child's eyes burned with venom as he spat at Frederick's feet. "*Englische Schweinhunde*!" he hissed, hands balled into fists, before fleeing back to his father's protective embrace. Frederick stood frozen, disbelief rooting him in place as the others marched on. From the corner of his eye, he saw a pistol raised in his direction, heard another shouted order. Swallowing hard, he forced his feet forward, each step dragging as if the insult had seeped into his very soles.

For miles they walked, a painful blister forming on Frederick's heel, until they reached Alexanderplatz and were ordered aboard a train. The station was dim, the air bitterly cold, and Frederick hesitated, wondering if he might turn and run. But where would he go? A soldier shoved him forward, and he climbed aboard with the others.

A military officer with thick black curls and beady eyes stood at the front of the compartment, one hand steady on his revolver. He barked once for silence and no one dared defy him, the only sounds coming from the creak of the carriage, the faint murmur of the train gathering steam.

Frederick felt queasy. He closed his eyes, trying to make sense of the day's events, but all he felt was anger. Anger for every decision that had led him to this moment. Anger for the cruel absurdity of the world.

The train lurched into motion and Frederick opened his eyes. Outside the window Berlin slipped past, the grey expanse of the city dissolving into fields and trees. It was not long before they slowed again, grinding to a halt sooner than he had expected.

"Where are we?" the man seated next to him asked, leaning over to peer through the dusty window.

Frederick scanned the horizon, searching for something familiar, but there were no landmarks, no sign of where they might be. Just the flat, barren stretch of November, trees bare against the dull sky. He shook his head. "I don't know."

Twilight was falling. They disembarked, trudging forward in uneven rows, their arms heavy with luggage, their disoriented feet dragging against the gravel-strewn path. In the dusk, Frederick saw gates towering overhead. He squinted as he neared, trying to make out the iron letters.

"Ruhleben," he muttered under his breath.

"What does it mean?" asked the man walking beside him. They spoke in whispers, their words curling like mist in the chill of the evening.

"A quiet life," Frederick said, but his translation seemed meaningless against the barbed wire that coiled atop the gates and the guards stationed at the entrance, their spiked helmets glinting under fading light, rifles resting like threats at their sides. "I've been here before," he added in a breath.

The gates closed behind them with a resounding clang. Swears and shouts rose from every side, ordering them to line up. In the chaos, Frederick shuffled around bodies and luggage to take his place in the lines that began to form. His heart stammered in his chest, his knuckles straining against the handle of his suitcase.

A man in a tailored grey uniform approached, his jackboots covered in a thick layer of mud. A shock of white hair fell from under his peaked hat, matching the grey handlebar moustache that clung to the cigar jutting from his mouth.

"Quiet!" barked one of the guards following closely behind, though few had dared to speak.

The first man raised his hand and nodded, slipping the cigar from his mouth. "Gentlemen," he began, his tone dripping with disdain. "You are no doubt wondering how you came to be in this situation. What grievous error you might have committed." He gave a wry smile. "Allow me to ease your conscience: you have done nothing wrong. No more than those Germans held captive in British prisons. Your government has seen it fit to detain them, refusing their return home in this time of great need, and now we must do the same. But rest assured," he added, his voice softening into something almost mocking. "You will not be treated as poorly as they are."

Frederick's jaw tightened, the words settling like a stone in his chest.

The Commandant puffed on his cigar with indifference. He gave a signal and the guards approached the lines of nervous men. One proceeded in the direction of someone to Frederick's left, tearing the luggage from his hands. He searched its contents, unravelling the folded clothes, the rolls of money, the organized medicine bottles. The man watched in horror as the guard pulled out a framed photograph and threw it to the ground, shattering the smiles of the woman and child in the image. The man opened his mouth to protest but closed it when the Commandant approached. Bending forward, the Commandant retrieved the photograph from the mess and handed it to the man.

"Kein Glas," he said dully before turning. *No glass.*

The guard tossed the opened suitcase to the prisoner's feet and moved on to the next person in line, leaving the prisoner to gather his things from the ground. He shoved the rumpled clothes back inside the case and snapped it shut with trembling fingers.

"Name?"

Frederick turned to see that a different guard had approached someone to his right. He was holding a clipboard and pinching a short pencil between his fingers.

The prisoner hesitated before answering. "Andrew Lewis."

The guard made a note without looking up. "Beruf?"

Lewis hesitated again. "Thirty-two."

The guard lifted his eyes slowly and glared. Frederick could almost sense Lewis retreat beside him.

"Beruf, nicht Alter," the soldier spat.

"I'm sorry," Lewis stammered. "I don't—I don't speak German."

The soldier shook his head, his jaw clenched.

Before he could stop himself, Frederick stepped forward. "Kann ich in seinem Namen—"

A bolt struck the air from his lungs. He stumbled back, looking up at the guard who had interrupted his offer to translate with his baton.

The guard who had been interviewing his neighbour sighed. "Mach das nicht," he told the second guard with annoyance. *Don't do that.* The baton was returned to its holster and the guard retreated without a word. The interviewer turned to look at Frederick. "Sprechen Sie Deutsch?" *Do you speak German?*

"Ja," Frederick confirmed, clutching his chest, the taste of copper in his mouth.

The guard motioned for him to continue. "Bitte übersetzen." *Please translate.*

Under the growing shadows of a bruised sky, Frederick translated for his neighbour, then for another, and yet another.

Once all their information had been gathered and bags searched, the men were told to stay in line for a head count. Darkness was falling quickly, greying their faces. Frederick closed his eyes, the weight of the day pressing down on him. He felt exhausted, emptied, but still his mind raced. He could hardly keep pace with everything that had happened since that morning. A knock, a cell, a prison camp. It seemed impossible. But there he stood, surrounded by hundreds of inmates, an enemy in an enemy country.

At last, they were told to pick up their bags. Frederick followed the others as they crossed the compound, dark buildings casting shadows across their path. One guard led a smaller group into a long, dimly lit corridor. The concrete floor was damp from the cold, the air stinking heavily of manure. He slid open an iron door and considered them for a moment before pointing to a handful of men from the front of the line. "You six in here," he ordered in German.

They shuffled inside. The line continued, shedding some of its men as they were directed into different rooms. From the back of the line, Frederick could not see much more than the iron and wood on either side of them. It was only when he finally passed by the first door that he confirmed his suspicion—the rooms were in fact horse stalls. Peering inside, he saw shapes of men trying to arrange themselves on the thin layer of straw scattered across the ground.

"There's still horse shit in this one," someone protested from a different stall.

Frederick's stomach churned. Could this really be where they would be kept? The cramped prison cell from that morning seemed almost a comfort by comparison. He felt a cold sweat breaking, dreading what he might find in his stall, but when they reached the end of the hall, the guard brought them outside.

"The rest of you will sleep in the hayloft," he said, pointing to the narrow wooden staircase that ran up the brick exterior of the building. When no one immediately stepped forward, he raised his pistol to the sky. A shot rang through the air. They all jumped, then obeyed, the stairs swaying dangerously under their combined weight.

Darkness enveloped them as they entered the loft. Frederick could not see more than shapes as he pushed and pulled his way across, narrowly avoiding the low beams that ran in all directions across the sloped ceiling. There was a sense of urgency in the air as they all desperately sought a place for themselves on the straw covering the ground.

Frederick sat down in his coat and scarf, his suitcase tucked at his feet. It was too cold to change and too crowded to unpack. He reached for the cloth bag in which he had stored his bedding but it was gone. Panic pierced through the fog. Had he left it outside? Had it been stolen? He racked his brain, running his hands among his things again and again before realizing that he had entered the camp carrying only his suitcase. He remembered it clearly, one hand gripping the handle with white knuckles, the other running the lining of his coat pocket to calm his nerves. He must have left the bag on the train. He felt himself deflate. Another blow to the day. One final incredulity.

He lay down on the ground, clutching his suitcase to his chest. Someone dropped down next to him, close, too close, while invisible feet stepped and stumbled over them. Fear permeated the air, sharp and metallic, settling bitterly on his tongue. Frederick had no blanket, no pillow, nothing but the brittle stalks of straw that rasped against his skin. He tucked his suitcase under his head and pressed his eyes closed, willing himself into stillness.

Frederick remembers it all too well. The smell of manure, the cold seeping through the unheated barracks. Perhaps he did not need to describe it for Koval to know why he wanted to talk.

He tries again. Introduces himself, mentions his mother, and without going into details, simply writes, *I often wonder how others who were interned have managed to weave those memories into the fabric of their lives. Perhaps a correspondence might help us both untangle the threads of what happened during those lost years.*

CHAPTER 12

"Good morning," Rose says as she enters the kitchen. The sun streams through the windows, casting a bright glow around the room. Rose inhales deeply and catches the scent of freshly baked scones and butter.

Jeanne glances over her shoulder from where she stands at the counter, kneading a lump of dough. "You slept in late."

Amelia is seated at the table with a book in front of her. Rose stretches her arms high above her head, leisurely making her way over to Jeanne. "I haven't slept so well in years."

"Must be the salt in the air."

"Must be." She picks up a peach from the counter and inspects it in the light, fuzz shining against deep red skin.

Jeanne gestures for Rose to take a seat. "Tea?"

"Yes, please." Rose settles next to Amelia. "Hello," she says softly.

Amelia smiles and retreats slightly.

Curious, Rose cranes her neck to get a better look at the book. It is illustrated but contains paragraphs of text that seem too advanced for a child of three. Rose reads a few slanted lines and recognizes it immediately. It is *The Wonderful Wizard of Oz*. She smiles at Amelia. "What a lovely book," she says, feeling a twinge in her heart.

Jeanne sets a pot of steaming tea and a plate of scones on the table. "So will you tell me about your outing?"

Rose chews on her peach, juice gathering at her lips. "Where is everyone?"

"Silas left for work hours ago. Émilie had a Women's Council meeting. I expect she'll be out all morning."

Rose nods slowly, setting down her peach. "Where are the other children?"

"They're in the garden."

Pouring herself a cup of tea, Rose reaches for a scone. She can feel Amelia's eyes on her and turns to make a face. Amelia giggles.

"Amelia, why don't you ask Aunt Rose about Uncle Freddy?" Jeanne says.

Rose offers a warm smile. "There's not much to tell," she says to the child, then turns to look at her sister. "We had a picnic in the park. He took me to a beach near his cottage. We searched for fossils."

Jeanne raises an eyebrow, her shoulders moving up and down as she pushes and pulls the dough apart. "Sounds riveting."

"I enjoyed myself."

Amelia reaches for her torn pieces of scone, and Rose reaches for the book, its pages now covered in crumbs. She dusts them off. "Would you like me to read to you?"

Amelia nods.

Keeping the book on the table, Rose flips to the first page. There, in tidy blue scrawl, is Frederick's name. She smiles, turns the page, and begins to read.

After breakfast, Jeanne takes the children to run errands in town, leaving Rose alone in the house. She wanders from room to room, her footsteps echoing off the polished floors. After weeks in the hectic household, she tells herself she is glad for the solitude, but in truth, she's come to enjoy the chaos, the way the constant noise drowns out her thoughts. Coming here had meant to be an escape, an attempt to shed the past, but at times it seems to cling to her tighter than ever. She had expected Jeanne to be too busy to concern herself with Rose's emotional state, but instead, her sister has been prying at the edges of her shell, asking about Anna and Leo. Asking about James, of all people. Rose had not thought of James in years.

She stops in the doorway of the drawing room, her hand on the frame, and for a moment she's back in a different doorway, the one that led to the makeshift hospital where she spent days tending to the wounded. The air is thick with the scent of antiseptic and blood, the groans of the men muffled by the sheer force of her will to remain detached. But she had never been able to detach completely, had she? She had been too eager when she arrived in France. Too naive. She had taken to her role as caregiver easily, and James's presence in her ward had brought a sense of familiarity to her life in France. Even Mae had quickly grown to feel like a sister.

She enters the room and takes a seat at the piano. Her fingers drop against the keys, the scattered notes echoing across the room.

One night, late in August of their first year in France, Rose and Mae had returned to the hospital after a quick outing in town to find a concert underway in the church hut, the audience a display of injuries: men with arms slung to their chest; men with eyes covered in crisp white gauze; men in wheelchairs attended by orderlies. Rose was surprised to see James seated near the back, a pair of crutches angled on the back of his chair. She could hardly believe he had made his way here on foot. Lower limb fractures were difficult to heal and required a prolonged period of immobility. James had already been at No. 1 CGH for two months, an unusually long time for a patient to stay at a field hospital, but it hardly seemed like enough. Men whose injuries required a considerable length of care were normally shipped back to England after a few days or weeks, but his physician, Captain Eaton, had been experimenting with a new treatment and had requested that James stay for close observation. Rose had been glad for it at first but now she wondered if he wasn't rushing his recovery.

Rose placed the vase of flowers she had bought in town on a nearby table and settled in to watch the entertainer scurry his hands across the piano keys, drawing enjoyment from her patients' smiles more than the music. The player finished with a flourish and the tent erupted in stalled and irregular applauses. Rose clapped louder to make up for the echo.

Mae appeared at her side. "I should go change before my shift."

"I'll see you in the morning. Bon courage!" Rose called out as

Mae hurried off. The two words they exchanged before every shift.

Rose picked up her vase and waited as the throng of men filed out of the tent.

James wobbled on his crutches, trying to make his way to her. "May I escort you home, Sister Avery?" He wore a shy smile.

Rose laughed. "Please. Allow me."

They followed the others outside. It was still light, the sun low on the horizon. The heat of the day had broken, a cool breeze now drifting from the sand dunes.

"Day off?" James asked as they made their way through the grounds, the sound of his boot heavy against the boardwalk as he alternated with his crutches.

"Yes. Sister Harper and I went to the beach and stopped in town after lunch."

"And you bought me flowers?" He gestured to the bouquet with his chin.

"For the ward. Aren't they beautiful?" She had stumbled upon a quaint little flower shop while searching for a hair salon. After Rose had introduced herself, the fleuriste had insisted on cutting fresh roses from the garden for her. "Roses for Rose," the woman had said. She was dressed entirely in black, a photograph of a man in a pale-blue uniform and an Adrian helmet perched between the bouquets on the table by the door.

"I thought they might bring some colour to the tent," Rose told James. "I've long thought about planting a garden somewhere in the compound. Wouldn't that be nice?"

"It would certainly cheer the boys up."

She glanced sideways, considering the sight of him in uniform. Since his arrival, she had only ever seen him wearing pyjamas. Someone must have helped him dress. "You're walking," she finally said. She had meant it to sound cheerful, but it came out like an accusation.

James sighed. "Doc says I should be released in a day or two."

"You're not even walking on two feet yet."

"According to him, I should be able to. That's all that matters."

Rose pressed her tongue to the roof of her mouth, sidestepping an uneven plank. "Is it still painful?"

He stopped, wavering on one foot, and looked at her. He didn't nod, but she saw him flinch as he blinked. "Yes."

It was all he needed to say. "I'll talk to him," Rose said, lowering her voice. Surely, she could reason with Captain Eaton. If not, she could always bring it up with the Commanding Officer. The CO was a gruff man who rarely listened to the nurses, but she could try.

"Thank you," James said.

She led him inside the tent, placing her bouquet on the table near the entrance.

"Something to remember you by, nurse?" The man in the nearest bed said, a British soldier with wandering hands and an arsenal of dirty jokes. He grinned beneath his bandaged head, a cigarette dangling from his lips.

"These will last longer than your charm, I'm afraid," she replied, and slipped out of the tent.

Mae returned to their tent the following morning after her shift. She sighed, pulling the kerchief from her head roughly. "I can already tell today will be warmer than yesterday. Sleep will be impossible."

Rose was seated at the table with an oil lamp, writing letters home. "I'll be quiet if you want to try to sleep now, before it gets too warm," she said.

"No, I'm too wound up. One of my patients hemorrhaged in the night. It was quite an ordeal." Mae fell into the vacant chair. "Any news from home?"

"Margot has decided to become a VAD."

Mae grimaced and her hand shot up to cover her mouth. "I'm sorry. That was rude of me."

Rose shook her head and chuckled. "No, I understand." Women who had never shown any prior interest in nursing were suddenly flocking to war as untrained members of the Voluntary Aid Detachment, seemingly more interested in adventure than in caring for the injured men. That was exactly what her sister was doing, though Rose could not fault her for it.

"And Leo?"

"Not a peep."

"Perhaps he was only trying to impress James when he said he planned to enlist."

"That may be," Rose said, though it did not seem like something Leo would do. She sighed. "James told me yesterday evening they are sending him back to the Front in a few days."

"Already?"

"I don't see what good it will do. An injured soldier on the Front, barely able to march in line with his battalion."

"Does he want to go back?"

Rose lowered her voice. "Do any of them truly want to go back?" Nobody would dare say it, of course, but it seemed to Rose that many soldiers who had volunteered their lives had quickly realized the horrors of war and might not be so quick to do it again, given the choice.

Mae wore a puzzled expression, her gaze far away. "I had a patient begging me to send him back last week. His sons were at the Front, and he was desperate to return."

"Was he badly injured?"

"A shell had exploded near him. Nearly blew his chest out. It was miracle he was still alive."

Rose was silent.

"We sent him back to England." Mae peered at her. "It's not easy, is it?"

Rose shook her head. "No. It isn't."

Rose arrived on duty to find most of the ward still sleeping. She prepared breakfast while the orderly washed and shaved each patient. She had hoped this particular orderly would not be on duty that morning. Patrick Blake had been at the hospital longer than Rose but had only recently been assigned to her ward. He was tall and lanky with a mess of dark hair and wore a constant expression of superiority. Most orderlies at No. 1 CGH were soldiers who had not qualified for duties at the Front due to age or physical and mental fitness. Rose did not know why Blake was deemed unfit, only that he had been a medical student prior to enlisting with the army, and therefore considered himself significantly more qualified than the nurses. He refused to recognize their rank as Lieutenant and resented having to take orders from them, frequently objecting when asked to do mundane tasks like sweep the floors or count the instruments, preferring to assist in the surgical ward. They had exchanged harsh words a few days earlier when Blake had refused to make beds. "That's a woman's job," he had protested, looking down at her over his hawk nose.

"I will remind you, Private Blake, that you were not sent here as a physician, which means you are under my orders," Rose had said, trying to keep her voice measured.

She was glad to at least see him attend to the patients without fuss that morning.

Sister Nicholls arrived shortly after. "Good morning," she said brightly.

Rose stirred the porridge. "Morning."

"We missed you yesterday."

"Did anything happen?"

"Nothing out of the ordinary. Privates Smith and Lockhart were returned from the surgical ward." She lowered her voice. "Corporal Marshall had another episode. Poor soul."

Rose began scooping the porridge into bowls.

"Did you bring those flowers?" Nicholls asked.

Rose glanced over her shoulder. She had forgotten about the roses. "I did." They already looked wilted. "I suppose I should give them more water."

"Colonel Hatfield is doing rounds this morning. Another large convoy is anticipated, so I expect he'll be issuing release slips."

Rose's heart deflated. "This morning?"

Nicholls nodded and checked her watch. "He should be here shortly."

Rose readied a tray with breakfast and capsules. She hurried through her patients, trying to make her way to James as quickly as possible. She placed the tray on the bedside table and brought her hand to his forehead. "Did you sleep well, Private MacLeod?"

The skin under his eyes was a shiny lavender. "Not a wink," he said.

"You feel feverish, Private MacLeod," she said in a raised voice. "Are you in pain?"

Blake looked up from his patient a few beds down, razor still in hand.

James looked at her quizzically. "I feel fine," he assured her. "No worse than usual."

"I should check your temperature." She placed the thermometer in his mouth and waited. The mercury levels barely moved. "High temperature," she announced. "I better take a look at your wound to make sure it hasn't reinfected."

James continued to watch her curiously but said nothing else until the orderly had moved on to a different patient farther down the tent. Nicholls was busying herself counting the stores.

"What are you doing?" he asked, barely above a whisper.

Rose was bandaging his leg. "Helping you." She stayed with him, feeding him mouthfuls of porridge. On his chart, she noted the incorrect temperature and made erroneous notes about his food intake. It was the only thing she could think to do. No one would question her records.

She brought him a hot water bottle before the Commanding Officer was set to arrive. "Take this."

James's eyes widened. It was already too hot in the tent, the air stale with sweat. He took it obediently, slipping it under the blanket. He flushed, his cheeks tinged pink.

When the CO arrived, Rose discreetly pressed the thermometer to the hot water bottle before sliding it into James's mouth.

"Sister Avery," Colonel Hatfield greeted her. "How is Private MacLeod this morning?"

"He appears to have taken a turn for the worse. I fear an infection." She showed him the thermometer. "Loss of appetite, loss of sleep. I've upped the dosage of his medication."

Colonel Hatfield barely glanced at the instrument. He sighed. "Well, it looks like you might stay with us a while longer, Private MacLeod."

James managed a curt nod. "Sir."

The CO turned to Rose. "Alert Captain Eaton."

"I will."

He moved on to the next patient. James took hold of Rose's hand before she left. His eyes bore into hers, conveying a look of immense gratitude. She gave him a quick smile. Neither spoke a word.

Rose made her way to the Matron's office after her shift. The end of summer had brought a wave of injured soldiers from the battlefields of Ypres, and a steady stream of convoys burred between the tents at all hours of the day, forming a cloud of dust that irritated Rose's eyes. She held her breath as one moved past her, blinking the cloud away.

"Come in," the crisp voice called when she knocked.

Rose entered to find Matron Grimshaw seated at her desk with a cup of tea and a pile of papers in front of her. "Good morning, Matron."

"How can I help you today, Sister Avery?"

Rose brought her hands together to keep from wringing them. "I have a patient, Matron. He has been with us for a while already but is not improving as well as we had hoped."

"Transfers must be discussed with Colonel Hatfield," Matron said, directing her attention back to the page on the desk.

"No, Matron. I wanted to inquire about possibly keeping him here longer. Not as a patient, but as a volunteer. I think it would help improve his health. To feel useful."

The Matron lifted her gaze, her head still bent. "What did you have in mind?"

"Perhaps landscaping or manning the stores. Or he could help the orderlies. They've been working day and night."

"The patient is well enough to care for other wounded men but too ill to return to his battalion?"

"I fear a risk of infection if he is returned to the trenches prematurely. The conditions are too unsanitary, and he is still only learning to walk on his injured leg. But I think he is strong enough to be of assistance to us." Rose waited for Matron to respond but was met with silence. She continued. "The orderlies are exhausted, Matron. We've barely allowed them to sleep all week."

Matron Grimshaw studied her. "Is this patient known to you, Sister Avery?"

Rose hesitated but gave a curt nod. "Yes. He's a friend of my nephew."

Matron inhaled deeply and set her pen down. She sat back, interlacing her fingers in her lap. "We cannot give preferential treatment to anyone, Sister Avery. We must treat each of our patients equally."

Rose nodded again under Matron's steady gaze.

"That being said…I agree we could use some additional help." She pulled a piece of paper from a drawer and started writing. "He can stay," she finally added, handing the slip to Rose.

Rose tried not to show her relief as she stepped forward to take it.

Matron cocked her head to the side, narrowing her eyes. "But I am moving him out of your ward. He can sleep with the orderlies if he no longer needs constant medical attention."

"Yes, Matron."

Matron sighed. "Heaven knows we will need the bed." She dismissed Rose with a wave of her hand.

Rose saw less of James after that. She was assigned to the night shift near the end of September and struggled to adapt to the change. The tent felt cold, and she missed talking with her patients, who slept while she tidied supplies and startled when she checked their wounds. On nights when they expected convoys, the stillness of the evening felt tense, minutes collapsing then moving with haste, leaving Rose to wonder whether the sun would ever break over the sand dunes again.

On one such night, as she waited for the bugle marking the end of her shift to sound, she slipped out of the tent for a breath of morning air. The grass was heavy with dew, the bruised sky threatening rain. She saw figures in the distance moving in and out of another tent, the last few stragglers of that night's convoy. Six men had been assigned to her ward, all of them horribly wounded. She rolled her neck, pausing to examine the sky.

"I thought that was you."

She turned to see James walking between the tents, his limp less pronounced now. He pulled on his cigarette and blew smoke to the wind.

She smiled. "I haven't seen you in a while. I thought you might have left."

"Without saying goodbye?"

She rubbed her arms to warm herself. "How is your leg?"

"Are you asking as a nurse or a friend?"

"A friend."

"Much better, thanks to you. But don't alert the CO yet." He offered her a cigarette, but she refused.

"I'm glad to hear it."

They were quiet for a moment, smoke drifting between them. The yolk of the sun cracked, spilling onto the horizon.

"Leo signed up," she said.

"I heard." James sounded grave. "I'm sorry."

A cold breeze blew past them, and the tent flap rustled behind her, the ropes straining and creaking. She studied him, considering his sombre expression. He had been such a cheerful boy. Shy, but energetic and kind. She had difficulty associating the young James she had once known with the man who now stood before her. "He thinks he'll get here by the end of the year," she said. "He's concerned the war will end before then."

James threw the end of his cigarette into the mud. "Weren't we all? It's been nine months since I enlisted. I also thought it would all be over before I got my chance."

"So did I," Rose said.

They let the words hang between them.

He turned away from her, his face half illuminated by sunrise. "You have a half day today, don't you?"

"How did you know?"

"Would you—would you care to join me for lunch?"

"We're really not supposed—" she started, softening the blow with a smile.

"I know. You can bring a friend. Or two. I would just like the opportunity to thank you properly."

Rose looked at the sky. "We might get rained out."

"We might not."

She considered it for a moment, then nodded. "That sounds nice."

His face widened into a grin. "Until this afternoon, then."

He left, hobbling on the planks as the sun all but disappeared behind clouds. Rose stayed a moment longer, until the sky broke, and she retreated into the tent, the sound of rain against the canvas roof drowning out the soft snores of her patients.

❧

James waited for them by the narrow trail that led through the dunes to the beach, holding a basket in one hand and a wool blanket in the other. Beside him was a man Rose did not recognize.

"Afternoon, Sisters," the stranger said, removing his cap.

"Good afternoon," Mae said, smiling widely.

"Sister Avery, I'd like to introduce you to Lieutenant Colonel Harold Archibald," James said. "My Commanding Officer. He was passing by, so he decided to pay me a visit."

"Yes, well. I wanted to make sure Private MacLeod here was still in one piece," Lieutenant Colonel Archibald said, slapping him on the back. "It's lovely to meet you, Sister Avery." He turned expectantly towards Mae, hand already extended.

"Sister Mae Harper," she introduced herself.

Archibald looked at James. "I can see why you're in no hurry to leave."

Rose hoped James's cheeks were pink from the sun.

James led the way down to the beach. His limp seemed more pronounced, trudging in the sand, but he refused Archibald's offer to carry something. There were a few children playing nearby but the beach was otherwise empty. The air was cool, the sun warm. James lowered the basket onto the sand and laid the blanket down for them to sit.

"This is lovely," Rose said, accepting a mug of sour wine from Archibald. "Where did you get all of this?" Fresh bread, soft cheese, tinned vegetables, preserves, and apples were spread across the blanket.

"Archibald took me into town this morning," James said. "We stopped at a farm for the wine and purchased the cheese and apples as well. This," he said, holding up a jar of crimson jelly, "my mother sent me a while back. I've been waiting for fall to open it."

Mae spread some of it on a piece of bread, her eyes growing with delight at the first bite. "What is this?" She drew her hand to her lips.

"Crabapple jelly. My grandmother's recipe."

"It's delicious."

Rose took a sip of her wine and stole a piece of cheese. "Truly, this was far more than necessary."

"It was the least I could do."

"Private MacLeod—" Mae started.

"Please, call me James."

"James, then," she repeated. "You're a friend of Leo's?"

"Yes. We've known each other since we were children."

"So you'll be frank when I ask if he is truly as wonderful as Rose makes him out to be?"

James chuckled. "She has good reason to be proud."

"Well, then I can't wait to meet him."

"If he heard you say that he might try to get here sooner."

"Is he on his way over?" Archibald asked, shading his eyes from the sun.

Rose cleared her throat. "Not yet," she said. "He's still in training. He only enlisted a few weeks ago."

"Good lad."

Rose forced a smile. She had received a postcard from Leo the previous week featuring a photograph of himself in his freshly pressed uniform, the gratification visible even in the sepia tones of the image. *Hope to see you soon!* he had scrawled hurriedly on the back. *Will a Lieutenant such as yourself still have time for a mere Private like me?*

She owed him a response, though she did not think she could acknowledge the possibility of his coming to France so soon. She wanted to tell him about her last bicycle trip through Widehem and Hubersent—to describe the sensation of the wind flapping in her veil as she cycled down the hill, Mae screaming as they swerved madly to avoid the flock of sheep crossing the road. It had seemed impossible that only fifty miles away, the same golden fields of wheat were being shelled, the soil swallowing men whole. She wished she could mention the eight hundred wounded that had lately passed through the hospital. She wished she could mention the sounds of the guns the wind carried from the Front, but knew the censors would blacken her words. She owed Anna a letter as well but could not think of what to say. *You can't keep us safe forever*, she had thought on the day she received her telegram from the CAMC. But forever had come to an end sooner than she had realized.

"We are in need of new men," Archibald said, turning to James. "And of old ones." The words were playful, but James remained silent.

"We had an interesting conversation about this very topic with the men at the Indian hospital recently," Mae said.

"The Indian hospital?"

"Yes, the one near Montreuil. Rose and I cycled there recently and visited the ramparts, where we met several soldiers from India."

The hospital itself was strictly off limits. Rose and Mae had found English sentries posted at the door when they rode by. The hospital was staffed by male doctors and orderlies only. Rose had thought the nurses' exclusion from the Indian hospitals was due to cultural or religious preferences, but the soldiers they had met at the ramparts suggested otherwise.

"It is a shame we are denied the ministration of a nurse," Sergeant Dast had said after introducing the rest of the group. They sported the same khaki tunic as the rest of the British Army, but instead of military hats wore turbans, their regimental insignia clipped at the front.

"Well, you seem to be getting on well without us," Mae offered. Only two of the four men were visibly injured, one walking with crutches while the other's arm rested in a sling on his chest. But Rose knew injuries could sometimes be concealed.

"It is true we have been lucky," Dast said, gesturing vaguely in the direction of the hospital. "The same cannot be said for other men in our unit." A shadow crossed his face. "And we might not be lucky again."

"Will you be returning to the Front soon?" Mae asked.

"You say it like we have a choice in the matter."

Another man, Private Khan, spoke. "We are as grain, flung into the oven a second time."

Dast nodded gravely. "It is unfair. We have done our loyal service once, and now they demand we do so again. That we risk our lives again. How many chances will we get?"

"The black pepper is being used up while the red pepper is being saved," said Khan.

Rose thought she understood his meaning. From their perspective, Indian troops were being sacrificed while British soldiers were protected. They might have thought otherwise had they seen the stream of British, Canadian, Australian, and New Zealand soldiers that passed through her ward, but how could they know when all they saw was their own wounded?

"And what did they have to say?" Archibald asked.

"They think it is unfair that they should be sent back to the trenches after they have been wounded serving the Crown," Mae said. "From their perspective, they have fulfilled their duty."

Archibald frowned. "A wound is not the end of our duty, Sister Harper. I rather think they should see this as a chance to prove themselves. Those who fight for the Empire earn a place in its future. You should know that as well as anyone." He looked at each of them in turn. "Besides," he added, taking a sip of wine, "if we returned every wounded man home, we would be left with no one."

"But perhaps it could be left to choice," Mae said.

Archibald raised his eyebrows, almost incredulous. "Allowing soldiers to decide whether they return to the trenches after being wounded would be absurd," he said. "Warfare demands consistency and reliability. Leaving the decision to personal choice would undermine both."

"Are you not concerned that soldiers who return to the Front before they are mentally or physically ready might endanger their battalion?" Mae asked.

Rose tried not to look at James.

"Those decisions are made by medical professionals such as yourself," Archibald said. "You decide when they return, do you not?"

"We do," Mae admitted. "But unless the injury is grave, we must always return them. The choice is hardly ours either."

Archibald gave a slight shake of the head. "These men signed up for this. And I believe they are in this together. Most of my men would not want to leave their battalion short-handed."

Mae shrugged. "I'm only offering a different point of view. One your men might not feel comfortable sharing with you."

Archibald turned to James. "MacLeod? Do you have anything to add?"

James swallowed a heavy mouthful. "The Indian soldiers might have a different perspective," he said after a moment. "They might see this war differently."

"Well, we are all fighting the same war, and if we want to win, we need to act like we are," Archibald said sternly.

Silence descended on the group. Rose peered into her wineglass, red swirling around the cup. When she glanced up, Archibald and Mae were looking in opposite directions, and James at the sand. She considered what she might say to ease the tension, but did not want to press the subject further. She was almost relieved when she felt the first few drops of rain, holding out her palm to the sky.

They quickly repacked the basket, Mae shaking the blanket a few paces away while Archibald lit a cigarette.

"Thank you," Rose said quietly to James before they left. "This was all very nice."

"My pleasure," he said, still looking slightly embarrassed. Rose reached for his hand and squeezed it before following Mae down the path to the hospital.

Along with the showers of autumn came a stream, a river, an ocean of wounded. Every night they received hundreds of injured men. Every morning, they sent more to England to make room for the ones who would quickly follow. Rose's ward filled and emptied, expanding and collapsing like a lung. There was no time to learn names, so they referred to the patients according to their bed number. Number six had a fractured pelvis. Number nine a bruised back from being buried by shellfire. Number twenty-two was paralyzed below the arms. Number thirty-four had a bullet in his shoulder and a blistering foot.

Rose felt exhausted. A tickle in her throat, a creeping fever, but she could not, would not, take time off. There was too much to do, barely any time for daily tasks, only dressings, dressings from dawn till dusk. With gauze slipping between her fingers, she tallied the number of wounded in her head. A hundred and seventy. Two hundred and twenty. Three hundred and ten. Five hundred. A thousand in less than a week. Was that even possible?

They knew nothing of what was happening at the Front, only heard the confused snippets shared by injured soldiers, but it was dreadful, a massacre—though apparently a military success. When she accompanied Mae to the quaint little church in town, they found only a few women in attendance, all dressed in black.

October folded into November with a glacial breath, and she and James grew closer. Now that he was no longer under her charge, Rose allowed their friendship to grow. On a few occasions, he had joined her and Mae on outings around Boulogne, and whenever either of them received a letter from Leo, they made it a habit to read it together wherever they could find a bit of privacy. It was a comfort to have someone familiar in France. Someone who knew the people and places that were synonymous with home.

She met him in the cemetery late one afternoon. James was waiting by the same wooden cross where they always met, the resting place of a young man who had died before either of them had landed at No. 1 CGH. Poor Officer Earl Moran, 1891–1914, was forced to chaperone their outings. Rose waddled through the thick mud, deliberately stepping in the puddles to clean her boots. It had been raining for more than a week, the sky a grey slate of steel. She imagined the walls of the trenches were sliding with muck. The number of cases of trench foot had ballooned recently. One Scottish patient protested loudly whenever she was in earshot, railing against the absurdity that trench foot was a punishable offence. "There are rats swimming at our feet!" He cried, incredulous. "When do we have time to change our socks or grease our feet?" Rose knew his rants might be the only worthy distraction from the pain of the edema in his foot and leg.

James held his cap in his hands, turning the brim between his fingers.

"Leo could have chosen a better day for his letter to arrive," Rose said, lifting her skirt to step around a patch of mud.

"There are two today. One from September."

Her heart gladdened. "The postal service must have known I needed comfort today."

"Shall I start?"

She nodded.

James read the first letter aloud. Rose averted her eyes, resisting the urge to close them entirely. She could almost hear Leo in James's voice, the way he emphasized certain words and expressed the note of irony that Leo always seemed to exude. James never interjected, not even when Leo described aspects of his training that James had no doubt experienced himself. There were moments when he would quiet, his eyes still roaming the page. Rose did not mind his censoring, though she wondered whether the verbal omissions were for Leo's benefit or his own. He finished the letter as he always did. "Give love to our dear Rosie. I'm writing to her next. Regards, Leo."

Rose shifted her gaze to James. "That must have been the one where he described the review with the horses."

He handed her the second envelope. "You may do the honours."

She hesitated. "Are you sure? He wrote it for you."

He nodded. She reached for the envelope, noting that it had already been opened. She slipped the pages from the sleeve and unfolded them.

"Dear chum," she started, the sight of Leo's familiar handwriting calming her. "Our daily routine continues as it has since the last time I wrote. There is nothing official yet, but it looks like we might sail before the end of the year. They said the war would be over before Christmas last year. I for one hope it won't end before this upcoming holiday season."

"We have been preparing for departure, being inoculated, etc. In a twist of irony, the worst baby of us all proved to be the doctor of our division. He has not stopped complaining of his sore arm since we received the last of our typhoid shots. It makes for good jokes, but his mood has soured."

Leo's letter continued for another page. Rose lost herself in the rhythm of his voice, the anecdotes he shared, until she reached the third page. Her name was there, inked in black, with the same familiar swoop of the R that adorned all her letters from Leo. She read the paragraph in silence.

With regards to your question about Rose, I can only say that you have my blessing. I always suspected you had your eye on her, and I will admit that the thought crossed my mind when I learned you had both found yourselves in the same place again. Be it fate or damn good luck, I can only say that I will never call you uncle.

I would say give my love to Rosie, but it sounds as though you already have.

Regards, your future nephew-in-law,

Leo

Rose felt colour rise in her cheeks. She glanced up. James's piercing green eyes bore into her, a look of hopeful determination on his face.

"James, I—"

"Rose," he interrupted, taking a step forward. "I felt that it was only right to ask him first, but I wanted you to know, to see, what he wrote, so that you could answer me without reservation." He reached for her hand, and she nearly dropped the letter. "I have always found you remarkable. Even as a boy, I was—" He chuckled. "I was completely enamoured with you. And finding you here after all I had experienced since coming to France. It felt like fate. Or damn good luck." He smiled, and she could not help but return the gesture. "I know this hasn't been the most ordinary of courtships, but I have enjoyed getting to know you better. And I think you've enjoyed it too." He didn't wait for her confirmation. "I want to make my intensions clear. I want you to be my wife."

Rose's mouth was dry. "James," she said, as softly as she could, wanting most of all to point out the absurdity of it all. To be propositioned in a cemetery during a war by a man she had only ever considered a child.

Something in her voice made him waver, but his hopes redoubled. "You don't have to answer right this moment. I understand I've taken you by surprise. I would only like for you to consider my proposal."

She squeezed his hand. "James, I'm flattered. Truly. But you must know I can't get married. Not now. I would have to leave my post. I would have to renounce nursing. I could never do that knowing Leo is on his way to the trenches. Knowing so many of these men need my help."

He shook his head. "We can keep it a secret. Or we can wait. I don't mind."

"That's very kind of you, but—"

"Will you at least consider it?"

She took a deep breath, studying the man standing in front of her.

He was right in saying she had enjoyed their growing familiarity. He was kind and made her laugh. But she had never thought of getting married, not even as a girl. She had always known she wanted to be a nurse and had pursued that goal alone, never thinking that she was renouncing anything else in the process. But now it was something else. Something more urgent. What kind of world was this for marriage? She had seen friends dash for the chapel as soon as war was declared, claiming that any morsel of joy was worth grabbing even in the face of death. And some part of her did believe that to find love and gladness in the midst of this inhumane war was to prove that all was not lost. And yet, she still considered it absurd.

She nodded. "I will."

A grin split James's face. He took the letter and brought the palm of her hand to his lips. She felt a rush at the sensation of his skin on her fingertips.

December arrived, and Rose's thoughts grew fragmented, the days collapsing together. Every morning, she returned to her ward to find new faces and discover more unimaginable wounds. Nothing could have prepared her for this, not even the lectures in military nursing they'd all had to attend on the passage over. She had turned to this profession with a desire to heal but could hardly believe all the ways men found to annihilate one another.

She awoke to a bitter breath of wind billowing against the walls of her tent one morning, threatening to blow it down. Rose pulled on the wool underwear she had recently purchased in Boulogne, knowing the summer garments she had packed in June would soon be unsuitable. Why had she not packed any winter clothes? Perhaps in the depths of her mind she had not expected to stay so long. It seemed a distant past now. Dressed in her layers, she opened the flap of the tent and paused, marvelling at the blankness of the landscape.

"What is it?" Mae asked, arranging her veil in the reflection of her small compact mirror propped on a stack of books atop her trunk.

"Snow," Rose said breathlessly.

It had fallen in the night, caressing the tent without noise.

Mae joined her. They listened to the stillness of the morning, the winter blanket muffling the noises of war. There were no thundering guns in the distance, no ambulances moving on the gravel road, no marching footsteps, not even the peep of birds. Everything was quiet.

"Well," Mae said after a moment, reaching for her coat. "It might be time for us to return our bicycles."

Rose stepped into the snow, leaving traces of herself behind.

She received no letters from Leo that month, though she thought of him more often as the year drew to a close. Would he be able to tell her when he arrived? Would he hint at it, if he was stationed nearby?

Winter dragged on, the days shrinking to little more than a blur of grey light. The hospital emptied as more men were evacuated to England.

"They're sending me back, aren't they?" James asked when she met him outside the church hut one blustery morning, the haunting notes of a piano drifting from inside.

There was a strange look in his eyes. It was more than concern. It was the sunken look of someone who knew he was condemned to die. Someone who understood that death had been added to the list of equipment he carried since the day he had slipped his arm through his khaki uniform. His luck had run out.

Rose nodded, unable to confirm his suspicion with words. Captain Eaton had already told her James was needed back in the trenches.

James cast his eyes towards the dunes.

She met him again at the entrance of her ward on the day of his departure. In the shadows of the tents, he bent down to kiss her cheek, his hand pressing into hers.

"There's something I want you to keep."

James pulled out a small leather notebook from the pocket of his coat, the same one she had seen him write in on numerous occasions. She knew it contained poetry from the few times he had read to her from it.

Rose reached for it and turned it over in her hands, fingering the leather string wrapped tightly around it.

"Won't you need it?"

"I'd rather it stays safe with you."

She heard in his tone the suggestion that it was himself he wanted her to keep safe.

"Take care, Rosie," he said with one final glance at her face, his eyes drinking her in.

He did not repeat his question and she gave him no answer.

She watched as he turned and gradually slipped from view, walking to the ambulance that would take him down the road to Boulogne, back to his regiment, back to the ditches of war. She knew at that moment that if he crawled into the trenches again, he would not come out. And she had been right.

CHAPTER 13

"What was his name?" Millicent asks.

"Mr. Hughes."

Millicent giggles. "Why Mr. Hughes?"

"I'm not sure," Rose says. "Your aunt Margot named him."

Rose had enjoyed sharing this childhood memory with Frederick, but now, with Millicent peering at her with Jeanne's perceptive eyes, it seems to bring her too close to Anna, too close to Leo. She worries for an instant that Millicent will ask her more questions, but she simply shakes her head, laughing softly to herself.

"Mr. Hughes," she mutters under her breath.

They are on the swing on the front veranda, seeking refuge from the growing midday heat. The rest of the family is at church, but Millicent sprained her ankle bouncing down the stairs that morning, and Rose offered to stay home with her. As soon as she had heard the child's wails, she had sprung into action, inspecting the injury and sending for bandages to wrap the quickly swelling ankle.

"Not broken," she had assured Jeanne, who had come running into the room with a fright. "Only a tumble," she added softly to Millicent, trying to ease her tears. It had felt good to be needed, even for a moment. To feel the familiar comfort of her nursing skills in action once more.

Rose had always liked working with children, and as she took care wrapping her niece's foot, she wondered if perhaps this might be a new professional avenue for her—nursing of a sort that she could bear return to. But a realization had immediately settled over her. She did not want to return to nursing. Not at all. She did not want to wear the uniform, did not want to answer to *Sister*. But perhaps, she thought as she clipped the bandage and dried tears from Millicent's red cheeks, there were other ways to use her skills. Perhaps even as a mother.

She had made some chamomile tea for pain relief and instructed the child to keep her foot elevated. It was now resting on Rose's knees.

"Have I met my aunt Margot?" Millicent asks, turning her head on the mound of pillows. The swing creaks under her slight movement.

"You have," Rose says. "She visited many years ago, when you were still a baby." Margot was the only one of the sisters who had managed to visit Jeanne after Millicent was born, Ellen too busy with work, Rose already in France, and Anna refusing to travel to avoid taking space needed by soldiers.

"Where is she now?"

"She lives in France."

"Is she the one who sent us those French books?"

"She very well might be."

"Grandma says she can teach me."

"So could I. So could Uncle Frederick."

"Do you all speak French?"

Rose nods. "Oui."

"What other languages do you speak?"

"Only those two, I'm afraid. But your uncle speaks many more."

Millicent looks away, contemplating the front yard blazing with heat. "I think I would like to speak many languages."

"Then you could read many books," Rose says, lifting the volume splayed open on Millicent's lap. *The Merry Adventures of Robin Hood.* She remembers it from her own childhood. Turning to the first page, Rose checks for Frederick's signature, but finds Silas's instead, along with doodles of arrows and forest animals. She looks to Millicent. Her eyes are closing, the heat embracing. Rose sets the book down and places a hand on Millicent's legs, holding her in place while she swings gently back and forth.

Every time Rose has entertained the thought of leaving nursing behind, it is quickly chased by another: who would she be without it? Nursing had been the cornerstone of her life. She has never imagined herself as anything else. A wife? A mother? Rarely has she envisioned having children, mostly because she never wanted to give up nursing for marriage. Never wanted to trade her work for the smallness of domesticity. But if she chose to let it go—not for marriage, but for herself—what then? Could she make space for more in her life? Was there still time? Already thirty. No longer a spinster, but a thornback.

She has no illusions about what it means to be a mother. Watching Jeanne these past few weeks has laid it bare. There is nothing tidy about it. It requires a significant change, a dismantling of the self to give to others, piece by piece. Most of the time, exhaustion seems to wear Jeanne down to the bone. She had been such a sunny, obliging child, but had grown into a woman who seemed, at times, to have misplaced herself. And yet, she was happy—truly, deeply happy. With a husband and children, she had made exactly the kind of life she always wanted. But Rose cannot think of Jeanne as a mother without thinking of Anna. Where Jeanne was giving herself away in pieces, Anna had been hollowed out all at once by the loss of her child. Why was there a word for a woman who lost her husband but none for a mother who lost her only child?

The others return from church, Oliver and Amelia tearing at their Sunday best before they even walk through the door.

Oliver darts up the steps to peer at his eldest sister. "Are you better?"

Millicent tries to stifle a smile, closing her eyes in feigned exhaustion. She pats him on the head. "I would be better if you brought me the magazines from your room."

Rose casts her a pointed look as Oliver dashes off, but she cannot fully suppress her smile. "Where are Silas and Émilie?" she asks Jeanne, taking Amelia's sticky hand to help her up the steps.

"Silas had to pick something up at the office," Jeanne says, fanning herself with her purse. A light sheen of sweat clings to her face, but she smiles as soon as she sees Millicent. "Darling," she says, her voice soft. "How are you feeling?"

Millicent sighs deeply. "Some sweets might help."

Jeanne and Rose exchange a quiet, knowing smile. "She's fine," Rose says in a low voice.

Jeanne nods. "Good," she says, just as Oliver comes rushing out the door again clutching a stack of magazines to his chest.

"I'll stay with them," Rose says. "You go change."

Silas and Émilie return an hour later, the sound of the door catching everyone's attention. Émilie enters first, her straw hat tipped at an odd angle, her cheeks flushed from the walk back. Silas follows a step behind.

"It is sweltering out," Émilie says, swiping tendrils of damp hair from her neck as she removes her hat.

"I nearly fainted walking back," says Jeanne.

"I hope you told Anna to pack lightly."

Rose, who had been watching Oliver attempt to teach Amelia new words with her wooden blocks, looks up sharply.

Jeanne hovers over Millicent, trying to make her more comfortable on the sofa. "I tried to persuade her to leave her mourning clothes at home, but I doubt she will listen." She catches Rose's alarmed gaze and straightens. "Did I not tell you? She wrote this week to say that she had changed her mind and would love to visit."

"You didn't tell me," Rose says, her voice thin.

"I'm sorry. I assumed I had—or that she would have told you herself." Jeanne's brows knit together.

Rose swallows, a sudden unease settling in her chest. She cannot bring herself to admit that she has not opened her last two letters from Anna.

"Well," Émilie says. "Hopefully the heat breaks before she arrives."

"When is she coming?" Rose asks.

Jeanne reaches for an empty glass by Millicent's side, already crossing the room to refill it. "I can't remember. Silas?"

"In two weeks' time, I believe," Silas says, stretching languidly in the chair by the window, pulling at his tie.

Rose keeps her eyes on the blocks for a moment longer. *CAT* becomes *HAT*, followed by *CHAT*, which Amelia pronounces *cat* again. Not wrong, Rose thinks before rising to her feet. "I'll go write to her now," she says, though she has no intention to.

In her room, she finds Anna's letters where she left them, in the top drawer of the desk. The first one is brief—an apology of sorts, for the way they left things, but the second is even shorter. *I have decided my boys can survive a few weeks without me. I look forward to speaking with you in person.*

Rose settles into the desk chair, her fingers absently brushing the edge of the envelope. Through the window, green leaves rustle in the tall trees. She should have known Anna would not want to be left behind. Not this time. Not again. And just as Rose was beginning to feel like herself again. Anna's presence would threaten that. Anna would be a reminder, always, of Leo—of everything Rose has not yet allowed herself to face.

How could she ever move forward with Leo always at the forefront of her mind?

He had sent her a letter at the end of 1915, announcing his arrival in London and detailing the passage over. Then, in early January, a few words to let her know he had crossed the Channel. He was tight-lipped about where he was stationed, though he seemed to hint at his also being in France. *I have finally joined you and Margot*, he had written.

Three of them in France. Three of them at war.

I can feel both of you here, Margot wrote on the back of a postcard featuring l'Hôtel-de-Ville in Arc-en-Barrois, a small town in northeastern France. *It comforts me to know you are close*. Rose could feel them too, that inexplicable sensation of proximity she had always felt at home, knowing everyone she loved lived nearby. Yet it was not comforting to have them near now. Not here. Not in France. Not in the middle of a war, guns sounding in the distance. What she felt was mild panic. Panic at the thought that this feeling of proximity might extinguish itself at any moment and that she would know, deep in her bones, that she had lost one of them. Surely, she would know—would sense it somehow.

Knowing Leo was less likely to write to his mother from the trenches, Rose had reinvigorated her own correspondence home. It had become more difficult as the months passed to find anything worthwhile to say, but she took the time once a week to sit and write. One evening in late January, her sodden feet propped on the iron stove, the wind howling outside, she opened a letter from Anna. The script slanted on the page unhurriedly as she detailed the activities of her women's group, which met every Monday and Wednesday to knit socks, plan fundraisers, share worries about their sons and husbands, and now, it seemed, to learn to defend the city in case of a German invasion, meeting at a shooting range at Long Branch to practice their shot.

The gun is much heavier than I expected, but nothing compared to what our boys carry every day, Anna wrote. Rose chuckled and made a mental note to fill Margot in. *Anna with a gun?* She read on, skimming the next few lines. More news about their father, who was busier than ever as younger colleagues left for war, and of Ellen, who had now taken on the care of a second patient, a young man who had lost both legs to a blast and had come home to a mother already grieving her husband. A note about Jeanne inviting them east that summer. Then, at the end of the page, words Rose had never expected from Anna. *I am so proud of each of you,* she wrote. Rose set the letter down, wondering when Anna had changed her mind about her involvement in this war.

Winter passed in a blur. In February, Rose and Mae were sent back to England for a temporary reassignment—a chance for rest, Matron said. Rose was disinclined to leave France but also recognized weeds of melancholy sprouting in her mind.

London was changed, the atmosphere grim, the nights as black as the border surrounding the newspaper page listing the dead. People seemed tired, overworked. The city had suffered considerable damage from air raids, but nothing would stop Londoners from going about their day. Everywhere Rose looked, women in uniforms had replaced men lost to war.

She found her spirits somewhat restored after waking in the warm bed of the hotel room on Great Russell Street but found it strange to be back among civilization. The luxury of locking a door or conjuring light with the flick of a switch came with an odd sense of guilt. It was an adjustment, but certainly an improvement. Reliable laundry facilities meant she and Mae no longer needed to hang their uniforms to dry around their beds, or lose a veil to stains, and, most importantly, could wash sanitary cloths instead of relying on wads of field dressings, which they had to sneak away from the wards. The work, too, was more regular. After a few days in London, they were stationed at the Duchess of Connaught Red Cross Hospital at Cliveden, where their patients had already been cared for by many capable hands before reaching them. There was less blood, less horror, less shock.

But no matter the comforts, no matter the ease, Rose only wished to get back to France, to be closer to Leo, especially after she received word from Lieutenant Colonel Archibald informing her of James's death. *You were such a balm to him,* he said. He must have been in a state when he wrote to her, because he said much more than they normally did. *It saddens me to have to share this news with you, perhaps more so than it did to tell his mother. I suppose it is different when you have met a loved one. When you can picture them receiving the news so clearly.* Then, abruptly—*My deepest sympathies, Sister Avery.*

The news was terrible, but not unexpected. She did not know how, but she had known. James had answered only one of her letters since his departure from the hospital. She had asked after his health, his well-being. *It is worse than I remembered,* was all he'd said.

Rose wrote and rewrote a letter to Leo, trying to find the words to tell him. She had learned to be the bearer of bad news, to tell strangers about the passing of young men whose names she barely knew. But to tell Leo that his oldest friend was lost felt beyond her.

For three weeks, she carried the weight of the news alone, at one point even considering sending him Archibald's letter instead. But the longer she stayed in England, in the world of the living, the more she remembered how delicate a task this was. In the end, she wrote a single page, informing Leo that she had recently learned of James's death, and that she was terribly sorry for his loss. She did not bother to say, as she normally would have, that James was brave to the last. Leo knew the truth of it.

They returned to Étaples in early spring, Rose feeling more restored than she had in months, but the feeling did not last long. She fell ill almost as soon as she stepped foot in No. 1 CGH, confined to her camp bed with the same raw throat, blinding headache, and wet cough that plagued her patients. Trench fever. She had long suffered through the inadequacies of the hospital by reminding herself that the men in the trenches had it worse, but now the trenches had come to her. It was a slow recovery, Mae sitting at her bedside after every shift.

"You should keep your distance," Rose told her between coughs. "I don't think I can care for you just yet."

"Nonsense," Mae said, stirring honey into her tea. "A dozen men on my ward are sick. If I was going to catch it, I would have already. Besides, I need to make sure you're recovered by your birthday."

Rose thanked her, tea steaming her face. "How did you know it was my birthday?" It wasn't for two weeks still, and she did not remember telling anyone. Birthdays seemed such a small affair, in the grand scheme of things.

"Margot told me, when I wrote that letter on your behalf. Said she'd try to send you something, but I told her I had it covered."

"You really don't have to."

"Of course I do."

"What did you have in mind?" Rose sipped at her tea, the water scalding her throat. She winced.

"How does a trip to the beach sound? Away from the hospital. Just the two of us."

"That sounds lovely."

"Good." Mae picked up her veil and secured it in place. She reached for Rose's hand. "Something to look forward to."

By the time her birthday came, Rose was only too glad to leave the hospital. They made their way to Boulogne, still undecided about where they might go. Mae insisted on going somewhere new, but they were somewhat limited by the lines marking the Front.

Pockets of men in dusty uniforms waited on the platform while Mae considered their options on the board, Rose only half listening. The fever lingered, fogging her mind. She turned her face away from the sun, squinting. There, she saw him.

He was standing a few paces away from them, a lit cigarette

dangling from his lips. He looked leaner than the last time she had seen him, his shoulders hunched under an invisible weight, but it was him.

Mae paused, noticing Rose staring. "What is it?"

"It's Leo."

Mae twisted around. "Here? Where?"

Rose stood transfixed. She said his name again, louder this time, waiting only long enough to see him turn his head before rushing to meet him. His face broke into a grin of surprise. He scarcely had time to flick his cigarette to the ground before she jumped into his arms.

"Rosie!"

His frame felt even smaller against hers, his muddy uniform ill-fitting. She embraced him tightly before letting go to peer into his face. "What on earth are you doing here?"

"Going back to England for a bit. On leave." He motioned to the man standing beside him. "This is Officer Warren Gillis."

Gillis placed an unlit cigarette between his lips and raised his hand in a sort of wave. Both looked worn out. Rose shook his hand, and introduced Mae.

"When is your train leaving?" she asked, turning to Leo. "Why didn't you tell me you were passing through?"

"Last-minute orders. You know how it is. I wanted to stop by the hospital, but we weren't allowed. I suppose I should have written."

"Do you have time for lunch? A cup of tea?"

"Our train leaves in half an hour." Leo hesitated. "But the boat to England doesn't sail until this evening. I suppose I could catch a later train." He turned to Gillis. "Care to join us?"

He shook his head. "Thank you, but I don't think I can stay on my feet much longer. I might take a room in town for a quick rest and a wash before going to England."

Leo nodded. "I'll meet you at the docks, then."

"What do you want to do?" Rose asked once Leo had exchanged his ticket. "We packed a lunch if you wanted to find a quiet spot along the water."

Leo smiled, the dirt enhancing the creases on his neck. "While I'm certain whatever you have in that basket is lovely, I feel I've been eating in sand for months. I was very much looking forward to a real meal."

Mae smiled, swinging the basket behind her. "We know a few places."

They took him to a small bistro in town. Leo devoured pastries and coffee, the sugar mixing with the dirt on his chin. Afterwards, they took him to a beach. Mae and Rose opened the bottle of champagne while Leo slid into the waves. He dashed and jumped, howling from the cold, and came out looking cleaner and much more refreshed than before.

"How were you that dirty?" Rose asked, seeing the dust fly from his uniform as he snapped it to the wind.

"I was buried alive a few days ago," he said simply, buttoning his coat. His tone was grave but he did not elaborate.

They sat on the beach talking until the sun started to dip in the sky, at which point Mae returned the empty bottle to her basket. "I should bring this food back to the hospital before it spoils." She bid them goodbye and went on her way.

Rose turned to Leo. His hair was drying in patches, lifting at the crown. "You're looking more presentable. Shall we grab dinner in town?"

Leo got to his feet, lending his hand to help her up. "I need to run a few errands first," he said.

They returned to town, dashing in and out of shops before they closed for the day, speaking of nothing, speaking of home. There was a question she had wanted to ask him, one she had pondered for months but never found the words to put to paper, and she wondered again if this was the time or the place.

"Why did you enlist?" she finally asked over dinner.

He looked surprised, pausing to take a sip of wine. "You were the inspiration," he said, as though it should have been obvious. "You were even braver than I. Than most of the men in my unit. You didn't even blink an eye when war was declared. It was as though you had been preparing your whole life, while the rest of us scrambled to catch up."

They sat facing each other over plates of veal cutlets with rice topped with a mushroom sauce and a side of green beans. Leo had already eaten most of his (his first substantial meal in months, he said) while Rose picked away at hers.

"I didn't know what I was getting into," she said.

"None of us did."

A waiter passed the table, casting a shadow on Leo's face.

"Your hand keeps twitching," Rose said. She had noticed it earlier that afternoon.

Leo was chewing. He waved his fork in the air, hand gripping the steel. "It's nothing. Just tired is all. And hungry." He took another bite, filling his cheeks.

Rose was quiet. Leo swallowed, took another sip of wine, and looked up at her.

"He said he left a notebook with you."

Rose furrowed her brow. "Who?"

"James. He said he left it with you before he returned to his battalion. For safekeeping."

Rose blinked twice. "He did."

Leo nodded, his eyes registering her reaction. She felt stunned. They had spoken only briefly about James in their letters, but Rose felt suddenly shy.

Leo was quiet for a moment. "Had you accepted him?"

Rose picked up her own glass of wine, bringing it to her lips before lowering it again. She shook her head. "I thought I might. Later on. But part of me knew. I was wholly unable to envision that future, even when I wanted to."

Leo nodded, casting his eyes downward. He resumed eating and finally said, "Did you read it?"

"The notebook?"

"Yes."

"No. I haven't." She had tucked it away, thinking perhaps James would ask for it again, although she knew he would not. In truth, she had nearly forgotten about it.

"I think he would want someone to read it."

Rose shifted in her chair, shaking her head at the waiter who had reappeared with a carafe of water. "I can send it to you," she said when he left.

Leo shook his head. "No," he said resolutely. "He didn't want it back in the trenches. He wanted you to have it."

Rose gave a small nod. "I'll keep it safe."

They returned to the train station on foot. Leo had offered to escort her back to the hospital, but she waved him off, saying she preferred to see him safely seated on the train that would take him back to England.

As they waited on the platform, he took out a small brown box tied in a white ribbon from his pocket and handed it to her.

"What's this?" she asked, smiling under her suspicious gaze.

"You didn't think I had forgotten your birthday, did you?" He grinned.

"It's not for a few days still." She unravelled the ribbon and opened the box to find a delicate gold locket, engraved with a solitary rose.

"When did you manage to get this?"

"When you were busy talking with someone outside the little green shop. I was planning to buy you something in England, but when I saw this..."

"It's beautiful." She reached for him and embraced him tightly. She had left him a boy who brought her chocolates and sweets for her birthday and now found a man, smartly dressed in his military uniform.

The train announced its arrival with a prolonged whistle. The crowd hurried to gather their things, stepping forward while the train continued to roll by, as though they would arrive at their destination more quickly if they were the first ones aboard.

"Write when you reach England. And write to your mother. She must be worried sick about you."

"About both of us," Leo said. He lifted his packed sack onto his shoulder. "It was lovely to see you, Rosie."

The train slowed. Rose waited as the platform emptied around her. The train idled until the clock struck seven-thirty, at which point it let out another misty wail and started forward. Rose waved to Leo through the compartment window and stood until the train had disappeared from view before making her way back to the hospital, clutching the locket to her chest.

Sitting in the guest room at Jeanne's house, Rose pulls the locket from inside her dress, turning it over in her fingers. She studies it for a moment, the weight of it familiar.

Could she ask Anna not to come? Could she try to explain that she needed more time? But Anna wouldn't understand, not unless she explained why, and the thought of telling her that she had failed Leo in every way filled her with a deep, sinking shame.

She can hear the children making their way up the stairs and thinks she should check on Millicent again. Slipping the locket back inside her dress, she takes a deep breath, letting it out slowly, and rises to her feet.

CHAPTER 14

It takes nearly a week for Frederick to hear back from Petro Koval, his letter travelling from Halifax to Ontario to finally arrive in Montreal, following the path Koval had taken in the years following the war. Frederick had not expected to meet him in person, but as soon as Koval suggests it, he knows he must. He packs a bag and heads to the station, purchasing fare for the next train. Before the whistle can sound, he ducks into the telegraph office to send two quick messages: one to Silas, apologizing for his sudden departure, and the other to Rose, informing her of his trip. WILL EXPLAIN LATER, he tells them both.

He settles into his seat, eyes scanning the scene outside. The platform hums with haste, the rush of bodies. So much has changed in the world, yet at times it feels like nothing at all. Frederick thinks back to the early days of his return to Nova Scotia, the way nearly every aspect of his life had felt like a jarring counterpoint to his four years in Ruhleben. The solitude of his own little cottage, a reversal of the crowded barracks. The simple pleasure of preparing meals to his own taste rather than suffering through the unpalatable food provided in camp. Even the act of turning a key in his own lock had felt, for months, like a treat. His freedom was richer for what he had once lost. Yet he had never revisited that time with conscious intent, looking directly at it rather than letting it loom in the periphery. He considers what he might ask Koval, how he might begin the conversation, and slowly, his thoughts slide into memories.

Frederick had woken that first morning in Ruhleben to the sound of tramping on the stairs, the first light of morning creeping through the gaps in the slated roof above his head. A guard burst through the door, shouting for them to get up. The bodies pressed at either side of him groaned, the air heavy with the smell of damp straw and sweat. Frederick's first thought was the slow, desperate realization that the world had come undone, and he had gotten caught in its unravelling.

"Aufstehen!" The guard shouted again, the word sharp as a whip crack. Frederick winced, remembering the sting of the baton. More quickly, the men rose to their feet and made their way outside.

All day, they moved under orders. To the roll call, to the barracks, to the mess hall. Breakfast was a cruel joke: a slimy cup of acorn coffee and a shard of black bread, so dense and stale it might as well have been made of stone. Then came the order to wash. The guards gestured towards a few horse-feed tubs, their water already crusted with ice. Frederick stood back, watching with mild disgust as men took turns dunking their hands into the murky water, scrubbing at their skin with a single, rapidly shrinking sliver of soap. He pulled at the collar of his shirt, cold air swooping in, before deciding he could wait.

The Commandant made another appearance during the third head count. He stood before the crowd, eyeing them with satisfaction, a cigar ever-present between his teeth. One of the guards at his side stepped forward to read the long list of rules, the conditions of their internment interminable. No smoking in the barracks. No drinking. No card-playing. No gambling. Anyone in breach of these rules would promptly be escorted to a solitary cell and deprived of anything but bread and water. Because they had been classified as enemy aliens rather than prisoners of war, they would not be forced to work. Newspapers were strictly forbidden. They were allowed to write home, but only on postcards for sale at the canteen near the grandstands. The postcards would pass through a censor, the Commandant added with a scrape of his throat. "So mind what you write."

Despite the warning, Frederick headed straight for the canteen, desperate for a way to reach his family. He imagined his mother learning of his internment in the papers—the panic she would feel. He had thought of alerting them to the possibility of his internment, but had been too hopeful, too naive to think it would actually come to pass. Now he only felt foolish.

He found the canteen exactly where it had been on his last visit. It had seemed impossible the night before, but here he was in the place where only six months earlier he'd lost two marks and ten pfennigs to Christopher in a bet. The Ruhleben Trabrennbahn, as it was known before the war, was a horse-racing track two miles west of Berlin. The crowd had consisted of a swirl of men and women in their finest then, voices bright with laughter, mingling freely under the warming sun. Now there were only distressed men in mismatched clothes searching desperately for any semblance of familiarity in the bleak expanse of their surroundings.

Frederick joined the line, making anxious conversation, but by the time he reached the front the shelves were nearly bare, the few remaining items priced beyond reason. Still, he reluctantly pulled out the money he had stuffed in his shoe that morning and purchased a postcard of horses racing around the track and his very own sliver of soap.

He looked for a place to write, not wanting to return to the loft. He settled for the grandstands, fingers frozen as he wrote. *Dear Father,* he began, the postcard propped on his knee. The letters took up too much space. He tried again, writing smaller. *This is where we are being kept for now. It has been converted to accommodate English civilian prisoners.* The tip of the pencil broke, leaving a streak of charcoal on the paper. Frederick cursed under his breath and looked up to see if anyone had overheard. Men were standing around, unsure of what to do with themselves. Frederick blew on the postcard and began again. *You can reach me at this address, though they might move us before you receive this.* He considered what he had written and pointed the pencil to the last empty space in the corner of the postcard. *Do not worry about me,* he added. He signed his name and barrack number (his new address, he supposed).

The following week unfolded in much the same way. Each morning, the men were roused at six, scrambled to the shared washbasins or to the open-air lavatories, swept their stalls, shook the straw sacks they had finally been provided, and joined the line for breakfast, spilling half the bowl of grimy coffee on their walk back before drinking its cold remains in the dark, freezing barracks. At noon they queued for dinner, always a miserably diluted version of soup, and returned at half past five for kriegsbrot and tepid tea. The hours in between were a patchwork of smoking, conversation, and roaming. It took all of ten minutes to walk from one end of the camp to the other, and numerous times a day Frederick spent those dismal few minutes trying to forget that he would soon be faced with another barbed wire fence.

The camp was loud, a discordant symphony of conversations, shouted orders, and the underlying hum of industry. Ruhleben, Frederick knew, was situated on the outskirts of industrial Berlin. All around them, there was only dull grey, and the unending stream of fumes pouring from the smokestacks of nearby factories. If he allowed his thoughts to linger on it for too long, Frederick could feel his throat constrict, the walls of the camp seeming to close in as even more prisoners arrived.

And every second of every day, rumours swirled.

"The United States are officially protesting our interment," one man told Frederick between bites of bread. It was mouldy and contained wisps of straw but was better than the blinding ache of hunger. He imagined a miniature bear had settled in the pit of his stomach, growling fiercely in complaint.

"The arrangements for our exchange are complete. It will only be a matter of days now," said another.

Frederick thought of chocolate melting on his tongue, of pastries dusted lightly with sugar, of thick slabs of cheese on warm bread slathered with butter.

"We're leaving on Monday," he heard someone say as he drifted to sleep one afternoon in the loft.

Someone else had said Wednesday. Another the twenty-seventh of November.

"I heard Friday," a second voice said. The voices were accompanied by the sound of cards snapping on the uneven wooden floorboards.

Card playing was forbidden, but they could usually hear the guards coming. Frederick wondered how they managed to see anything in the low light.

A chuckle. "Care to make this more interesting?"

The wind howled through the holes in the roof.

"What did you have in mind?"

"Even money we're out of here a week from today."

Frederick dreamt of lamb smeared with mint sauce, of a tall glass of merlot, of a steaming plate of duchess potatoes, drool soaking through his straw mattress.

Over a bowl of watery cabbage soup, Frederick heard another man say, "I'll bet you the best dinner you can order in London, *with* a bottle of wine, if we get there later than December first."

Frederick pretended his bowl contained lobster, cream, and an array of herbs. The bear in his stomach protested, the rumble now a thunderstorm.

I'm here, he wrote Klara when he got his hands on a second postcard. *I think of you every day. I look towards the city and wonder if you're safe. I can hardly believe you're so close, yet so far out of reach. Will you write to me?* He lifted his pencil. Will you acknowledge this mess, he wanted to add, but instead wrote, *Please assure me you're well.*

He did not know why he felt such an urgent need to hear from her. They hadn't spoken for weeks before his arrest. And yet, all he wanted was for someone to acknowledge that he was here, that what had happened to him was real. All he wanted was for someone to remember who he was, for someone to recognize this as the terrible injustice it was.

He also hoped Klara might be able to share some news, however covertly. He had not heard anything about the war since landing in the camp. They were completely isolated, and the only insight they could gain came from the trains that passed on the tracks outside the camp. Trainloads of ammunitions, cannons, and large iron cylinders rumoured to contain gas passed daily with troops.

Later, Frederick learned to read the direction of the trains as indication of whether the Germans were directing their efforts against the West or East towards Russia, but at the start of the war, they only corroborated the immensity and intensity of the war effort. He wondered if they had been right in their estimation of a swift blow of victory and felt a guilty sense of hope that they were, so that he might be released. It had not occurred to him yet that a German victory over England might not in fact result in his freedom.

As the days passed, the camp's atmosphere shifted, the initial shock of internment giving way to a restless energy. Men became impulsive, their daring fuelled by boredom and desperation. Uprooted from their former lives, they clung to one another. Talking endlessly, talking idly. "Where did they get you?" they asked, most eager for a reply only to recount their own capture. Some had been at home. Others at work. One in a disreputable club, which the officers had only been too glad to raid. They talked without listening. They talked to talk, to fill the air, to pass the time. They talked to see their experiences reflected in the stories of others.

A chant rose that first week.

"Are we downhearted?"

"No!"

It became a ritual, defiance in unison, shouted as though repetition alone could stave off despair.

When he received word from Klara, Frederick felt relieved that the frigid breeze that had preceded his internment had thawed. *It is torture to know that you are so near, yet impossible to reach,* she wrote with more passion than she had ever shown in the past. *Father forbade me from writing to you but I simply had to let you know that I am fine, if heartbroken by your forced absence.*

And with those words, the anger he had started nursing, imagining her receiving his letter only to discard it, laughing at him, dissipated. He was seen. He was no longer alone. *You cannot know what your support means to me,* he replied.

As November gave way to December, Frederick allowed himself

a fragile hope that the new year would bring his release. Everyone said it would. That once the year had turned, the Germans and the English would come to an understanding and release all civilian prisoners. With this promise in mind, Frederick allowed himself to follow the crowd. He laughed and joked, joining in the silly songs, a sense of cheerfulness rising in his chest.

They sang, loudly and without care for melody. They sang "John Brown's Body" and "Tipperary." When the old marching songs grew stale in their mouths, they invented new ones, bursting out lyrics until topical verses caught the ears of the crowd. They cheered for nothing and everything, driven by a desperate urge to defy, to object, to perform this small, shared act of resistance.

The guards responded with shifting rules and petty punishments, imposing new regulations as quickly as they forgot them. It made no difference.

"Are we downhearted?"

"No!"

But in the evenings, as they returned to their dark horse stalls and cramped lofts, the air of exuberance that filled their days quickly deflated. Melancholy returned as the men sat down over pitiful dinners. More quietly, they begrudged the food, reminiscing about meals they had once taken for granted, and thought of home. One by one, the men would settle down, their faces growing dejected in the greying light, and try to escape in sleep.

Frederick finally heard from his father three days before Christmas. *The world has become a strange place, my son, where even the innocent are caught in its tides*, he said. Frederick felt a pulse of relief. For some reason he had imagined his father might be mad at him for getting caught in the fray. He quickly wrote back. *Do not worry about me yet. I am certain I will be home soon.*

He did not mention the rats that scurried through the barracks while he tried to sleep, nor the worms he had found in his soup the previous day. He did not mention the itch on his scalp or the rash on his hands. He did not mention the furry feeling of his teeth or the lice he had found in his pubic hair when he had been marched to the public showers for his biweekly wash earlier that day, the water like ice down his back, his own body foreign under his curious gaze. He did not mention the unheated barracks, the way he woke every morning with chattering teeth. He did not mention his hunger.

The train pulls into Montreal early the next morning. Bleary-eyed, Frederick disembarks and makes his way to a nearby hotel to inquire about a room.

"How many nights?" asks the clerk behind the desk.

"I'm not sure," Frederick says, glancing at his watch. He is scheduled to meet with Koval in a few hours, but could he expect to leave the following day? "Can I start with three?"

"Certainly," the clerk says, jotting down his details.

He finds Koval's address easily, in an old building in need of repair. The flat is small, but large enough for Koval and his new bride. Olena hovers in the background of their conversation, preparing tea in the cramped kitchen, while her husband slowly unspools his memories for Frederick.

"It was easier to leave," he says when Frederick asks what brought him to Montreal.

They speak in hushed tones of German, the only language they share. Koval suggested it so that he might speak more plainly than he could in English, as Frederick knows no Ukrainian and only scraps of Polish.

"For a while, I even considered leaving the country," Koval says, taking a drag of his cigarette. "I wanted to return home, but I had no home to return to. I tried to immigrate to the United States, but that proved impossible. So, eventually, I came here. At least, I thought, there was a community here, where I might perhaps blend in."

Mrs. Koval brings over two cups, followed by the teapot. Her husband throws her a smile before pouring. Frederick leans over his cup, his eyes intent on the man seated across from him. *Where did they get you?* He wants to ask, but instead, he says, "Could you tell me what brought you to Canada in the first place?"

Koval eyes him, open but cautious. "That may take a very long time."

"I have time."

After a moment, Koval nods. "Sehr gut," he says, pulling on his cigarette again. Smoke prepares the way for his words. "I came to Canada few years before war, in 1912. Life in Galicia...it was not easy. Not for us." He sits back in the chair, his gaze drifting somewhere beyond Frederick's head. "We were Ruthenians, you see, which means that, most of the time, we felt like unwanted guests in our home. Vienna saw us only as peasants, as labour. The Poles, as intruders. And the Russians only thought of us when it suited them. No one cared for our language, our traditions, our way of life. We lived well enough, but always under someone else's shadow."

He takes a sip of tea, then another. "My uncle was a good man," he continues. "A generous man. He had left, made something of himself in Germany, and he did what he could to keep our family from poverty. We always had a roof over our heads and bread on the table. But there was no future in Galicia. We worked every day, but still were left with nothing. I wanted more. Like my uncle."

He reaches up to scratch his forehead, cigarette still glowing between his fingers. "We heard much about Canada in those days. We were told it was a place where a hardworking man could own land, could gain wealth. An old school friend of mine had immigrated a few years earlier, and he wrote to me about the opportunities to be had here. I was determined to come and make something of myself. For a time, it worked. My English was poor, but I was able to find work in a foundry. It was good work. Honest work. It allowed me to send money home to my family, to my sisters, all while living comfortably here myself."

Koval pauses, his brow furrowing. His voice grows quieter, more sombre. "Had I known then what I know now, I might never have come. Before the war, I had felt welcomed—or, if not welcomed, then at least tolerated. Those who did not want to see me simply looked away. But with the war, everything changed."

Frederick recalls how quickly his neighbours and friends had turned on him. "You became a target," he offers.

Koval nods slowly. "Yes. Though I was not initially concerned for my own safety. My thoughts were with my family back home. But then I lost my job. My employer told me he had no choice. There were so many men without work, and he could not, in good conscience, continue to employ an immigrant while men here were struggling. I suppose it had become something of an act of patriotism to dismiss us from our positions."

He shifts in his seat, flicking ash into the tray. "I wrote to my family, but I knew they could not help me as I had helped them. My uncle sent some money. But that was a temporary solution."

"How did you manage?" Frederick asks.

Koval gives a half shrug. "I did as I was told. I went to the police, I registered as a foreigner. I agreed to stay in the city, even though there was no work. But as the months passed, I decided I had to leave. There were rumours circulating that there was work in the United States, so I resolved to go. I knew crossing the border would be difficult—impossible, even. But I thought that if I could only take a train close to the border, I would be able to walk across. I only needed to get across. Then I would be free."

Mrs. Koval places a plate of half-moon pastries on the table. Her husband thanks her, then waits a moment for her to leave. He lowers his voice. "Some friends thought that I was risking too much, but most were intrigued. Willing to wait and see if I made it before trying for themselves. We were all desperate enough to consider it. But I was distracted. I got on wrong train, and when I asked the conductor in my poor English about our whereabouts, he called the inspector. They sent me back to Halifax, where I was arrested. They took what little I had left, including the watch my father gave me when I was a boy, the one thing I had brought with me across the sea. Within days, I was sent to a camp, along with the rest of us they called Austrians. I told them that I was not Austrian, that I had no loyalty to Austria. Austria was the empire, not my home. But it did not matter to them."

"You were an enemy alien," Frederick says softly.

"I was an enemy alien."

They observe each other for a moment, eyes searching. Then, Frederick asks, "What were the camps like here?"

Koval raises an eyebrow. "What were the camps like in Germany?"

"Awful."

"For us, too." Koval sighs. "We were held in an old iron foundry, confiscated from a German owner. It was large but in ruin—its walls crumbling, the air heavy with rust. The conditions were poor, though I might have tolerated them had it not been for the work."

"You were made to work?" Frederick asks.

"Yes."

Frederick opens his mouth but hesitates. Suddenly he does not want to point out that he, in fact, was not. Instead, he asks, "What kind of work?"

"Hard work. Clearing land, maintaining rail lines, farming." Koval gives a wave of his hand. "Whatever they needed. In all kinds of weather, under every condition. It might not have been so bad had they fed us properly. But, of course, they did not. Hunger makes even the smallest task feel impossible. And our tasks were never small."

That, Frederick remembered all too well.

"Though things did improve once your mother got in touch with me," Koval continues, his tone light. "A kind woman, truly. I appreciated her parcels of food more than she could know."

Frederick offers a small smile. "Yes, I can imagine. She tried to send me some food as well, but it spoiled before it could reach me."

He had been fortunate that others were willing to share their parcels with him, once families were allowed to send them food. Later in the war, the Red Cross had been granted the right to feed them, but only after the camp rations had dwindled to such a degree that they might as well have been starving them.

"Was it only Canadians in your camp?" Koval asks, grinding the end of his cigarette into the ashtray.

Frederick shakes his head. "British," he says, though the term seems absurd given the mix of men that landed there. Fishermen from Hull, sailors from the Caribbean, and traders from South Africa all shared quarters with tailors from the East End, jockeys from Hoppegarten, and businessmen from London, Cape Town, and Melbourne. The languages spoken were as varied as their backgrounds: Arabic, French, Spanish, Hebrew, Italian, Welsh, Yiddish, Russian, Afrikaans. Some had only the faintest ties to the Empire, their connection a mere passport or a distant ancestor, but all were bound together in this strange, unchosen community. "Though there were other Canadians, which I appreciated," Frederick adds.

Koval makes a noise of approval. "Yes," he says. "I understand. There were many different men in my camp, but some were from Galicia. It was a comfort to be with people from home." He looks suddenly wistful. "In the evenings, we found ways to be free, to travel home in our minds. One man was able to keep his accordion, and we played music. With whatever we could find. Spoons, pots. Anything to make noise. Anything to make music. And then we danced the Hopak, the Kolomeyka, on rotted floors."

Frederick thinks of their own chants, their own marching songs. *Are we downhearted? No!*

"I found other men who read," Koval continues. "We shared books, ideas, words. It was a small freedom, at the end of those long days." His voice trails off and he looks up at Frederick, his eyes filled with a quiet resignation. "I suppose it was not all bad."

Frederick nods. This was, at least, one way in which their experiences mirrored each other. The men of Ruhleben had also found small ways to be free.

Only a few weeks after their arrival, Frederick had seen an advertisement posted to the exterior wall of one of the central buildings. The poster was rudimentary—a scrap of paper with rough pencil lines inviting them all to a concert the next day. When he ventured outside that evening, Frederick was surprised to find a small part of camp transformed. A makeshift stage had been installed in the space between one barrack and the barbed wire fence that ran alongside it, crude wooden boards resting on two iron benches.

He joined the crowd, listening as they spoke about the five men seated on the stage. Professional musicians, they said, used to playing in the largest concert halls in Europe, who now sat in battered sweaters and clogs on a makeshift stage holding neglected instruments in their frozen hands. It was an odd sight—a desperate sight. But as the conductor drew his hand in a flourish and the violinists tucked their instruments under their unshaved chins, the details slipped away. The opening movements of Henry Purcell's *Golden Sonata* resounded through the crowd, bright and clear. Despite their ragged appearance, the performers seemed to be possessed by a divine bent, their fingers curling and skating on the necks of their instruments as they obeyed the twirling hands of the conductor. Strings were set ablaze. Sound waves rippled through the air, filling every corner of the desolate camp with a rich tapestry of notes. Frederick blinked back sudden tears, feeling the swell of the rhythm in his chest, in his fingers, on his lips. Embarrassed, he looked to the man standing next to him only to see that his face was also slick. They stared at each other for one strange moment. The notes were words of a shared language, the music a manifestation of the range of emotions they had suppressed for weeks. Then the man smiled, the melody wrapped up in silence, and Frederick felt the urge to laugh with relief. Perhaps beauty had not gone from the world entirely, he thought.

After that first concert, the camp had exploded with activities. Societies were assembled. A camp school was organized. A library was opened in one of the barracks, the men pooling their resources, and space was carved elsewhere for religious observances of all kinds. Some of the men, seeking diversion, started advertising their services on the central boiler-house, plastering its walls with scrawled bills. Mr. Abbott of Barrack 4, Loft B, was willing to exchange French or Spanish conversation for German. Mr. Westwood of Barrack 2, Box 25, promised to mend clothes and darn socks better and cheaper than anyone in the camp. Mr. Fernley was available to blacken shoes every morning between nine and eleven o'clock near the canteen. All those interested in forming a literary society should communicate with Dr. Ingram, Barrack 5, Box 9.

But these were only minor distractions, small ways to fill their empty days. It was not until negotiations for their release fell apart that they truly, finally settled.

The news came in March 1915, on a week of steady rain that left the camp glazed in winter. Chill winds nipped at Frederick's ears as he listened to the groans and curses volleyed at the Commandant when he made the announcement. The Germans had insisted on a one-for-one exchange of prisoners. But Britain, it seemed, held more than twice the number of prisoners and saw no reason to let them go. It was difficult to tell who was more incensed—the Commandant, for this political slight, or the inmates, who had been so clearly marked as pawns in the game of war.

A cloud of anger and disappointment had hung low over the camp for weeks. But as the men slowly came to terms with the fact that they would not soon be released, they set out to improve their living conditions, writing to the United States Embassy in Berlin to ask for medical supplies and other necessities, petitioning the guards to clean the latrines, organizing a mail delivery system—even assembling a small police force. If they were stuck in this place for the duration of the war, they reasoned, they might as well make themselves comfortable.

Frederick wanted no part of it. He refused to participate. Why should they accept this fate, settle into such a pitiful existence? He had been so certain of his impending release it was impossible to accept, quite suddenly, that it would not come. He resented their willingness to adapt, to make do, as if they could ignore the fact that every good thing in their lives had been ripped away. He didn't know where to direct his anger. At the Germans, for keeping him here, or the British, for refusing to negotiate? Or, even at himself, for not realizing how serious things had been until it was too late?

For months, Frederick stayed in bed, trying to drown out the grim reality of his life by plunging into news of the world outside. Newspapers were a recent allowance—in early spring, the Commandant had finally approved the sale of two dailies in the camp. Both were German, and naturally biased in their war news, but they were less sensational than some of the others Frederick had seen on newsstands in Berlin at the beginning of the war. And though English newspapers were still forbidden, they seemed to make their way into the camp with increasing frequency. Rumour was a guard bought them for one mark, sold them to a prisoner for ten, who subsequently rented them out at one mark per hour to other prisoners. This was one of the reasons, Frederick knew, the guards did not openly object to their improvement of camp. Many of them found ways to profit from it.

The price of the paper dropped a few days later, which was normally when Frederick borrowed the circulating copy, now crumpled and out of order. The news was out of date even by the time they entered the camp, so what difference did another week make? But rather than offering any comfort, they only made him feel worse. The news was always bad, always twisted. While the *Zeitung* dailies naturally boasted of German victories, the English newspapers clearly exaggerated their defeat, each one shaping the truth to fit their narrative. It was on the day that Frederick read contradictory accounts of the same battle—one claiming victory for the Germans, the other for the English—that he realized how malleable truth was.

He was disgusted with the world, disgusted with the war, disgusted, even, with himself.

Nothing could pull him out of it—until one day, a man approached him during dinner and asked if his name was Frederick Munro.

"Yes," Frederick said, chewing the single piece of spoiled potato he had found in his soup.

"I have been told you have a knack for languages." The man appeared older than Frederick, perhaps by fifteen years or so. He had short brown hair greying at the temples and lines around his eyes.

"I suppose I do."

"How many do you speak?"

"Fluently?"

The man laughed. "Or otherwise."

"Well, four fluently, but I'm rather good at Latin and Greek as well and have basic understanding of five or six more. So, I suppose a dozen."

A smile crept on the man's face as Frederick spoke. "I could use your help, Munro," he said.

"I'm sorry—who are you?"

He extended his hand. "Ira," he said. "Ira Gordon. Pleased to make your acquaintance."

Ira had been kept in Ruhleben far longer than the others, having been arrested in front of the British Consulate in Berlin the morning following Britain's declaration of war, the media pass meant to protect him serving instead as a target. Having suffered the camp in its most primitive state, he now navigated it with quiet authority, listening to everyone, offering comfort where he could, and trying to impose some order onto their lives. He had been instrumental in the establishment of the camp school, and spoke of it with such reverence that when he invited Frederick to join the voluntary group of teachers, Frederick found he could not refuse.

It was hardly a school. More of a stable loft, hastily partitioned into classrooms. The walls were thin, the noise from one room bleeding into the other, Italian clashing with French. But after those miserable few months Frederick had spent sulking on his own, it was a relief to find a community. The eager look of his students trying to grasp the grammatical rules of German, the gendered nouns of French, or conversational Italian was for a time the only thing that gave him any sense of purpose. But gradually, Ira convinced him to attend a lecture, then a play, until Frederick was fully engaged in camp life.

It would have been easy for him to slip further into the hole he had been digging for himself, to continue to seethe with resentment and rage. But who was he harming but himself? The Germans cared not for his mood. It made no difference to the war.

Spring seemed to lift everyone's mood. They spent more time outdoors, away from the cramped quarters of the stables. By summer, they had even managed to acquire enough equipment to form sports leagues. On the yellowed grass of the former racecourse, footballs interrupted games of croquet while runners tried to avoid misdirected baseballs flying at their heads. Frederick joined the baseball league and was glad to find an outlet for his nerves. For a while, he could focus his thoughts on something other than the war and move his body in familiar ways. Bending forward, baseball in hand, he felt a fleeting sense of freedom, a lightness to the weight of the year.

With time, Ira also invited Frederick to move from the dark, cramped loft to his stall on the ground floor. The stall, which he shared with four other men (Amos Harris, Wilfred Morley, Bill Richardson, and John Webb, all listed on the card by the door), was small, but a significant improvement nonetheless. As with other aspects of camp, the men had been allowed to purchase items through the special orders office to make their lives more comfortable, at their own expense. The stall contained six bunks in all, arranged in two tiers along each wall. The bedsteads were old, with bent legs and worm-eaten boards, but Frederick was grateful to finally have a bed—a real bed, not the straw sack he had slept on in the loft. In the middle of the stall stood a small folding table with mismatched chairs and stools, where he could more comfortably sit to read or write to his family, though their correspondence continued to be stilted.

For months, Frederick had lamented the fact that they were only allowed postcards, which gave him insufficient space to say anything. But even once they were allowed letters, their correspondence felt restricted. He hardly knew what to say, knowing it would pass through multiple censors, and then be delayed in the post. Anytime he wrote, updating his parents and brother on what had happened since his last letter, he knew he would not receive a response before the next three were sent. But still, he wrote. It was the only thing he could do.

He had tried to reconnect with Klara as well, after he had stopped responding to her letters that winter. What would he even have told her of his misery? She was the reason he was in here—partly, at least, as a German. But then she never replied, which was just as well.

Frederick also sent the first issue of the camp magazine, *In Ruhleben Camp,* to Silas. He had thought it would help convince his family that he was doing well. He always assured them in his letters, but he wanted them to know that things were not as bad as they might have seemed. Not as bad as they had been. The magazine showed that the school and library were expanding, that the Dramatic Society had planned a year of plays, and that there were sports tournaments, literary competitions, and other activities to occupy his time. *We've built a bustling metropolis,* he wrote Silas. *It's rather impressive.*

When he received Silas's response a month later, Frederick was surprised by his concern. *It's good I had the inclination to read through the magazine before sharing it with our parents,* Silas wrote. *What a cruel joke this is.*

Frederick had not expected his brother to understand the humour of the magazine, but he had not thought his confusion would extend to such consternation. He thought back to what was mentioned in the magazine. There were undoubtedly aspects of his life in captivity that would have shocked his parents. But the magazine had been an offering—a way for Frederick to explain what he was living through. What they might have found shocking had become second nature to him.

When he tried to defend himself and assure his brother that things were not as bad as they seemed, Silas accused him of romanticizing the detention camp in which he was, he pressed, *a prisoner.* It was clear to Frederick that no one outside the camp could understand.

No one, that is, except Koval.

They fall into a contemplative silence, the tea now cold. There is more Frederick could share about his own experience, but it feels like enough to have exchanged these few thoughts and to have been met, for once, with understanding.

Frederick takes his leave, asking Koval if they can meet again. Koval agrees.

The day is fine, so Frederick decides to walk. It has been years since he has wandered along bustling city streets. Though he might have expected the hum of activity to unnerve him, he is soothed by the noise. Like Koval, he appreciates the anonymity of the city.

He meanders from store to store, eventually stopping at a specialty bookstore. The bell jangles softly as he enters, but the man behind the counter barely looks up. It is cooler inside, the air stuffy with hints of ink, paper, and varnished wood. Dust motes swirl in the sunlight slanting through the tall windows at the front, landing on the books crowding the shelves from floor to ceiling.

Rose had mentioned a book to him during their last conversation. What was it? Something about the damned? He wanders towards a shelf at the back. French and English titles mixed together, in no order Frederick can decipher. He slides a few from their place before a blue-green volume catches his eyes, white lettering on the front of the wrappers. *Ulysses.*

Frederick has heard of this book. He had read an excerpt in magazine a few years ago, before it was banned. He remembers the strange, lilting prose, the verbal leaps and bounds.

"An ambitious choice," the shopkeeper says in French when Frederick brings it to the counter.

"Linguist by trade, I'm afraid."

The man's lips curl into a smile under his thin mustache. "I see. Well, this might be the perfect book for you. I don't keep many copies on display. Just in case."

The day is still light, so rather than return to the hotel, Frederick ventures into a park to find a place to read. Heavy book in hand, he turns to the first page. He begins three times before he resolves to trace the lines with his finger, occasionally muttering the words under his breath. The syntax dances—jarring and syncopated. He has read voraciously throughout his life, in as many languages as he speaks, but he has never encountered anything like this. It is rhythmic—almost incantatory. Children squeal nearby and Frederick looks up for a moment, stunned, but as soon as he turns the page, the world blurs again.

CHAPTER 15

Seated in the back garden, Rose swings her feet back and forth, feeling the soft blades of grass against her skin. The oppressive heat has broken, softened by a gentle breeze. Rose is watching the children while Jeanne mends a pair of Silas's pants in the chair next to hers, a pitcher of cold strawberry-leaf tea sweating on the table between them.

Émilie approaches Rose's chair and gently places a hand on her shoulder.

"Quelle belle journée," she says with a half-sigh.

Rose looks up and covers Émilie's hand with her own. They smile at each other in quiet understanding.

Frederick had told Rose that his mother had started speaking more French since her husband's passing. It was as if his death had led to a revival of her old self, her true self. She no longer needed to be Mrs. Michael Munro. She could simply be Émilie Melanson, that young Acadian girl from New Brunswick whom Michael had met at a football game. His team had been playing against Émilie's brother's at the neighbouring Collège St. Joseph. Émilie had only recently returned from finishing school in Québec, but her lessons in modesty must not have taken, for when the ball had flown off the field and landed near her feet, she had effortlessly thrown it back, directly into the hands of an impressed Michael. Four months later, he had brought her home to meet his family, bringing her back to the valley her own ancestors had tended for generations before being forcibly expelled. Though she had worried his family might disapprove, as it turned out, the Munros were far less scandalized by her lineage than by her Catholicism. But Michael was nothing if not persuasive, and his family had relented once Émilie had satisfactorily polished her accent and converted to the Church of England. She had managed to retain her language, but only by a thread. It was why she had been so adamant about passing it on to her own sons, Frederick taking to it more eagerly than Silas, who understood his mother perfectly but preferred to respond in English. Rose, who had learned French in school and polished it in France, was only too glad to serve as a conversation partner, though she was careful about not making Jeanne feel left out.

"How was your meeting?" Rose asks in English.

Émilie sighs. "Productive, I suppose, though there is disagreement among our members regarding the proposed memorial."

"Memorial?"

"For the fallen soldiers. Various ideas have been put forward, but we can't seem to settle on one. I try to maintain the peace, given neither of my sons will be included, but it's an emotional topic for many."

"Yes, it must be," Rose says.

"In any case, I have agreed to go to an unveiling this afternoon in Hants County to see what they have done. Some of our members believe we're not moving quickly enough, but it's not a competition, is it?"

"It shouldn't be."

"Perhaps I should take you with me, to provide an outsider's perspective," Émilie suggests.

Rose glances at Jeanne, who looks up, apparently surprised to be included. "I think that's a great idea," she says. "Rose can go. I'll stay here with the children."

Émilie glances at the children. "Yes, probably not the best place for them. But you'll come?" She turns her hopeful eyes towards Rose.

"Yes, I suppose I could go."

"Lovely," Émilie says. "We can leave after lunch. Now, I think I need to lie down for a while."

With a final squeeze of Rose's shoulder, Émilie leaves. Jeanne continues her mending, the children still playing in the yard. Millicent seems to have grown tired of playing with her brother and sits by Amelia, plucking wildflowers while chatting animatedly in that sweet voice she reserves for her younger sister. Oliver, content to play by himself, sprints forward, crouched down, then makes a move to pull the imaginary trigger in his hand. For an instant, Rose thinks he is pretending to hunt, but then he clasps his hand over his heart like he has been shot by an invisible bullet and collapses onto the grass, stretching his other hand towards the sky.

A buzzing fills Rose's ears, growing louder.

"Is Oliver playing soldier?" she asks.

Jeanne looks up from her needlework, distracted. "Oh, yes. He came home with one of those American pulp magazines last week. It had a soldier on the cover, so I suppose there was an adventurous war story in there. Last month it was cowboys."

The buzzing persists. Rose thinks of her other nephew, who had not played soldier but donned the uniform and ammunition, who had fallen not in the soft cushion of grass but in treacherous mud. The grass stains turn to festering wounds, the clump of dandelions clutched in the boy's round fist transform into a bayonet. It is Leo she sees, consumed by a smoking pit of ash and mud, until Oliver laughs and leaps back into the world of the living. Rose startles. He has risen to his feet and joined his sisters, joyfully running circles around them, his wartime fantasy already forgotten. Rose looks down to find that her hands are still clenched.

The park is crowded, people gathered around an enormous circular cenotaph covered in the largest Union Jack Rose has ever seen. Only the white cross at the top remains uncovered. Flowers have been placed at the base of the monument, and as they arrive, men in uniform bring more, poppies shining bright red against the green summer grass. Rose's eyes linger on the face of the young man in khaki making his way to the front. She wonders if she knows him, if any of these faces would be familiar to her covered in rust bandages and mud. Would she be able to identify them at all?

"I suppose we could have brought the children," Émilie leans in to whisper, surveying the children in shrunken suits and bouffant dresses crowding their parents' feet, likely unable to see anything but knees and tailcoats.

Rose thinks of Oliver playing soldier in the grass, oblivious to the world. Could this have been an instructional outing for them? An opportunity to gain deeper insight into their history? *Where were you during the war?* Millicent might have asked. What would Rose have said then?

By the newly erected monument is a hastily assembled stage topped by four wooden chairs. Men in dark robes cluster nearby, papers clutched in their hands. One by one, they mount the creaking steps, their presence alone enough to hush the gathered crowd into an expectant silence.

A man with a trim white beard and round spectacles approaches the front of the stage, his face as lined as a child's drawing.

"Ladies and gentlemen," he says in a voice that seems too loud for his small frame. "We are gathered here today not just in remembrance, but in deep admiration. Admiration for the men who faced the war with unwavering courage. Admiration for the way they stepped forward in our hour of need. Let this monument be a symbol of their bravery."

He seamlessly transitions into prayer and the women in the crowd instinctively bow their heads, already clutching handkerchiefs. Rose's gaze drops to the scuffs on her shoes but she cannot help but steal glances at the stage as the prayer drags on, wondering why no men in uniform are seated among the older gentlemen, none of whom, she would wager, have seen anything of war.

The prayer closes and another man stands to deliver a sermon about the bravery of the sons, the brothers, the husbands who have given their lives. He lists a few by name, recounting the heroic deeds they had supposedly done in the name of God, their valour unmatched by any. Rose tries to keep track of the number of times he mentions valour or bravery, but quickly loses count.

It was not valour she had seen in France, nor later, in Belgium. The men she had cared for weren't heroes. They were ordinary men. Men who had volunteered, believing their cause to be just, only to realize there was no justice on those battlefields. She presses the tips of her nails into her palms, attempting to divert her attention from the mounting pressure in her spine.

"These men fought not for the glory of battle, but for the triumph of peace," the man continues. "Their victory was not just in the fields of conflict, but in securing a future where peace might reign." Then his tone shifts, his sermon taking an unexpected turn. "They defeated the enemy, and we can find solace in knowing that those fiends, drunk on the bloodlust of conquest and utterly devoid of any shred of honour, have been vanquished. Civilization has been dragged back from the brink of barbarism. Your sons saved us from savagery. Your husbands shielded us from the clutches of beasts. Your fathers stood tall against the enemy. Today, as we gather to honour our fallen, let us remember that their sacrifice was not in vain. They laid down their lives in fierce defense of those principals which all good citizens regard as worth preserving in the best interest of humanity, and for that, we thank them."

Rose looks around her. Was this truly what everyone believed? She thinks of Mr. Winter's outrage at dinner. What she had seen during war had been horrific. But at whose hands? Whose fault was the bloodshed, the horror? The soldiers on the other side, who died just as horrifically, or the men who sent them there?

By the time the cenotaph is unveiled, the flag slipping down from its stone height, Rose is fuming, rage rising, a fierce tide against this varnished rhetoric that glosses over the blood and suffering. How quickly they had strayed from the truth. How easily they forgot the carnage, the shattered lives, the brutal reality of conflict that did not fit neatly into their heroic narratives of brave fools.

She had been a fool. They had all been fools.

Where was her memorial? Her name would never be etched in stone, despite stitching pieces of these men back together, and suddenly, that seems a crueller injustice than this sanitized version of history, because she can see clearly the capriciousness of who gets remembered. Only the names of those unable to speak are honoured. Only the names of those long silenced, those who could never rise to refute the distorted narrative, are preserved in stone.

Except Leo.

Leo would be omitted from these neat, tidy myths of remembrance, and then Anna would know. This had not occurred to her.

How the silenced might speak the truth for her.

Rose staggers, anger eclipsed by panic, and Émilie reaches out to steady her.

"Are you all right?"

Her voice, barely above a whisper, seems too loud.

Rose nods, head swaying. "It's too hot," she manages to say.

Émilie hands her the programme. Rose accepts it, fanning the heat rising on her neck.

A week after their chance encounter, Leo had sent word to say he would soon be returning to France, going back up the line and into the trenches. His note arrived on the same day as rumours that Canadian troops were taking part in a heavy operation near Ypres.

Patients arrived en masse, telling frightful stories of entire regiments being mowed down by artillery fire. Canadians lost then regained their trenches. Rose asked after Leo, speaking with every patient lucid enough to recall fragments of the Front. She had no way of knowing when he would be sent back, only the grim certainty that with every wounded man brought into her care, more would be sent to take their place. If Leo was not already knee-deep in mud, it was only a matter of time.

Every morning after her shift, Rose made her way to the bulletin board by the nurse's recreation tent to join the others struggling for a glimpse of the daily casualty list. Though she knew there would be others she recognized, she only ever searched for Leo's name. She could not bear anything more than knowing his was absent from the list.

In her ward, she overheard one of the other nurses asking a patient if he knew where her brother was. The patient, half drugged from surgery, only said, "The last time I saw him, he was face down in the mud."

One evening in June, Rose stumbled back to her tent, utterly spent, her body weary and her spirit bruised. She had been summoned to the operating theatre three times that week and could still taste, smell, and see blood everywhere. Nursing took on a harsher edge in a tent with saws, scalpels, and clamps, the body cast in a different light. She could not help but think of her father every time she worked with a surgeon and wondered how he had managed all these years. She removed her shoes with a low, involuntary groan, then peeled away her sullied dress. The stains on her apron seemed to pulse faintly as if the life they bore was ebbing away.

Once in bed, she reached for the letters tucked in the drawer of her nightstand. She wanted to read Leo's latest note again and again, to savour the description of his leave in England, to picture what he had seen and eaten and smelled. Anything but the red seeping into the fabric of her dress. Picking up the stack of letters she kept tied together, she spotted the small leather journal hiding beneath it. Her fingers brushed the cover, and she felt an immediate wash of relief knowing *James Cyrus MacLeod* was no longer a name she had to fear encountering on the bulletin board.

The thought passed like a flash but left her horrified. Rose reached for the journal and brought it to her chest. Tears of exhaustion and frustration came, but she brushed them off and untied the knot of the journal. She hesitated for a moment, unsure if she could read his words knowing he would never need them back. But Leo had said James would want someone to read it. To remember. To witness the life it contained.

She sat, moving her finger over the dusty paper to decipher the hurried pencilled notes, careful not to smudge the letters. His voice sounded in her head, a low, intimate murmur. James's notebook was a scribble of notes, poems, and half-thoughts, mostly written in those early months in the trenches. But the way he described the war. The way he framed it. She had never seen anyone dare to put such words to paper. These were words of decay, of ravage, of apocalyptic panic. He wrote of the *drowning mud*, the *iron smell of fading life*. Men *shell-wracked and gaping*. His words had none of the heroism and fanfare of the letters and poems printed in newspapers back home. They were brutal. They were raw.

It was nearing midnight by the time Rose flipped onto a blank page, and the immensity of the loss came crashing around her. It had ended nearly mid-thought. The final entry had closed with a note on the weather, and then he was gone, never to write another word. She flipped through the rest of the blank pages, desperate for another entry, for a final word aside from *sleet*. Nothing came.

Rose closed her eyes, swallowing the soreness in her throat. She knew there was truth in James's words. Though she had not experienced trench warfare, she had witnessed its direct aftermath. This slaughter of men. James had obscured it. *Told it slant,* in the words of Emily Dickinson. But the disturbed truth was captured there in the sonnets, the rondeaus, the elegies for the dead. A poetic account of a shattered body, of a shattered world.

It must have helped him, in some way, to put such bleak thoughts to paper. James had seemed so resigned to the war, but Rose could see how the journal gave him the space to probe his emotions without fear of judgement, shielded from the haunting gaze of war. Writing had been a way for him to maintain a sense of connection to his old self, she knew. To enter into conversation with the poet he had been before the war, to find words for the dislocation, the disorientation, the constant threat of death. To name it was to impose control over it.

What would she name it, she wondered. This chaos, this loss of faith.

Rose fell asleep with the notebook on her chest. When the sun filtered through the canvas, the larks singing their ignorance of the world splintering forty miles from the coast, she awoke with a thought fresh in her mind.

No convoy had arrived the previous night, and the morning was quiet. She snuck out of the tent and made her way to her ward. It was hours before her shift, but the night nurses barely blinked an eye when she entered. Rose walked between the rows of occupied beds toward a man who had been in their care for nearly a week. He smiled when she approached.

"Morning, Nurse. A bit early for you, isn't it?"

"Good morning, Private Thompson. May I sit?"

He nodded, his breathing laboured. He was one of fifteen cases suffering from gas poisoning. "You know," he started, catching his breath. "I've asked you to call me by my name many times."

She smiled. "Victor, then. How are you feeling this morning?"

"They said I'm being shipped out to England later today. A lot of us are."

"That's good news," Rose said enthusiastically, though she knew it meant quite the opposite for her. "Well, before you leave, I thought I would ask you to sign my book."

His face lit up. "Me, Nurse?"

She offered him the small red notebook that she had bought for herself when she first arrived in London, before realizing that she had neither time nor energy to relive her days on paper. Victor accepted it, plucked the pen from her hand, and wrote down his name, regiment, and hometown in the uppermost corner, leaving space for others to follow suit.

"My sister had one of these when we were growing up," he said. "An autograph album. She got everyone to sign it. Some even added bits of poetry in there. Popular ones, usually, but I always preferred to come up with my own rhymes." He grinned, taking a deep breath between his teeth. "More fun that way."

"Would you like to add something to mine?"

He waved his hand. "Couldn't think of anything good if I tried."

She nodded and lowered her voice. "There is something I would like to include with your name, if you'll allow me."

"My address?" He hadn't shaved yet and his smile stretched the stubble on his cheeks.

"An account. Of what happened to land you in here."

His smile faltered, his gaze turning to suspicion. "What are you keeping there? A record of injuries?"

"Perhaps," she said, looking him straight in the eyes. "Or perhaps simply a true account of this war."

He held her gaze a moment longer, then sighed, nodded, and began his story. She had heard it before, but she paid closer attention to the details this time. The pale green colour of the gas approaching, quickly drifting on the wind. The sweet odour of pineapple and pepper reaching them before they could move. The horror it carried. Victor and a few of his colleagues were able to put on their masks before they suffered too much damage, but they struggled to wake the men around them as they tried to retreat. Many never woke again.

The recollection had cast long shadows over his face, but he thanked her when he was done.

"What for, Victor?"

"For listening."

She continued to record patients' stories, taking the time to sit with them between her shifts. They were desperate to tell someone about their experiences. It always came stumbling out in a flurry. Neither nurses nor soldiers were allowed to keep journals for fear that sensitive information might fall into enemy hands, but James had known what would result from this censoring. If all that remained from this war were the statistics of battles won and lost, if all that remained from the dead was a number, if all that remained were the sanitized stories sent home, then they would all forget the true cost of war. They would all forget the face of sacrifice.

And so, he wrote. And so would she.

Hers was different from the clandestine diaries kept by other nurses. Rose knew what they wrote. They frequently sat together in the nurses' quarters, chronicling their travels, making note of letters, of parcels, portraying the men as brave and cheery, even the shattered, the bleeding, the dying. Many avoided writing about the boys altogether, only briefly mentioning the injuries or deaths that marked them.

"Why dwell on the loss?" Rose recalled one nurse saying. "That's not what I want to remember from our time here."

What was worth remembering, if not the loss? Rose was keeping men alive on the page. No matter what happened when they left her hospital, at least a piece of them would forever remain imprinted on the pages of her book. The same way James was immortalized forever.

This push gave her a sense of purpose as the number of convoys continued to increase that summer, often bringing hundreds of men at once. Rose studied them, looking for the tufts of flaxen hair that she had clipped with sewing scissors as a child. Looking for Leo. Every time, her relief came with a reminder that each of these patients had people waiting anxiously for news of them at home. The rapid pace of her work in recent weeks had made nursing feel much more impersonal than she was used to and adding signatures to her journal was a way for her to disrupt this. But it was more than that. Her experience of war was inseparable from the experiences of soldiers. Her role existed only in relation to the wounded, and compiling these stories allowed her to reconstruct a history with which to reconcile the mutilated bodies she so frequently encountered.

As the hospital overflowed, the stream of information from the Front seemed to dwindle. Assurances that outcomes of battles were favourable flew in the face of the countless bodies pouring through their doors, and Rose jotted down details of even the most gruesome injuries, preserving the price rather than the outcome of the campaign. Imposing individuality on the faceless mass of soldiers recorded in the official accounts. On those times they heard bombs or heavy gunfire with no official word on their meaning, Rose knew that her little notebook was a necessary rebel of war.

She received a letter from Leo in late July. He didn't say where he was, only that he had not been injured. She slipped the letters and her notebook into her nightstand, where they remained as she was thrust directly into the aftermath of the Battle of the Somme.

Convoys arrived in droves, filling the hospital's beds to capacity. The nature of her work had always ebbed and flowed depending on efforts at the Front, but it seemed impossible that so many men were charging at the Germans.

"This is murderous," Sister Nicholls whispered early one morning as they tried to find more beds for the endless surge of wounded.

The skies turned grey as the days grew shorter. The influx did not abate. Mud returned, rain softening the distant sounds of gunfire. The heavens cracked daily with star shells lit by searchlights.

In late autumn she found a young man crying in his sleep, trembling beneath the thin blanket that covered him. She paused at the foot of his bed to see if he would wake. His face crumpled before he regained his composure, the pillow damp. He opened his mouth. "Tom," he whispered in his sleep. He was quiet for a moment, tormented by dreams. "We're nearly there," he said. "Hold on."

His head shook on the pillow. His hand jerked over the blanket. Rose considered giving him a sleeping draught but did not want to wake him. He was one of her recent shell shock cases. His foot was in a cast, but his wounds ran much deeper.

She found him sitting up in bed the following morning, looking morose. He ate his porridge slowly, too tired to even lift the spoon to his lips.

She brought him a fresh carafe of water. "Good morning, Private White."

He barely looked up, bruised circles under his eyes. When she returned for her shift later that evening, she found him staring into space.

"Would you like something to read?" she asked. "We have books, or I can send someone to fetch a paper for you."

He gave a curt, quiet response which Rose missed entirely.

"Pardon?" she asked, stepping closer.

"It's Eddie," he said louder, finally looking up at her. He was Australian.

"Eddie then. Would you like anything to read?" He shook his head, and she nodded. "Very well. Let me know if you change your mind."

He stayed in bed, staring ahead or down at his hands all evening. Even after most of the men had fallen asleep, there he sat, his eyes open. Rose approached him again. She busied herself with his chart, pretending to pay him no attention.

"Would you like something to help you sleep, Eddie?" She replaced the chart and pulled out her watch. It was nearly midnight.

Eddie shook his head.

"You need rest," Rose urged. "You didn't sleep well last night."

His eyes flashed up. "How do you know?"

"It's my job to look after you. You seemed restless."

"So, *you* heard me too."

Had another patient said something? Mocked him? She pulled a chair and sat down. "You can't avoid sleep to avoid nightmares."

He kept his eyes defiantly forward.

Rose waited a moment before asking, "Who's Tom?"

Heat rose from his neck to his cheeks. He tried to maintain his expression of defiance, even as his eyes filled with tears.

She lowered her voice. "The others are asleep if you want to talk."

He was silent a moment. Keeping his eyes on his hands, he blinked, and a heavy tear fell down his cheek. He took a shaky breath and exhaled. "Tom was my friend," he said. "I met him on the boat over nine months ago. We were the same age, from different towns. Didn't know each other but we became friends. We saw it all together. I don't think we left each other's sight since we landed in France." He lifted his hand to wipe tears and frowned, trying to keep his voice steady. "We were each other's good luck charms—that's what he said. So long as we stuck together, nothing bad would happen."

His face closed and he wept, his shoulders quaking. "Part of him might have been right," he added. "Because when we were injured in the field last week, we needed each other. My foot was shattered, and I couldn't walk. Couldn't feel my legs at all. Thought I might have lost them both. Tom was blinded. The side of his face had been blown nearly to bits and he couldn't see. We were both injured, but together, we made a whole person." Eddie accepted the tissue that Rose handed him and blew his nose.

"Is that how you were able to get back to the trenches?"

Eddie nodded, sniffling. "He managed to find me in the mud. He carried me nearly three miles as I guided him with my sight. But then a shell exploded near us, tearing us apart. I must have lost consciousness because it was dark when I came to. I crawled around looking for him. I reached for his hand, shook his shoulders, until...until I realized that his head was missing from his body." He brought his fist to his mouth.

Tears welled in Rose's eyes, but when she reached for his hand, Eddie pulled away.

He shook his head. "I didn't want to leave him. I laid down in the field, waiting for the shells to find me, but someone else did, and brought me down to the dressing station. I didn't want to leave."

He wept openly, Rose alongside him. She had never cried in this tent. Not once. But Eddie looked so defeated. She had never met anyone who regretted being saved.

"I'm very sorry for your loss," Rose said.

She stayed with him in quiet contemplation for close to an hour before offering him a sleeping draught, sending Eddie into what she hoped would be an empty, dreamless sleep. Rising to her feet, she brought the rest of the draught to the medicine station, where Private Blake, the orderly, was busy organizing bottles.

"That was nice of you," he said softly. "How you were able to calm him. He refused me all day."

"Sometimes they just need a bit of help."

"How did you know to do that?" Blake sounded genuinely curious, a change from his usual demeanour.

"I didn't," Rose said, lifting a bottle to inspect its label more closely. "I followed my instinct." She turned to face him. "We mend more than bodies, Private."

The following morning when he woke, Eddie found a small notebook and pencil waiting for him on his bedside table with a note that simply said *Write*. Rose had brought him a new journal rather than her own, suspecting there was much more to this story that Eddie needed to keep close to his heart.

Rose thinks of her journals now, heat bearing down as the robed men on the platform drone on.

Those patients who had left traces of themselves behind in her pages, desperate to be immortalized, as if they knew, as if they expected, to die. Was this how they would want to be remembered? Those men who landed in her hospital on the brink of death, calling out for their mothers. Would they have considered this stone monument, devoid of life, a fitting tribute to the senseless spilling of their blood?

Rose had told herself there would be time for grief after the war. But this public mourning had always seemed more a performance than a genuine reckoning. They were mourning the immense loss of life, certainly. Mourning the loss of the future they had all envisioned for themselves. But no one seemed willing to question why they had lost it. If it was worth it. If war was ever worth it. And now, here they were, her role already forgotten, Leo already forgotten. Men now cold names etched in stone.

On the way home, Rose is silent.

"I feel I owe you an apology," Émilie says once they are off the train and walking in the direction of the house, the sun still blinding even in the late afternoon.

"What for?"

"For asking you to come today. For not considering how it might affect you."

Rose is struck. She looks up at Émilie, her face soft, her gaze incisive.

The one thing Rose had yearned for the most after returning from France was a mother. She had rarely missed her own mother growing up. She barely remembered her. Anna had filled that role seamlessly, never leaving Rose to feel wanting. But after the war, after Leo, Anna was also in need of mothering. She had rarely considered how things might affect Rose, even after everything.

"Thank you," Rose says, because it is the only thing she can think to say.

Émilie reaches out to squeeze her hand. "I could sense your frustration. And though I don't want to pry—this is precisely why I asked you to come. To gain perspective from someone who has been to war."

Rose nods, tears stinging. "I was. Frustrated. Disappointed."

"May I ask why?"

Rose tries to steady her breathing, considering the question. "I suppose…" she begins. "I suppose it feels absurd to watch the world celebrate war as a victory, even while they acknowledge the loss. It seems paradoxical." She takes a deep breath. "I went to war thinking, as so many did, that we were doing something noble. But it didn't feel noble once we were there, once we were in it. Years of fighting, the frontlines shifting back and forth like a cruel tide, each wave bringing more bloodshed. It seems absurd to me to cling to those old myths of glory when the truth was a wasteland of bodies, shattered and forgotten in the mud."

Émilie hands her a handkerchief and she accepts it, wiping silent tears.

"Thank you," Émilie says, stopping them both in their tracks. She holds Rose's hands in her own. "I appreciate you sharing these thoughts with me."

Rose looks down. She wants to tell Émilie that the prospect of Anna coming for a visit, of the truth spilling out of those monuments, worries her. The weight of this realization still sits heavily in the pit of her stomach. But even this—even this brief, bitter reflection is a relief. She can feel it almost as the words leave her, the tight coil in her chest unfurling.

Émilie lets go of her hands and links her arm through hers as they resume walking. "I can see how difficult this all is for you. But would you perhaps be willing to share these thoughts with others?"

"What do you mean?"

"I would like for you to join me at our next committee meeting. One of the women has already arranged for an officer to come to discuss a few options. But I think your perspective might be as valuable."

The house is within view. Within minutes, they will return to the chaos of family life. Millicent will pull Rose away, Émilie sweeping in to relieve Jeanne from her duties. Rose will be saved, once again, from the silence and the thoughts that accompany it. But in this moment, with the sound of the wind coursing through the trees, wind chimes singing in the distance, Rose basks in the stillness and considers Émilie's proposal. It was one thing for her to share these thoughts with Émilie, but would she be able to voice them in front of others? She had always been wary of criticizing the war openly—even while in the midst of it she had only done so covertly, with pen and paper. And never had she intended for those journals to become public. But was there a way for her to make herself heard now? Could she be critical when lives were not at stake—only their memory?

"Yes," she finally says before they turn into the garden. "I will."

Émilie smiles gratefully at her. "That's wonderful, Rose. Thank you."

CHAPTER 16

Mr. Koval shakes his head violently. "No," he says decisively in German. "No, I cannot." Then he turns to his wife and speaks urgently in Ukrainian. Her eyes widen, hands wringing her damp tea towel. He is still shaking his head when he focuses on Frederick again. "No."

"I understand this might be difficult for you," Frederick says, leaning forward. "I did not mean to offend you." He places a protective hand over the typed article sitting on the table between them. "If I did, I apologize. Truly."

Koval refuses to meet his eyes. "No. I did not agree to this."

Frederick can tell the man wants to say more, and wishes he spoke Ukrainian so he could give Koval license to speak freely. He lets out a short breath and looks down at his hand splayed out on the table. He retracts his fingers slowly, uncovering the words.

He had returned from his last meeting with Koval feeling inspired to write something in his defence. For hours, Frederick had sat on that park bench reading *Ulysses*, until the sun began to sink behind the trees and he found himself, quite suddenly, thrust back into the present moment.

Frederick had enjoyed few books since the end of the war. Going through the boxes Silas packed for him after he had left home, Frederick found all the cherished volumes that had once lined the shelves of his childhood bedroom. Homer in Greek, Goethe in German, Beaudelaire in French—the rest in English. Once, he had felt as though these authors were showing him a world steeped with meaning. But returning to them after the war, he felt their words rang hollow. Homer's heroism a farce. Whitman's exuberance distant, almost mocking—Wordsworth's odes to nature too soft, too delicate. All of it seemed lost, anchored to a past that offered no solace. Frederick might have once believed that history moved in cycles, but the last few years had followed no script he recognized. It seemed they had veered into uncharted territory, these authors no longer able to guide him. But Joyce. Joyce had seen this uncharted world.

There was something about the book's unflinching ordinariness, its fixation on the small, physical characteristics of daily life. To some readers, it had seemed absurd, even pointless—but to Frederick, the minute details of Bloom's day felt oddly, painfully familiar. His own life had been reduced to the same kind of monotony in Ruhleben. Time had slowed to a crawl, until seconds felt like hours, hours like days. And the book's intimacy—its exposure of private moments, even embarrassing ones. Frederick had spent years in close quarters with other men, surrounded by open latrines, shared bunks, infrequent showers. The smells, the sounds, the sheer lack of privacy—these had been the realities of his existence. And in Joyce's world, all of it was granted a kind of dignity. This might have been, Frederick thought, the most honest thing he had ever read.

But what resonated most deeply was Bloom himself. A man who hoped for understanding. Who sought to bridge divides, to erase the barriers that continued to tear people apart, even after such a war as this.

It's a patent absurdity on the face of it to hate people because they live round the corner and speak a different vernacular, so to speak.

He saw the world as it was and yearned for unity. That, Frederick realized, was what he wanted too.

So, he had returned to the hotel and started writing. He began with the harsh reality: thousands of so-called enemy aliens interned, thousands more under the constant scrutiny of the police. These were men who had been invited to Canada, encouraged to partake in the building of a nation, often settling in areas few others wanted to inhabit, all to avoid the looming threat of annexation by the United States. Canada had a moral and political obligation to those it had brought to its shores, Frederick argued—a responsibility that had been callously cast aside.

What had Canada fought for during the war? Was it not for justice, freedom, and independence? And yet, these were the very rights they had denied the men who had languished in internment camps throughout the country. Frederick pointed out the bitter irony of it all: rather than embracing these individuals and offering them the chance to become part of the community, the nation had chosen to ostracize them, alienating them from the ideals Canadians claimed to uphold. Would it not have been simpler, more just, to naturalize them, to integrate them into the fabric of society?

It had been one thing for Frederick to accept that his country had done little to help him when he was interned. It was quite another to come to grips with the fact that they had done the same to others, under worse conditions. So many claimed the war had been the real birth of their nation, Canada unified through its sacrifices and victories on the battlefield. But it was rather a false unity, Frederick thought. One forged as much through the exclusion of those deemed not fully Canadian. They had simply narrowed the definition of national identity. The mass internment policy had been based on the assumption that these men's loyalties lay elsewhere, yet these were individuals who had chosen to make this place their home. They had crossed an ocean, leaving behind all they had ever known, in search of something new. Why would they risk that for the sake of old-world conflicts? For many, Canada represented a fresh start, a place removed from the tensions of Europe. Did it not speak volumes that so many of them, when faced with hostility and exclusion here, had attempted to move to the neutral United States rather than return to their homelands?

It was then Frederick had focused on Koval. Labelled an Austrian, though he did not identify as such—only a man from a contested region where his language and culture were suppressed, a man caught between shifting borders and conflicting national aspirations. How could Canada claim to have interned the enemy when it didn't even know where the enemy was from? The war had made synonymous for many the idea of foreigner, immigrant, and enemy. Koval's story was a clear example of that.

Frederick had not named him in the article, simply referred to him as a man from Galicia, but Koval had begun shaking his head the moment Frederick mentioned including him in the piece.

"Could we perhaps change a few of the details? Make it anonymous?" Frederick suggests, though he knows it might put his whole argument into question.

"I cannot," Koval insists. He finally stops shaking his head and instead begins tapping his fingers on the wooden table. "It is too dangerous. For my family—my wife—" He throws a look over his shoulder. "No." He gets up, hesitating for a moment, and leaves the room.

Frederick sighs, wondering how this meeting has gone so poorly. He begins to gather his papers, reaching for his briefcase.

Mrs. Koval approaches hesitantly from her spot by the stove. "There are things he did not say to you," she says quietly. Her English is halting, but stronger than her husband's.

Frederick wonders if she speaks English rather than German so her husband will be less likely to understand.

"What do you mean?" Frederick asks.

She takes a seat, hovering at its edge, washcloth still in hand. "I cannot say I know all the details. Only small parts," she says. "He tells me little. I know it was hard for him. When he spoke to you, he spoke of dancing and books." She shakes her head. "But life in the camp, it was not easy."

Frederick stills. Evidently, her husband had not told her he himself had been interned. He says nothing, only nodding for her to continue.

"There were beatings," she says, her voice almost inaudible. "That, he told me. Punishment, for such small things. Once, my Petro fell ill—very ill. He could not work, could hardly stand. But the guards would not let him rest. They forced him to the fields, and when he fell..." Her breath hitched. "They threatened to shoot him, then locked him in a cell for a week. His fever worsened. I do not know how he survived."

She exhales sharply, and glances at the washcloth in her hands, twisting it between trembling fingers. "May I say one more thing?"

"Of course."

She takes a moment to gather her words, still avoiding his eyes. "Life in the camp. It was not easy. But life outside of camp was no easier. I did not know Petro then. We were not yet married. But I was here. I had come with my brother, who was watched, but not interned, mercifully." She looks towards the window, blinking rapidly. "I heard things. From the women in our community. They often spoke of what happened to those of us left behind."

She stops, her fingers tightening around the cloth. "All of us were scared. Without husbands, many women struggled. Children went hungry. We did what we could to help, but..." She hesitates, a flicker of bitterness passing over her face. "There was no help to be had. The men were taken away, yes. But the women, too, were abandoned."

Frederick watches her in silence. While there had certainly been physical abuse, threats, and harsh confinement at Ruhleben, for the most part the guards had left them alone. And the women. He had known some of the men in the camp had wives and children waiting for them outside the gates, but he had rarely thought of them. The situation had been different for him. Klara was better off. What could he have offered her?

But was there more he had not seen? Or worse, refused to see?

Even within the confines of Ruhleben, he thought, where all bore the weight of suspicion, there were groups who were set apart—by class, by faith, by the colour of their skin. Some had borne more than their share of suffering. It had not happened instantaneously. During those first few weeks, the anxiety they all shared had banded them in unity. But gradually, the norms of society had returned. That old adage that if stranded on a deserted island, the first thing British men would do is form clubs and exclude each other, was nothing if not true. The old boys from certain colleges fraternized exclusively. Doctors joined in weekly discussion, as did lawyers, and professors. Those from the same countries or regions found each other as they always did. Discord arose, the men now starkly divided. It irked Frederick. Wasn't this the same kind of division that had landed them here in the first place?

One morning during roll call, the Commandant had asked all Jewish prisoners to step forward. Frederick had sensed Ira stiffen at his side. A few men had stepped forward first, then a dozen more.

Ira did not move. The Commandant was unsatisfied, eyebrows knit under his cap. He addressed them again, explaining that this was for their own good—that a Jewish soup kitchen in Berlin had petitioned for the right to send them kosher food. "We have granted them this one allowance," he said, as though it was of great trouble to him.

More men joined the ranks, gathering at the front, but Ira stayed put.

"There is really no need to concern yourselves," the Commandant assured them with a vexed chuckle, a cigar smoking between his fingers. But there was a sense of mistrust humming among the men, a low murmur of suspicion. Frederick turned his head away from Ira, surveying the remaining crowd. He suspected Ira was not the only one to have stayed back.

After a third call, the Commandant turned to address the new collective and the guards dismissed the rest.

"Why did you not step forward?" Frederick asked later that evening as they made their way to dinner.

Ira was silent, his face gloomy. Finally, in a low voice, he said, "This kind of isolation—it never ends well."

Frederick had not pressed him further, but Ira's concerns had quickly materialized. The next morning, they found that the men who had stepped forward had been relocated to Barrack 6—the oldest, most decrepit stable in the camp. Ira visited them a few days later to find them using garments and the straw from their beds to fill the holes in the walls of the barrack. The food they had been given, driven all the way from Berlin, had spoiled and caused many to fall ill. Though they were told that they had only been identified for this one purpose, Jewish men became an easy target, subject to frequent raids on the accusations of smuggling and illicit trading, often fuelled by the jealousy of fellow prisoners who falsely believed that the food from the soup kitchen was better than what they received in the camp.

Class had proved as stark a division, as had race. Men interned in Ruhleben came from all walks of life, and even in his own stall, this caused tension. Webb, an Oxford man, was mistrustful of Richardson, the sailor from Grimsby, and was open about his distaste. The atmosphere was always tense when they were both in the stall. Frederick had sensed it from the beginning, and had followed Ira's example in trying to keep the peace, but Webb, and to a lesser degree, Harris, seemed determined to look down on Richardson.

"They once asked Richardson if they could hire him to do their laundry and clean the stall," Ira had told him. "You can imagine how that went over."

When Richardson had refused, Webb had hired Thompson, an inmate from Jamaica, who now came every morning to sweep their floors, take out the garbage, and make the beds. It had not escaped Frederick's notice that Webb was anxious to reinstate a certain social order on the camp. There had been some degree of integration in the camp early on, particularly in sports and occasionally in music, but the Black men were now segregated in Barrack 13, often referred to simply as the Black Barrack. There had been instances of hostility towards them, similar to what Jewish prisoners faced. But what struck Frederick most was the condescending attitude towards the men in Barrack 13. Many of the other inmates dismissed them, assuming that their unfamiliarity with English indicated a lack of intelligence or education, even though they were not the only non-native English speakers in the camp. Frederick found it troubling and irrational that his fellow inmates would emphasize solidarity based on race when it was amongst predominantly white nations that this war was being waged.

"You don't have to tidy my things," Frederick told Thompson one day, offering a smile, but the look Thompson gave him suggested he had understood his meaning differently. "I only mean," he rushed to clarify, "Webb and Harris pay you, not me. You don't need to help me. I can clean my own side."

"They pay me to clean the stall, so I clean the stall."

"Yes, well." He didn't know what to say, so instead he made sure to clean his bunk before Thompson came every morning. He had not grown up with servants and felt strange about the ease with which Webb and Harris paid people to do the chores of daily life in a place where they had no real responsibility. Richardson's dismissal of their status had strained ties between the stall mates, but it had endeared him to Frederick.

He understands why Koval is unwilling to share his story publicly, even nameless. There is always the risk that he will be found out, that he will be cast out, as he was before. Frederick was able to leave the country of his internment. Koval was not.

Frederick looks down at the papers gathered in his hand. Why had he thought it would be a good idea to write about him, without his express permission? He had gotten carried away with the argument. He had tried to get to the heart of the matter with a precision that left little room for rebuttal. He had not really thought of Koval at all.

"Could you apologize on my behalf?" Frederick asks Mrs. Koval, feeling remorseful.

She nods. "I will."

CHAPTER 17

Rose can hear the blood rushing in her ears, so she keeps her focus on the hats. The silk hats, the feathered hats, the blooms that threaten to take over fabric. There are an array of styles and colours atop the heads of the women in attendance at Émilie's group meeting, and Rose examines each one. This summer seems to have brought colour back to the world, and she takes it all in, trying to forget about the task that lies ahead.

They have gathered in the parlour room of one of the women's homes, a Mrs. Purdy whose husband has been in office sixteen years and who is certain, she tells the others, will be able to help them establish any memorial they want. Rose cannot be sure but she discerns from her tone and her age that Mrs. Purdy is unlikely to have had either son or husband in the war.

The meeting is called to order, one woman in the corner taking careful notes in a small black notebook. After introducing Major-General Jost, the man who had for a time commanded the battalion that included the sons of many of the women in the room, Mrs. Purdy asks the group if there is anything else to add to the agenda.

Émilie clears her throat. "Yes, there is. I also invited a guest to speak to us today." She turns towards Rose, holding her gaze. "Sister Rose Avery served in France for three years and was for a time stationed at a field hospital near the front lines in Belgium, where she cared for countless injured soldiers. She saw the war first-hand, as a woman, and heard their stories, their hopes, and their fears in their most vulnerable moments. I asked her to join us to share those experiences with the group in the hopes that she might provide some insight into what these soldiers might have wanted for themselves."

Mrs. Purdy bows her head slightly. "Welcome, Miss Avery. We look forward to hearing from you. I'm sure you'll add much to our discussion with Major-General Jost."

Rose looks across the room to find Jost smiling forcibly under his thick moustache. He is wearing his military uniform, two pips and a crown on the epaulettes of his khaki tunic. Rose tries to return his smile, wishing for a brief moment that she, too, was wearing her uniform, to give her more authority than her yellow striped dress.

"There were many suggestions at our last meeting. A cenotaph was discussed, as well as a sculptural pathway in the park. All good ideas. Has anyone given it any more thought?"

The woman with the black notebook begins writing quickly, her pen dashing across the page while her eyes remain on the group. Someone to her left raises a tentative hand and Mrs. Purdy invites her to speak.

"I liked the idea of a sculptural pathway, but the more I considered it, the more I thought we should do something more...lively. A memorial garden, for instance. Or perhaps a tree-lined pathway rather than sculptures. Something that blooms. Something that could represent the various seasons of life."

A few nods.

"Perhaps even a bed of poppies," another woman suggests.

Rose remembers dashing through a field of poppies in France, Mae at her heels, the sweet smell of citrus and vanilla wafting through the air. That had been at the war's earliest beginnings, before the bodies, before the destruction. Whenever she encountered poppies, even as symbols of remembrance, it was this moment that came to mind. She liked the idea of a bloom representing the loss, the fleeting brilliance of life.

Jost clears his throat. "If I may," he ventures in a quiet voice. "I wonder if you would not prefer something more traditional. You said a cenotaph was already discussed?"

Mrs. Purdy puts down her teacup. "Yes, there was a rather heated discussion last week as to whether we should do the same as has already been done in nearby towns, or create something of our own."

"The cenotaph is a common act of remembrance," Jost agrees, nodding solemnly. "But perhaps it is so common because it is the most fitting. I know many of you lost sons or husbands to the war." His gaze lingers on a few of the women. "I had the privilege of serving alongside them. And I must admit, one of the most difficult parts of my job has been accepting the fact that I came back while so many stayed. It was difficult for many of us to return home and leave the fallen behind. And yet, we must." He looks across the room. "You may know, of course, that cenotaph is a Greek word. It means an empty tomb. I rather think it a fitting symbol for those men whose final resting place is so far away from home."

A few women nod in agreement, one holding a discreet handkerchief to her cheek.

"And we could inscribe it with the names of our men, as I suggested last week," a woman adds, the peacock feather pinned to her hat quivering as she turns her head.

"Certainly," Jost says. "I have seen some cenotaphs remain unadorned, serving more as a symbol of the collective loss without focusing on individuals. But some do include names, and citations as well. The one in London, for example, says *The Glorious Dead*." His tone turns reverent.

Rose stirs in her seat. The war—her war—was not glorious, and yet she cannot bring herself to tell these women, these mothers, the truth. That their sons died scared, in terrible pain, and sometimes alone.

Jost continues to answer the women's questions until gradually they all come to the conclusion that a cenotaph is indeed the best option.

Once, in the years before the war, Rose had attended a memorial unveiling for the Boer War on University Avenue. She had found it beautiful—four bronzed figures, with two soldiers near a base, and a female figure between them. Canada sending her sons to war. At the top of the tall obelisk stood a winged figure. Victory, holding a golden crown in her outstretched hands. Rose had been struck when she had first seen it. And yet, now she knows the truth of it, it feels inadequate. A falsehood. A romantic ideal.

She understands the appeal of a cenotaph made of stone. It endures. A hundred years from now, the memorial will stand, the names still visible. No one will be able to forget. And yet, will the names be enough? Will they have any meaning once those who now whisper them in grief, who remember the lives behind the names, leave this world to join them? What about the stories, the sacrifices that left no names to carve into stone? What about the living?

"Miss Avery," Mrs. Purdy says. "Is there anything you would like to add?"

Rose looks up, alarmed. The conversation has continued without her and she is unsure of what to say. "These are all great ideas—beautiful ways to commemorate your loved ones," she says, too quietly. She clears her throat. "But I wonder if there is a way for this memorial to reflect more of the sacrifices made."

"Meaning?" asks Mrs. Purdy.

"Meaning..." Rose's mouth is dry. "Meaning the war impacted everyone, including yourselves. It left behind widows and orphans, fractured whole families. And those men who came back, injured or otherwise—how do we honour them?"

She had thought about it often since the memorial unveiling. About what she felt was missing. It had captured so little of the war. So little of the loss.

The room is quiet. Rose can feel the weight of their gazes on her.

"What might a memorial of this scale look like?" Mrs. Purdy finally asks.

"I'm not sure," Rose admits. All she knows is that the war has taken from everyone in this room, one way or another. Was there a way to capture that? A way to memorialize the loss of innocence, of hope, of self? Was there a message they could send into the future that did not glorify war but revealed its wounds? Was there a way Leo could be remembered alongside the others?

Rose presses her hands together in her lap. "I only think it is important to include everyone," Rose says in a low voice.

Major-General Jost clears his throat. "It sounds to me as though you mean yourself."

Rose blinks. "I beg your pardon?"

"I apologize if I misunderstood," Jost says. "But your insistence on wanting to include *everyone*—well, I can only assume you mean yourself. Or rather, nurses."

Rose begins to shake her head. "No, I only meant—"

"Let us be clear," Jost interrupts, his voice firm. "While we certainly appreciated your care, those boys faced death head-on, with nothing but their courage to shield them. There is a distinction to be made."

"I was not making a comparison," Rose bristles. "Nor was I asking for recognition. Though would it be so unfounded? Nurses were there. In the thick of it. We saw the same horrors—"

"From the sideline," Jost says coldly.

Rose is taken aback. The sideline? Nurses had died for this war as well, on torpedoed ships, or in hospitals. Even No. 1 CGH, where Rose had spent most of her time in France, had been bombed, blasted from the sky. Eight patients had been killed, dozens more wounded—and three nurses. Three nurses had died trying to care for the wounded. The first Canadian nurses to die in action.

Had they not faced the same dangers? Rose had watched men die. Men who would have lived if she had only been able to get them help in time, or to get them away from the Front, away from the mud. Who would have lived had she not been instructed to send them back to their deaths. She had held them in her arms, felt the life leave them, as life faded from her as well. There is much she wants to say, but it sticks in her throat like ash.

"Well," Mrs. Purdy begins carefully. "Perhaps there is room for more than one kind of recognition. I do appreciate you sharing your thoughts with us, Miss Avery." Her gaze sweeps the room. "But I think I speak for everyone here when I say that the loss of our sons and husbands is more important. Perhaps your ideas might find a home elsewhere, in some other way."

Before Rose can utter another word, Mrs. Purdy suggests they take a break, pointing the group to the refreshments table.

With the women occupied, Rose excuses herself, telling Émilie she feels unwell.

"Bien sûr," Émilie says, her voice low. "Would you like for me to come with you?" she offers in French.

Rose shakes her head. She would rather be alone.

Major-General Jost's words cling to her as she makes her way home. *The sideline*. How many times had Rose refused to leave her post? How many times had she remained near the frontlines even when offered the chance to leave?

When in 1917 Matron had presented nurses who had been at the hospital longest a new post in England, Rose had refused. She could not imagine leaving for England while Leo was still in France. She knew it was irrational, but there was a gravitational pull keeping her in place. Rose felt increasingly paralyzed at the thought that Leo might land in her hospital, bloodied and broken, but she was even more concerned that he might land in a different hospital, and that she would not learn of it until it was too late.

Almost daily there was a parade of blue skirts moving from the hospital to the Red Cross office to enquire about missing brothers, injured cousins, lost neighbours. The flood had returned, bodies upon bodies crowding the tents of the hospital, marking either success or loss at the Front—one could never tell from the bodies. Rose found herself calling to Leo in the slivers of fitful sleep she managed to fit in the remnants of her days, beckoning him. She had not heard from him in months, but knew he must have been there. Surely, he was taking part in the offensive. She had once prayed that death may never come for him, but seeing these mangled, severed bodies, she now prayed that if it must, it be swift and effortless.

Mae left for England, along with most of the other nurses they had been working with since returning from their last leave. Rose was left alone with strangers.

Matron called her into the office the morning after the others left. "I understand you did not want to transfer to London, but I really must urge you to take leave," she said, eyebrows drawn together. A rare show of concern. "Doesn't a Scottish holiday sound lovely?"

Rose had looked down at her palms, her skin flaking. "Does it need to be Scotland?" she asked. Margot was in France. Nearly a day's travel away, but if Rose had to be anywhere else, it had to be with family.

"I'm so glad to see you!" Margot exclaimed, throwing herself at Rose with wide arms.

Rose stumbled back, unused to such close affection, but in an instant melted in her arms. Margot smelled vaguely of bleach and powder, but Rose could still distinguish hints of her sister's familiar scent. Hints of home. It was such a relief to see Margot after so long.

Margot pulled back, keeping her hands on Rose's shoulders. Maybe she could sense Rose needed steadying. "It's been ages!"

"Too long," Rose agreed, and Margot pulled her in for another short embrace.

"Come, let's put these in water." Margot took the flowers from Rose's hands. She had almost forgotten them—a bouquet of verbenas, ageratums, and hollyhocks that had travelled with her from her little garden at the hospital to now rest in a tarnished copper vase that suspiciously resembled a cocktail shaker in the kitchens of a castle turned convalescent hospital in northeastern France.

"I'm sorry we don't have a better vase," Margot said, primping the flowers with her fingers. "I think every *blessé* must have at least one bouquet by his bedside."

Rose had not taken the time to look at her properly, but she did so now. The VAD uniform was similar to her own, with little, truly, to distinguish them despite their difference in qualifications. Margot's dress was of a lighter shade of blue, without the fussy brass buttons and belt, and her apron emblazoned with a red cross. But they could have aptly been called bluebirds, too.

Mae resented the blurred distinctions between trained and untrained nurses, saying the VADs were tarnishing their reputation, but Rose had difficulty mustering the same level of contempt for women like her sister. She had often wondered why Margot had not chosen this profession herself—Margot, who had been older sister to her, Jeanne, and Leo, a little helper for Anna. Perhaps that was the reason she had not pursued nursing. Perhaps she had rejected the role she had occupied at home.

Margot was fanciful and driven to try new things and would have undoubtedly resisted the constraints of military nursing, though she seemed at home in this environment, where she was a companion and advocate to the wounded. She had sent Rose an article published in the Toronto papers in which she thanked the generous folks at home for helping her raise funds for an artificial limb for one of her patients, a most deserving man and father of three who had bravely fought for two years. This was where she shone. In society. And though she had still shown no sign of wanting to marry, Rose suspected she would return home to find something else to occupy her time, while Rose continued nursing.

"How many men do you have here?" Rose asked.

"Oh, not many. We have capacity for fewer than two hundred. I would say it gets hectic when we receive large transfers, but I suppose it's much worse for you."

Rose wondered what a large transfer entailed here. Perhaps twenty, thirty patients at most? All of them bandaged and sutured already. No need to assess bloody wounds or change dressings. No urgency.

She returned Margot's smile. "All French?"

"All French. Though the staff are mostly British. I suppose that's why I'm here, terrible though I feel my French is at times. It does make for some interesting conversations, I must say." Her eyes glinted. "Come, I'll show you around."

The temporary convalescent hospital had been established in the château of the Duc de Penthièvre, Margot explained as she led her outside to explore the grounds. "It's really an ideal place for the patients. Such a lovely area." Margot bounced on her feet as she walked.

Rose had to admit that the rolling uplands and vast forests surrounding them were magnificent.

"The townsfolk are so kind. We join them in church on Sundays, and the priest visits to conduct service for the men." She waved at another VAD passing by and pointed to a cluster of men in the distance. "They also get to enjoy the views and the fresh country air. I expect it's quite a relief for them to find themselves here rather than back in the trenches."

There was a man in a wheelchair and another with the sleeve of his missing left arm tucked neatly to the side of his jacket. The aftermath of the amputations and surgeries Rose normally saw.

"Are their families allowed to visit?"

"Many do, if they live nearby."

That was one advantage the French and British soldiers had over the colonials.

They turned a corner and strolled to the front of the massive castle, its large windows reflecting them as they passed. A group of men stood smoking on the front steps, laughter drifting with the smoke. They nodded and some even took off their caps as Margot approached.

"Bonjour," she said brightly.

"Bonjour, Soeur Avery," two replied in unison, though Rose could tell from their accents that they were English. They wore uniforms but none seemed to bear injuries.

"Is Docteur Cyr in today?"

One man standing near the back shook his head. "Emergency in town. He left early this morning."

Margot looked disappointed. "Do you know when he'll be back?"

The men exchanged glances, shrugging. "Sorry, Sister."

Margot brushed off her disappointment, her cheery self returning. "Not to worry."

One of the men opened the heavy oak door to let them inside.

"Who's Docteur Cyr?" Rose asked as the door closed behind them.

"The local physician. He comes in to help our volunteer surgeons." She motioned to the door they had just passed through. "A wonderful man. I would have liked for you to meet him."

Margot led the way through the ornate halls of the castle. Most of the furniture had been removed to make space for the hospital equipment, the large rooms occupied by cots and trolleys filled with medical gear. The space was much nicer than the tents Rose had grown accustomed to, and she envied her sister these small comforts. How many times had Rose's hands cramped from the cold while trying to administer a needle because the tent only had one stove? Here there were large, embellished fireplaces, now dormant, but enticing nonetheless. And baths—they must have had bathtubs, while Rose had to make do with the rough Channel waters most of the time.

"And here he is, mon patient préféré." Margot moved between two cots to take her favourite patient's hand. He was smiling, his hand eagerly reaching for hers as he lay in bed, the sheets neatly tucked around him.

"How are you this morning?" she asked in French.

"I'm well. How are you, Nurse Avery?"

"I'm wonderful, seeing as I have a visitor today." Margot motioned to Rose. "Oumar, I would like you to meet my sister, Sister Rose Avery."

Oumar's eyes flickered briefly to Rose but he quickly looked away. "Enchanté."

Rose nodded. "Pleased to meet you as well."

"And this is his faithful companion, soldat Niang." Margot smiled at the man seated on the other side of the bed, who nodded at Rose.

"They are serving with the tirailleurs sénégalais," Margot explained. "Oumar was injured during the Battle of Verdun, and Niang has only recently arrived."

Rose had been surprised to learn that French colonial soldiers of colour were allowed on the frontlines. When two soldiers from the British West Indies regiment had landed in her ward the previous month, they had noted they were primarily responsible for digging trenches and loading ammunitions—jobs they argued were more dangerous than fighting. Privates Jones and Barrow were both from Barbados, both terribly young. Their charts said they were eighteen, but Jones had let it slip that he was actually seventeen. Some of the other nurses had started calling them the Tar Babies, though Rose had never heard them use such infantilizing terms with other young soldiers. It confounded Rose that these Black soldiers were at once infantilized in hospital and given the most dangerous tasks on the battlefield.

One of the orderlies, a former soldier himself, had complained that they should not have been treated in the same tent as the white soldiers. "Are you offering space from the orderlies' quarters?" Rose had asked, pointing out that there was not enough free space in the hospital to separate soldiers by race. The orderly had said nothing else, but Rose noticed that he started attending to Jones and Barrow last, so she made a point of giving them their medication herself, usually taking a few minutes to sit with Jones at the end of her workday. He reminded her of Leo: he was animated, funny, and had been an avid football player before the war. "I was desperate to come," he told her one evening. "To prove myself. To represent my country." In some ways, she saw her own early enthusiasm reflected in his. "I wanted to win something in honour of my race," Jones had said.

Barrow, more cautious, had refused even to sign her notebook, but Jones had willingly shared his story. He had been a sugar cane cutter before the war. Beyond recognition, Jones had hoped the war might offer financial and social capital and had eagerly gone in search of it. His eyes were bright when he recounted the warmth with which he had been received in France. "I went to a cinema and the crowd erupted into applause at images of the Senegalese riflemen at the Battle of Verdun. I felt a swell of pride, even knowing I would not myself be in a combat role. I thought at least someone was showing them we could. I thought at least some of us were regarded as brothers."

Rose wondered whether Oumar and Niang understood the pride they had instilled in Jones, or if the racial climate of France was colder than Jones could ever know.

Margot flitted from bed to bed, speaking with her patients in that light tone of voice that suggested they had nothing to worry about. And here was the most important difference in their work, Rose realized. It was not that Rose had three years of training that Margot lacked, or that she was being paid for work that Margot volunteered. It was that, in her role as a VAD, Margot was able to focus solely on her patients. To heal, to console. Her only goal was to improve their health. She was secondary to the war. Rose, on the other hand, was a cog in the war machine. She healed men to send them back down the line. By healing them, she was killing them. Not for the first time, Rose found herself envious of Margot.

"Have you seen him? Since your last birthday?" Margot asked when they were seated in the garden, glasses of port in hand. The buds on the trees were nascent, the earth in the vegetable patch freshly tilled.

Rose shook her head. "Have you heard from him lately?"

"Not for a while," Margot said. "Anna mentioned in her last letter that he had grown quiet of late. I thought he might have been writing to you instead."

Rose fingered the stem of her glass, averting her eyes. She wished she could say that Leo had written.

"I'm sure he's fine. He'll write soon. He wouldn't miss your birthday," Margot said.

Rose's hand automatically lifted to the rose necklace hanging on her chest. She could hardly believe it had already been a year since he had given it to her. She never wore it on duty but had made a point of wearing it for her visit to Arc-en-Barrois. She had thought it might make her feel as though he were here with them, but they had all been away for so long that she could no longer recall the feeling of them all being together.

Time away had prompted her to develop individual relationships with each of her family members. She remembered how, years ago, during the summer she and Jeanne had spent with a great aunt in Montreal, they had addressed all their letters *Dear family*. Now Rose wrote to each of them separately, told them different things about her life in France. With her father she discussed medical trials and advances happening at her hospital, reading through his lengthy scientific responses with little time to fully absorb their concepts. With Anna she shared social news, speaking of the friends she had made in France and those she had left at home, absorbing the many ways Anna seemed to have gotten involved in the war effort since she had left. To Ellen she sent shorter versions of the news she relayed to her father, conscious of the fact that Ellen had once tried to work in this environment herself but had been denied. With Jeanne she wrote little about the war at all. Her youngest sister, a new mother with another little one on the way, seemed to live a life entirely removed from the war. It was only ever with Leo and Margot that she was able to share her true feelings, and even then, she obscured it. Perhaps because of this, Rose found that she could not envision a time when they would all be together again. The feeling had grown more acute in the wake of Leo's silence.

She took a deep breath and smiled at Margot, lifting her glass to her lips. "I hope not."

Her visit with Margot had refreshed Rose, but not for long. By the time autumn arrived, she was stationed at a casualty clearing station near the Front, as close to the firing lines as she had ever been. She had proven her skills in the operating theatre and demonstrated that she worked well under pressure.

That was how Matron framed it one morning after breakfast.

"As one of the most senior nurses here, we trust you will be a great asset to the physicians at the Front."

Rose had nodded, feeling numb. Casualty clearing stations were a few rungs down the ladder of evacuation for soldiers, but the first fully equipped with surgical facilities, and nurses had been banned from them at the start of the war. After the clearing stations, men were sent to stationary hospitals or general hospitals, like No 1 CGH. These were the largest and usually the last stop before patients were returned to England. Because clearing stations were situated only a few miles from the firing lines, they had initially been deemed too dangerous for women. Rose wondered what had changed but dared not ask.

She arrived at No. 2 Canadian Clearing Station in the middle of October 1917. Bushes and trees greeted her at the entrance of the gravel driveway while wooden passageways twined between the tents and the wooden barracks. The complex was much larger than Rose had expected, a small city sprawling in the shadows of Ypres Salient. To her surprise, it looked almost identical to the general hospital she had just left, apart from the tents, which were stained brown rather than white.

"Camouflage," the lorry driver explained when Sister Hume, her companion, enquired. "We get bombed pretty regularly around here."

The distant booming of guns reminded Rose of the roar of surging waves breaking against the side of a wharf. When she stepped out of the cab, her feet sank deep into the mud.

There was no time to get settled. Rose was shown to her tent and immediately put in charge of triage. Every day, she sorted the wounded as they were unloaded from ambulances, their broken bodies held together by rust-coloured bandages. The stretcher bearers gathered them in her hut, the wind blowing the penetrating smell of steel, blood, and disinfectants that pervaded the enclosed ward every time they opened the door.

Rose fluttered about the room, checking tags, feeling clammy skin. It was her job to decide whose life was slipping away quickest, to distinguish the dying from the nearly dying, but it was not as easy as it had been farther down the line. These soldiers all had the same pallid, vacant look in their eyes, the same muddied and bloodied uniforms, the same ragged breathing.

As she read the scrawled notes of the dressing station surgeon on the back of one patient's tag, the soldier suddenly reached out to touch her hand, caressing her skin. Rose looked up, startled, but did not move. A voice rang in her ears. "You're the first woman they see coming out of those trenches," one of the surgeons, Captain Kerr, had told her shortly after her arrival. "Their angel in white," he added ironically. She had looked down at her apron, permanently splashed with blood. Nothing stayed white in a clearing station.

She blinked at the patient and tried to smile but noticed his eyes were bandaged.

Time at the clearing station dissipated, days tumbling forward. Rose counted the weeks with the growing and shrinking slivers of the moon as she wore a path between her tent and the hut every night, the darkness somehow darker here. She longed for the time she had shared a tent with Mae, her presence a comfort even when they had been like ships passing in the night. The loneliness of her empty hut extended to the entire clearing station, where she was one of only a few women.

The sodden earth sank under her feet as Rose hurried from one man to the next. She started referring to them, like Margot, as *blessés*. It was the most suitable word for what they were: wholly, entirely wounded. They did not even look like men, but rather pieces of men. Masses of limbs bundled in cloth painted deep red and rich brown. Bodies twisted and bent, skin of a petrified hue. War had broken them, misshapen them. Moulded them. From the mud of the trenches a new species had been born.

They did not sound like men, swearing and groaning and screaming for their mothers. Mewling like wounded animals. It was excruciating to listen to, but Rose was certain those who remained quiet were the least human of all.

She then learned to refer to men not as patients but as injuries. Knees, lungs, abdomens. That was all the surgeon needed to know. That was all they had time for. There was no time for names, for regiments, for hometowns. Another patient would surely die in the time it took to mention them, or note them down in her journal.

The orderlies returned to fetch more cases for the operating theatre. She pointed, her fingers still despite her constant agitation. "Two Abdomens, one Lung, and one Knee. The Elbow can wait."

The orderlies bent down to pick up the Abdomen. He whimpered, begging for a drink. "I'm so thirsty." He licked his cracked lips. "Can I have some water? Just one sip?" The contents of his stomach were exposed.

Taking a step back, one of the orderlies tripped on a body on the ground, narrowly avoiding the Head with his muddied boot. The Abdomen yelled his agony as he slid from the stretcher to the floor. The commotion nearly startled half the men out of death. Rose rushed to grab the other end of the stretcher.

"I'll help you carry him," she said, hiking her skirt to her knees.

The other orderly looked at her with wide eyes but proceeded out the door.

These were not men. She need not be a woman.

The bombs arrived a few weeks after she did. Aeroplanes swirled in the skies above their heads, dropping explosives that shook the huts and the people inside to their very core. Bright moonlight guided the aircrafts, which dipped and disappeared behind windswept clouds, hiding from view of the anti-aircraft guns that thundered below, the noise a constant companion as Rose worked, a canon lullaby as she tried to sleep.

Are we hearing the same guns? She wrote Leo, alone in her tent in the early morning hours. She wrote him more often, though she rarely managed more than one line at a time. *Father writes that his cousin's son has been missing since September*, she scribbled. Then she tried to think of something other than the war. *I voted against the Union Government of Canada this morning*, she added, though of course that was as much about the war as anything else: was she for or against conscription? *I wonder what Anna would make of the servicewoman's vote.*

Leo replied, *My mother wrote to say that she intended to use her vote as the mother of a serviceman, but for the Unionists. This war seems to have turned her into quite the radical.*

It had felt like a triumph for military nurses and the mothers, sisters, and wives of men in uniform to have been allowed to vote in the federal election, but it was somewhat tarnished by the circumstances under which it had been granted. The government trying to garner more votes for conscription, thinking women could only support sending more help for their sons, husbands, and brothers abroad. But Rose could not in good conscience accept that they should send more men, unwilling men, to the Front.

Sometimes I close my eyes and am reminded of all the horrific things I've witnessed, all the lives I've seen extinguished, Leo scrawled on a piece of paper ripped from a notebook, its edges frayed. Rose had noticed that he had stopped mentioning Gillis, the man with whom he had frequently gone on leave. She wondered if he had died but dared not ask. Rose felt relieved that although they had seen different sides of this war, it was also the same. They understood each other in the silences, the omissions. Leo wrote less often, and his tone was different, but at least he was writing.

One morning in November, Rose had reached into the pocket of a patient and slipped out a small notebook. She inhaled sharply. It had the same dusty leather exterior as the one James had left her, had the same weight to it. She almost thought for an instant that it might be the same one—but no, that journal was tucked away in the folds of her clothes in the bottom of her trunk. She had promised James she would keep it safe. But here she was, closer to the trenches than she had ever been.

Most nights, enemy planes hummed overhead like a hive of vexed bees, dropping bombs to the north, and then to the south of them. She would often pause her work, holding her breath, thinking—knowing—that missiles were moments away from falling on her hut. In those long minutes, she regretted she had brought all the men she had promised to keep safe to the line of danger. She regretted not having sent her journals to England with Mae.

The air raids continued throughout winter and spring, reaching farther into France as the rain melted the snow. Yellowed grass lifted itself from the damp earth in the distance, shedding its frost and eagerly soaking up rainwater until it turned green. Buds sprouted on the trees. Rose glanced at the horizon one morning and was shocked by the thick, vibrant foliage that sheltered the branches. Flowers had sprouted, growing wild in some areas of camp. Rose missed her garden in Étaples.

How are the magnolias, the delphiniums, the peonies? she asked Anna in a letter. *Describe them to me in full detail. There is only mud here. A sea of mud, swimming with coils of iron.* She lifted her pen, read what she had written, and dashed her hand across the page, soaking the words in ink. She picked up a new piece of paper and wrote, *Please describe the flowers to me. I miss you.*

CHAPTER 18

Émilie hands Rose a telegram.

"What's this?"

"It appears to be a note from my son."

A rush of warmth floods Rose's cheeks.

"Don't mind me. He would have to be daft not to recognize how great you are." Émilie gives her a playful wink. Despite the debacle at the meeting, Émilie still showed her as much warmth of feeling, if not more. Rose was grateful.

She accepts the telegram. "Thank you."

ROSE STOP DINNER TONIGHT? STOP FREDERICK.

She cannot help but smile. He was back from Montreal at last.

He arrives promptly at six, and they are on the road by seven, the children unwilling to let this surprise visit from their uncle slip by without acknowledgement. Oliver had been enthusiastically showing Frederick the fifth of his latest set of trading cards when Silas had swept in to say, "All right, that was very kind of you to share with your uncle, but I believe he has somewhere to be. Don't you, Uncle Freddy?"

Frederick had nodded, guiding Rose to the door with a hand on her back. "Yes, we do, thank you, Oliver. I'll see you all again soon."

"He admires you," Rose says as they settle into the motor car.

Frederick arches his eyebrows, still seemingly surprised by this fact. "I know. Hard to imagine there was a time I was barely a presence in their lives."

Frederick had not specified where they would have dinner. Rose thought perhaps he would bring her to a restaurant, but she is glad for the privacy of the cottage. He gives her a tour, moving from the living room to the kitchen in a few short steps and gesturing vaguely to the stairs leading to the second-floor bedrooms.

Soon, the savoury aroma of butter mingling with the salty scent of the sea fills the air as Frederick begins frying haddock. When Rose offers to help, he refuses. "I spent years dreaming of all the things I could eat if I only had access to a kitchen and fresh ingredients," he says with a smile. "Trust me, I enjoy this."

He pours her a glass of grapefruit juice and invites her to take a seat at the table, but Rose stays leaning against the countertop, too enthralled by the smells and the sight of a man standing over a stove.

"Where did you learn to cook?" she asks. She has certainly never seen Silas cook.

"I suppose I picked up a few things over the years when I was travelling. Whenever I discovered a dish I enjoyed, I wanted to bring it home with me, so I often asked for recipes. But most of my practice came after the war, living alone." He waves his spatula in the air. "One has to learn to fend for himself."

"Did your father cook?" Rose knows very little about his father. She remembers meeting him at the wedding, a tall, gruff man who laughed boisterously from the centre of a thick beard. He was a man who seemed cold but melted as soon as he opened his mouth. She could tell, now, how easily he would have made Émilie happy.

Frederick shakes his head. "No. I suppose that was a different time. What use was cooking to folks who had cooks? That was his family, I mean. When he was growing up. I don't think my mother wanted hired help in the house, so she took on the responsibility herself." He flips a piece of fish, revealing golden brown.

"I don't think my mother did either," Rose says, then catches herself. "Actually, I'm not sure. Anna certainly didn't."

"So, you had to learn to fend for yourself." He turns to look at her, a strand of hair falling in his eyes.

Rose smiles. "That was by choice."

He looks at her with contemplation. "Sometimes I wonder what my father would make of this changed world."

"I also wonder. About my mother. And about Leo," she adds.

Some days, Rose thinks the war has changed everything. Certainly, empires had crumbled, and old social orders torn apart. But it was more than that. Rose had started working at a time when it was unusual for a woman of her station to work for pay. She had done it out of passion rather than need and had been allowed simply because her father did not disagree. But the war had allowed many more women to do the same. To venture into public life, to make themselves visible in the world. Before, she would have been expected to remain in her father's house until she married. But she had left home—had lived abroad, in a tent. She had been exposed to new ideas and cultures. The change in society had given her the ability to make choices for herself. Or, at least, the illusion of it. But even this—her ability to be here, alone with Frederick. It would have been unimaginable before the war. Scandalous, even.

Sometimes, she envies the younger generation, the one coming of age in this changed world, this new reality, who have known nothing of the world before. The push for change often seems to be coming from them; though, in truth, they are only the first ones to fully enjoy the freedoms others fought for—and the first to ask for more. Rose feels ancient when she thinks of this, as though she has lived through lifetimes.

"Did Leo share your concerns for a more just world?" Frederick asks, his curiosity sounding genuine.

"I don't know," Rose admits. "That was not something we ever discussed. That was not something we had the words for—not then. The changes we wanted to see in the world were those we were told to want, in order to go to war." She contemplates this for a moment, the sizzling of the butter in the pan the only noise in the room. "I often wish we would have had more time to talk. Afterwards. Once we had both seen what we had seen. I took it for granted that I would have someone to speak with about all of this, once it was over. Even then, I knew I would not be able to confide in Anna, or even Margot. Only Leo. But we never got the chance."

"You can speak to me," Frederick offers.

"I know. I've come to realize that."

Seated in front of steaming plates of fish, potato croquette, and scalloped tomatoes, Rose asks Frederick if he hunts or fishes.

Frederick shakes his head, chuckling. "I would much rather swim in a lake or stroll through the forest than engage in either of those activities."

"What about painting them?" She points to the various landscapes hanging on the walls.

"My mother painted those. Every last one." He takes a bite of his fish, then adds, "Surely you must have seen her paint during your time here?"

Rose chews thoughtfully. "I'm not sure I have."

"She used to paint in that large room upstairs, the one overlooking the garden. It had the best light in the house, she said. But the children seem to have taken it over, so she must have relocated her things."

"Yes, she must have." Rose wants to ask if he has seen his mother paint since the war, since the death of her husband, since his internment, but does not.

"Do you paint?" Frederick asks.

"I used to. I haven't picked up a brush in years. Not since before nursing school."

"Watercolour?"

"Oils, actually."

"Maybe this is your chance to pick it up again."

"Yes, maybe. The views here are quite spectacular." She gestures to the windows overlooking the sea in the backyard, the sun no more than a string of orange at the far end of the sky.

Their conversation continues as the candles dwindle, leaving drops of hardened wax on the brass holders. The light grows dimmer, the room more intimate.

"How was your trip?" Rose asks once she has cleared her plate.

"Enlightening."

"I have found Montreal to have that effect."

Frederick laughs. "I went to visit someone. A new acquaintance." He considers his words. "My mother told me recently that they helped a civilian interned in Canada. She and my father. It was strange..." He gives a slight shake of his head. "While I was in the camp, I knew, of course, that there were interned civilians in Britain. They were, I suppose, part of the reason Britain refused to negotiate our release. They held significantly more men than Germany, and it would have been unwise to release them. That's what we told ourselves, at least. Even as we resented being used as pawns, we only ever saw them as pawns ourselves. I never considered that they had families and lives waiting for them, too. I never considered the men who were imprisoned by my own country."

Rose waits for him to say more, but when he remains quiet, she asks, "What was his name?"

"Koval. Petro Koval." Frederick shifts in his chair. "He was the nephew of one of my father's business acquaintances. My mother says this man requested my father's help, but I suspect my father tried to use him as a bargaining chip. To see if he could exchange one prisoner for another. He was kind, my father, but also calculating. You don't get very far in business without thinking strategically. But of course, the Germans would have had no use for a Ruthenian. It was likely my mother who insisted they help him nonetheless."

"And did they? Help him?"

"I think so. They sent him care packages, at least. Some money."

"Why did you visit him?"

"More for my own sake, I suppose. I wanted to meet someone who had gone through the same thing I had."

Rose reaches for her glass. "There must have been others you could speak to, from your camp."

Frederick gives a half shrug. "I have not kept touch with anyone." He is quiet for a moment, then continues. "There was one person I considered a dear friend in Ruhleben. Ira. I'm not sure I would have survived those four years without him. He was Canadian, but he chose to stay in England when we were released, to record the end of the war. He was a journalist, you see. Last I heard from him, he had gone back to Germany. He wrote me a handful of letters. One to explain why he felt the need to return, and the others to speak out against what he found there. He was part of the reason I was so adamant about defending Germany. I had a trusted source who, like me, had been imprisoned at the hands of the Germans and yet still found it in his heart to forgive them and fight for their survival. What he described…it was not my Germany. It was not the country I had loved, the one I had called home. Nor was the Germany I had lived in for the last four years. And I want to see that Germany again. I want to see it flourish once more. Not wither on the vine of this war."

Rose tilts her head, studying him. "What happened to Ira?" She is cautious with her questions, and yet he seems so willing to share.

Frederick shakes his head. "I'm not sure. That's the worst part. I don't think he ever left Germany. I don't think he…" Frederick rubs the back of his neck, his words lost.

Rose tries to catch his gaze again. "I'm sorry."

Frederick nods stiffly, his voice barely above a whisper. "Thank you."

"Was your visit with Mr. Koval helpful?"

Frederick looks at the space above her head, eyes narrowing. "I don't know. I don't know what I was hoping to gain. It was helpful to speak with someone who had gone through a similar experience as I had. And yet, his experience was different than mine in many ways. Neither of us deserved what we got. But in hearing him speak, I implicitly understood that I had privilege he did not. I had a family I could rely on, who sent me money when I had gone through all of mine. I had stayed in Germany willingly, even after war was declared. I was treated decently, not made to work—which was both a privilege and a curse at times. I spoke the language. I understood what was happening to me. I trusted that my country had my best interests at heart, even when they seemed to forget about me. Koval could not say the same. Koval was afraid—is still afraid. I've returned home, but he has no home to return to, and rightfully doesn't feel at home here either anymore."

Frederick sighs. "I got away from myself while there. I heard of his experiences and immediately considered the ways I could share them with the world in order to make my point. The point I've been trying to make all along. This idea of enemies, defined purely by race or class, this division between *our kind* and the rest—it's a fabrication. A story we tell ourselves. The myth of our being one, as a nation, it means we exclude others. I've experienced that exclusion. And I wanted to show society the other side of it. I wanted to share Koval's story so they could see the other side as I experienced it. But Koval did not want to share his story, understandably. I regret pushing him. I thought, perhaps naively, that if they saw the truth—his truth—they might understand, might change. But now I see that I was expecting too much. Some stories, no matter how crucial, are not ours to tell."

Rose hums with approval. Then, she asks, "Why not tell your own story?"

"What do you mean?"

"If you're trying to show others what it feels like to be cast aside and treated as if you don't belong...why not share your own experience?"

"I have tried. I've written in defence of Germany based on my unique perspective as a civilian prisoner of war."

"But have you provided the extent of your experience? Have you shown them that you defend them in spite of what they put you through?"

"I suppose not. I suppose I've never wanted to."

"Why not?" Rose's voice softens.

Frederick bites the inside of his cheek, his foot tapping the floor under the table. Suddenly he leans forward, resting his elbows. "It's difficult for me to explain," he says, his eyes roaming the table, as though a script might materialize in the grain of the wood.

"Don't you feel that the world deserves to know about your experiences?" Rose asks.

Frederick shakes his head again, but this time, he looks directly into her eyes. "They won't understand. Nobody understands."

"You could help them understand."

"No," he says softly. "What we endured—four years of imprisonment, of uncertainty. The loss of any life we had known. It was real for us. It's real for me. But to the rest of the world, it seems as if we merely waited out the war, safely tucked away in enemy territory, never made to fight, never made to work. I can't begin to describe what it was like, and I fear they'll diminish our pain if we try to explain. Our freedom, our livelihoods were ripped away from us. We were malnourished, housed in horse stables, and told to wait out the war within four barbed wire walls. The mental anguish was unbearable. But to others, it will still sound better than the trenches. It will still seem safer than the battlefield. Even though we didn't know if we would remain safe, of course. We were at the mercy of the enemy, after all. Anything could have happened. But compared to what others lived through, compared even to what Koval endured, my own hardships seem...insignificant."

Rose reaches out, placing her hand on top of his on the table. "I understand. You don't want to explain yourself, only to have the world reduce your experience to nothing."

Frederick looks up. "Yes. Precisely." His eyes search her face. "I don't think anyone has ever heard me the way you do. It's as though you catch the things I don't say—the ones I barely know how to put into words." He laughs, embarrassed. "What a thing for a polyglot to say."

Rose smiles, her thumb brushing the edge of his hand as their eyes meet. She wants to speak, wants to bare her soul as he has, but once again the words lodge in her throat.

Frederick sits back in his chair and clears his throat. "Dessert?"

He brings out a blueberry pie. "I can't take credit for this one." He gives a quick laugh, and Rose smiles, but something in the air has shifted. They eat in silence. Everything they have shared that evening hangs between them like an elastic band, stretched to its limits.

As Rose savours her last bite and takes a sip of tea, Frederick glances at his watch. "I suppose I should take you home now."

"Yes, I suppose," she says. But a tightness grips her chest. She does not want to leave, does not want to let go of this moment, this rare opening between them. "Though I'm not sure I'm ready to say good night."

His eyes lock onto hers, and in that shared gaze, a thousand words go unsaid, and the elastic snaps.

That night, she tells him about Leo. Tells him the truth. Tells him what she has yet to tell Anna. When he asks about the last few weeks, she confides in him her disillusionment with the memorials—their hollow ceremonies, the way they deepen her sense of fading away. She unburdens herself, piece by piece, and with each confession, feels the weight lift, until she is almost light.

When Rose wakes in the morning, the space next to her is empty, save for a note resting on the pillow beside her.

Gone swimming. - F

She can hear the rain drumming on the roof, can see only grey through the thin white curtains covering the bedroom window.

In the kitchen, she finds a pot of coffee already brewed, a mug waiting for her beside it. She pours herself a cup and gazes out through the windows. The rain seems to have subsided, the grass a brilliant shade of green against the dull sky, the distant waves carrying only a hint of blue. Gulls drift on the wind, screeching their greetings. The warmth of the coffee in her hands feels like comfort, and for the first time since her arrival, she is glad for the quiet.

She is halfway down the steps leading to the sea floor when she spots Frederick, limbs cresting gracefully over the waves in the distance. Frederick had mentioned he swam in the ocean every day, another of those small pleasures he now enjoyed. Rose's heart swells at the sight of him. The bottom steps are covered in water, so she sits down somewhere in the middle and marvels as the movement of the ocean, the damp salty air caressing her skin.

She had not intended to stay the night. Jeanne, she knows, will have noticed her absence, though the rest of them would likely leave the house before she might have woken up. She hopes Émilie had a meeting this morning. Rose can't bear the thought of Frederick's mother knowing she spent the night with her son.

Spent the night. It seems an odd thing to say.

Rose understands the facts of life, having grown up in a house with an extensive medical library that neither her father nor Anna policed, her training as a nurse filling in the gaps. She knows how to prevent pregnancy and how to rid one. That knowledge had never driven her to seek out intimacy, but nor had it caused her to fear it. Most men, she knew, engaged in premarital sex. She had encountered enough cases of syphilis during the war to know as much. For women to be shamed for the same urges seemed a poor reflection on society. She had only been intimate with one person before—a physician on the Front, a friend with whom she had found comfort, especially during the end of the war, bombs falling on hospitals. It had provided a source of solace against the constant threat of death.

But her experience with Frederick feels different.

She smiles warmly as he emerges from the water, her eyes lingering for a moment. "I should have brought you a towel," she says.

Beads of seawater cling to his eyelashes. He looks clean, refreshed. Alert. He leans in for a damp kiss.

"I should leave if I want to get to work at a reasonable hour," Frederick says once he is dressed. "Silas will be wondering where I am."

Rose is at the stove frying a pair of eggs. "You should at least have breakfast first."

Frederick gives her an odd sort of smile, as if he is amused by this play of domestic bliss.

"You're welcome to stay here if you want. Or I can drive you back home." He takes a sip of his coffee.

She looks up, then turns to the sea. The clouds are parting, the tide receding. "To tell you the truth, I could use a break from the children. War was not as loud as they are in the morning."

Frederick chuckles into his mug. "Then, please, by all means, stay. Enjoy the quiet."

Sliding the eggs onto a plate, careful not to break the yolk, she hands it to Frederick. He eats quickly, seemingly famished, and plants a tender kiss on her cheek before rushing out the door.

Rose takes a deep breath and exhales, straining to hear the distant crash of the ocean. She is glad to be here. Glad to be home. Surprised, even, at how deeply at home she feels here—not only in Nova Scotia, but here, at this cottage. She feels at ease for the first time in a long time.

The clouds disperse, the rain seeping into the earth. By noon, Rose is hard pressed to find any evidence of the grey weather that greeted her that morning. Dispensing with shoes and stockings, she ventures into the backyard. She delights in the sensation of the earth beneath her feet, the tickling blades of grass, and the rough edges of rocks. They force her to look attentively, to step carefully.

Approaching the wooded area that borders the house, Rose peers through the window of the shed. Inside, she can see tools lining the walls, wood scattered on tables. This must have been where Frederick did most of his woodworking—a talent he acquired in Ruhleben, as she has come to learn.

Amidst the trees, she perches down, keeping her eyes peeled. She finds herbs she has only read about in books, plucking them delicately and twirling them in her fingers before tucking them in the fold of her skirt, pinned above her knees. This is a hobby she has picked up since returning from France. A way for her to think of medicine differently—to heal small matters with teas and tinctures rather than clamps and saws. Once her skirt is brimming with colour, she returns to the house and leaves the herbs in the kitchen to dry.

Not wanting to let the afternoon slip away indoors, she heads outside again, veering towards the cliffs. On the beach, she meanders around the puddles that have formed, the rocks still wet from the sea. She casts her eyes in the distance, wondering how much time she has until the waves reclaim their shore.

It remains a wonder that she can walk the very path Frederick swam that morning, her toes squelching in the mud. In the distance, she spots a few silhouettes. She wonders if they are looking for fossils. Slowly, she approaches, curious about their potential discoveries. Only when she draws near does she recognize the neighbour she met with Frederick a few weeks ago, accompanied by a young boy. The child crouches, diligently turning over rocks one by one. As the man's gaze meets hers, she hesitates momentarily, uncertain if he will remember her, before offering a wave. He waves back. Not wanting to disturb their peace, Rose diverts her path, her eyes keenly scanning the ground. It is pebbled, red rocks nestled amongst grey and black. Curiosity gets the best of her, and she stoops down to retrieve a jagged piece of copper rock, inspecting each side in search of fossilized imprints.

Before she can register his approach, the boy is beside her. "Did you find one?" He is pink-cheeked and eager, eyes brimming with enthusiasm.

Rose suspects he is around Millicent's age, perhaps a few years older. She shakes her head and smiles. "I don't think so, but you might be better qualified." She hands him the rock.

"I'm only a boy!"

"Are you? You seem quite knowledgeable to me. I'm relatively new to the world of fossil hunting."

The child nods solemnly. "I have been doing it for a few years." Taking the rock from her hand, he begins to scrutinize it.

The man approaches, apologetic. Rose shakes her head and lifts a hand, and he relaxes. "Clyde, did you introduce yourself?"

The boy looks up. "My name is Clyde. I live down the road. Where do you live?"

"It's a pleasure to meet you, Clyde. My name is Rose. I'm just visiting a friend." She motions behind him. "Mr. Munro. Do you know him?"

Clyde nods eagerly. "Yes. He gave me a fossilized fern."

The man seems to recognize her now, and he smiles.

Clyde looks at the rock again and says, "Sorry, ma'am, I don't think this one's special."

"Well, that's perfectly fine. There are plenty more here to search from."

Clyde points to a larger rock a few feet away. "Did you know those were fossilized tree stumps?" He has an almost imperceptible lisp, catching on the word fossilized each time, but determined to say it at every opportunity. She likes this boy.

"I did not."

"Many, many years ago, scientists discovered a host of new species in fossilized trees in a town nearby."

"Is that so?"

"People often mistake them for rocks. But they're really trees."

"They do look like rocks from afar, don't they? How do you know they're trees?"

"Well, you see, these rocks have distinct patterns and textures that resemble the rings of a tree trunk. If you look closely, you might even see bark imprints on the sides. I learned about it from a book."

"That's fascinating," Rose says, and she means it. She is impressed by the breadth of this boy's knowledge.

Clyde looks proud. "Do you want to help us look for fossils? I could teach you."

"I think we need to head back soon, Clyde," the man says, looking towards the sea.

Disappointment briefly flickers across Clyde's face, but he brightens. "Next time?"

Rose nods. "Next time."

"It was nice to see you again, Miss Avery," the man says, tipping his hat. Clyde waves goodbye, turning to look at her even as he walks away, stumbling on the rocks. Rose raises her hand in a farewell. As she stands there, the salty breeze gently rustling her hair, Rose feels a renewed sense of hope.

She begins to walk back towards the stairs. A glimmer catches her eye, and she turns in the direction of the cliffs, searching for a moment caught in time. There is something there, a gleam in the crook of the cliff. With her fingers, she begins to dig, feeling the dirt pushing the skin under her nails. The glimmer shifts, loosening around her fingers. She twists and pulls it free, covered in mud and hardened soil. She walks a few paces to a shallow pool of water. The colour brightens as she washes away the dirt, revealing a white stone cracked to a deep purple centre. She turns it over in her hands. The stone reminds her of the cenotaph, and she wonders what would happen if she cracked the monument open.

She holds it up to sunlight and considers it. How long had it been nestled there, caught in the cliffs? How many tides had washed over it, how many years had passed, unnoticed, as the earth held it in its grasp? How much else had time quietly uncovered? She thinks of the small revelations that have now been shared between her and Frederick. The things that had been buried, only half-formed, until now. She feels something inside her, too, shifting, unsettled, yet strangely whole. She drops the stone in the pocket of her skirt and returns to the wooden stairs, the waves pressing on behind her.

CHAPTER 19

Since that night, Frederick has been unable to shake Rose's words. She was right. He needs to consider his own internment before using someone else's to make a point.

The heavy trunk is exactly where he left it, inside the wardrobe in his bedroom, tucked away behind old winter coats and boots. He pulls it out and lifts it onto the bed.

The last time Frederick opened this trunk was the day after he returned home at the tail end of 1918, when he had wobbled up the stairs to the attic, searching for a place for all the memories he had brought back from Ruhleben—memories he was glad to put away, at least for the time being. The trunk had been tucked in a forgotten corner, filled with little more than a few old garments. He had removed it to the cottage later that year, and it had not crossed his mind since. But if Rose could be so honest with him about her experiences, he owed it to himself to be equally honest.

He unhooks the latches and the lid snaps back to reveal a sage-papered interior, edges frayed at the corners. Inside the trunk are layers of relics—stacks of letters above photographs and magazines, an array of small leather-bound books. A mess of memories. He pushes the records to the side, digging deeper, sifting through the folds of his past. A stack of photographs show men in mismatched clothes standing in front of a brick wall. A dusty baseball game on a large barren field. Dark, sparsely furnished rooms. He can hardly believe, studying those photographs, that they are of him. That this had been his life. But there he stands, hair sheared short, wearing an odd ensemble of a jacket and short pants, staring solemnly into the camera. What would Rose make of this man?

He is surprised by the swell of emotions that rises in him, reaching for a bundle of envelopes tied together with string. Letters from his family and friends. It dawns on him that somewhere in this stack are the last words his father ever wrote him. He cannot even remember what he said. One day, Frederick had received yet another letter from his father, and weeks later, the news from Silas. It strikes him as unfair that those final words should now be inextricably tied with the memories of his internment. That he should have to revisit the war every time he wants to remember his father. He puts the letters aside and peers into the trunk once more. At the very bottom is another stack, topped by a postcard of a horse-racing track. His own letters home. He picks them up, remembering the panic of that first postcard, and then sits on the bed, carefully untying the string.

Details return to him as he reads through his own letters. Though they mention little of his living conditions or mental state, a flood rises. He recalls with sharp clarity how cold, how miserable he had been when he wrote them. His mouth turns sour from the taste of mouldy bread, his eyes itchy from the sand. He can smell the mildew, quickly replaced by the scent of freshly turned earth, can hear the rats racing on the floorboards at night.

What strikes him most, all these years later, is how vividly his melancholy bleeds through the carefully chosen words meant to conceal it. Each phrase, meticulously crafted to obscure his anguish, now betrays the very despair it sought to hide. He is almost surprised by how despondent he seems. He had always considered himself resilient, and now he can only see profound vulnerability.

Day by day, moods shifted. One moment, certain of his imminent release, Frederick would be joyful, almost wild with hope. The next, he would be darkness itself. The evidence of his unravelling was right there—the fluctuations showing just how precariously he had teetered on the edge, clinging to hope one morning, surrendering to despair the next.

It had been worse at the beginning, before he found a sense of purpose, before he met Ira. But even when Frederick had settled into acceptance, the days had felt long. Long enough for mournful contemplation. Long enough for waves of misery.

It had affected them all. Even Ira, who had steadied everyone. Ira, who had always brought him back from the brink whenever Frederick retreated into misery, who had always urged, always pleaded, "We *need* to occupy ourselves. We must keep busy, or else the darkness will swallow us whole." From the beginning, he had been a pillar in the camp, helping others navigate the confusion. But when the promise of release was snatched away from him, he too had become unmoored. Near the end of 1916, the Commandant had announced that all men above the age of forty-five would be leaving shortly after Christmas, a group that included Ira.

"How will I survive without you?" Frederick had asked him, his words slurred. They had received their usual bottles of sour beer for Christmas, but New Year's Eve had found them all swimming in liquor. Frederick did not know where it had come from, only that bottles were passed to him, and their contents made him feel warm for once.

"You know," Ira said, placing a hand on his shoulder, "I don't know how long any of us will have to stay here. But I do know that we all must be able to create our own realities. To make peace with our circumstances. To find purpose and happiness where we can. Because even if we weren't here, son, there's still a war on. And at least your bed is not made of mud."

Everything had been arranged, plans made. Those slated for release were given passports and told to pack their things. For weeks, anticipation had grown—then months, seasons, dragging on without a word. Darkness swallowed Ira. He slowly withdrew from camp life, spending most of his time in the stall. If Frederick knew how to snap him out of it, it was only because Ira had done the same for him. He pulled Ira out from under the covers, dragging him on brisk walks around the frozen field, neither of them speaking as they focused on keeping warm. Buoyed by an unexpected cover of snow in early March, Frederick spent all morning wandering the camp, asking anyone he encountered if he could borrow a pair of skates. Having procured two pairs, he brought Ira outside to join an impromptu game of hockey on the flooded sports ground. Ira laughed in a way Frederick had never seen.

"I haven't skated in years," he exclaimed, holding on to his stick for dear life.

But, like Frederick, the tide of his emotion was unpredictable, and soon the darkness returned. The next day, he found Ira smoking in the YMCA hut, an unopened book resting on the table in front of him. Frederick peered at the title. *Twilight of the Idols.* "Nietzsche?"

Ira pulled on his cigarette. Frederick had never seen him smoke until recently, when Ira seemed to have lost his appetite for life.

"Pulford recommend I read it. I haven't started yet."

"I've read it."

"Any good?"

"Depends on how you feel about philosophy."

Ira was silent for a moment. "I studied it. A bit. In university."

The men at the next table were engaged in a game of chess, the pieces moving on the board with soft scrapes. There was none of the excitement that had accompanied chess games in the early days of their internment. There was a muted quality about everything now happening in the camp, especially in winter. It took everything, every ounce of energy, just to keep warm and to not let the hunger take over.

"He does have an interesting philosophy in this one," Frederick said.

Ira glanced at the book as he tipped his cigarette into the ashtray.

"He who has a *why* to live can bear almost any *how*." Frederick watched Ira's face for a sign of recognition but found nothing. Ira had told him almost the same thing on several occasions, but now it no longer seemed to resonate. Ira, who had found so many reasons to improve camp life, so many *whys*, had grown tired of his own efforts. In preparing for his departure, he had been pleased to find that things would run smoothly without him. He had done what he could to improve life for others, and it had worked. At first the realization that he was no longer needed had come as a relief, but slowly it had morphed into something ugly. He was no longer needed. There was nothing left for him to do. No more *whys*.

There were days when Frederick recognized the old Ira. But most of the time he seemed weighed down by indifference.

Frederick looked about the room, trying to find another way to lift Ira's spirits. "Didn't you say once that you wanted to write a book about Ruhleben? A memoir?"

Ira was quiet for a moment. "Not a memoir. A sociological exploration of what we built here."

"You wouldn't be able to do that if you were gone. Not properly, at least."

"I suppose not." Ira ground his stub into the ashtray next to three more. Frederick wondered how long he had been sitting here, smoking.

"So why don't we?"

"Write a book?"

"Yes!"

Ira's eyes scanned the table. "They barely let us write about the camp in letters. You think they'll let us write a book?"

Frederick shrugged. "They let us publish magazines. Even let us poke fun at the Commandant."

"I don't think the censors understood that joke." Then Ira's eyes flashed up to his face. "You want to write a book?"

Frederick offered a smile. "Who else but us?"

They started at the beginning, collecting stories from men about their arrests and arrivals. They tried to write about those cold, bleak days in November 1914 but found the task too daunting. Even as the snow melted and the mud dried around them, they shivered at the thought of that terrible first winter. Instead, they created a timeline of all the improvements the prisoners had brought upon the camp. The opening of the library, the first concert, the first play, the building of the YMCA hut. When they were done, they decided the only way to write faithfully about the camp was to experience it all first-hand.

Frederick joined the horticulture society, throwing himself into the task of tilling, sowing, and watering the soil until seven thousand vegetable plants had been planted. Carrots, turnips, radishes, and beans filled one side of the plot while spinach, cauliflower, potatoes, and peas filled the other.

Ira started attending religious services, concerts, entering into conversation with musicians. He joined the staff of the camp magazine, printing ads asking for prisoners who had kept diaries to help them build a narrative.

Frederick joined a woodworking class, learning to build a birdhouse, a chest, then a chair.

Ira was cast in *Twelfth Night*. He spent his mornings in the stall reciting lines with their bunkmate Morley, who, though too shy to step on the boards himself, held a deep appreciation for theatre.

The summer months found them busier than ever. Frederick found, to his surprise, that he enjoyed working with his hands. There was something about digging his fingers into the soil. Something about moulding, shaping, and altering the mud that had plagued him for nearly three years. It revived him, a seedling of hope growing inside of him. Once the garden was complete, the horticulture society shifted its focus to flowers, cultivating them from seeds procured from Berlin and overwintered in the greenhouse they had built near the grandstands.

Frederick had noticed the cheerful splash of pansies and geraniums beneath the windows of some barracks in previous summers but had been too preoccupied to appreciate them. Now, however, the camp was beginning to bloom with purpose. Antirrhinum, nicotiana, penstemon, and salvia were planted in flower beds around the barracks. Dahlia and rudbeckia added height, while canary creepers climbed frames installed to cover barrack walls and trail over arches that spanned the walkway. Lobelia, petunia, and cyclamen were carefully arranged in window boxes. Hundreds of ornamental shrubs were spread across the camp, transforming the weary views into something surprisingly beautiful.

Frederick's efforts felt more tangible than the time he had invested in the camp school. He could count on one hand the number of students who had genuinely taken to one of the languages he had taught. Most had only been looking for distraction. But the flowers, vibrant with colour and fragrance, and the garden filled with vegetables, offered undeniable proof that he was doing something worthwhile.

He learned more experimental wood-carving techniques, creating spoons, bowls, then figurines. He entered one of his pieces, a small bird, into the art exhibition. He allowed himself a humiliating loss at a public debate, where he argued in the affirmative, with strong conviction, that *All citizens, regardless of gender or social status, should have the right to vote in national elections.*

Ira was praised for his role in *Twelfth Night*. The camp magazine published a glowing review of his portrayal of Maria and he insisted to everyone who congratulated him that they must have only written such positive feedback because he was on the magazine staff.

They joined the baseball team, made up primarily of Canadians, and found themselves a small group of acquaintances who spoke in a familiar accent. Neither Frederick nor Ira returned to the school, though they continued to attend lectures. They now kept copies of the pamphlets and announcements in a wooden box Frederick had constructed to help inform their writing. In the evenings they sat together at their rickety dining table and organized their thoughts for the book they had still not started writing. But the intention was there. The purpose ever-present in their minds. They had found a *why* to endure their *how*.

Frederick had set out to revisit his memories with the intention of writing about the feeling of exclusion—the distance, the isolation, the way he had been cut off from the world. But as he dug through the pamphlets, the notes, the scraps of his past, something else emerged. *This* was what he wanted to remember from his time in Ruhleben. The society they had built. The way these men, thrown together, stripped of their freedom, had still sought ways to create something structured and purposeful. They had formed a school, started a magazine, organized sports leagues, cultivated gardens, and practiced art.

They had been deprived of their freedom, their homes, their livelihoods—their lives interrupted. And yet, they had still found ways to contribute to the collective good. Yes, these had all been ways to maintain a sense of normalcy, but they had also been an act of resistance.

He remembers Koval telling him about the music, the dancing. The small ways they had found to return to themselves. The fact that they had tried to do the same, in whatever capacity they could, under even more adverse circumstances—did that not say something about the human condition? That even when all else is taken away, people still search for ways to contribute? To make meaning of their lives? In these places designed to strip individuals of their humanity, they had managed to forge new forms of it. And was that not worth commemorating?

CHAPTER 20

Rose steps out onto the platform. The sun is peeking through the clouds, casting a golden glow over the vast expanse of marshlands. She has barely crossed the border into New Brunswick but already the landscape looks different, wind rippling through the tall grass, birds swooping over the copper mud. A lively group of university students spills out from the train, animated conversations filling the air. They pile into waiting wagons and head off towards the centre of town.

Mae stands eagerly by the side of the station, waving her arms with excitement. Rose quickens her pace to meet her.

"How long has it been?" Mae's voice is tight as they embrace.

"Far too long," Rose says.

Rose raises a glass of lemonade once they are seated in Mae's living room. "I suppose congratulations are in order." She gestures to their surroundings—the home, the husband, the two beautiful children. A slice of lemon bounces inside her cup.

"Oh," Mae says with a wave of her hand. "Old news."

"Still," Rose insists. "I haven't seen you since you got married." She hadn't seen her, in fact, since France. Mae had remained overseas long after the war, caring for the soldiers returning from the trenches, many ill from influenza. They had all signed up for the duration of the war, but for nurses, that extended far beyond combat, its effects echoing long after the last gun had sounded. *The war is far from over for these men,* Mae had written to Rose in 1919. *Maybe it never will be.* Rose had long pondered over those words, wondering when it would be over for her.

Mae nods. "I always intended to visit you in Toronto when I returned. I had even planned it for the spring, but by then, I was already engaged!"

It had seemed quick to Rose, but perhaps less so after learning that Mae was marrying someone she had known since childhood. Alfred Scott, like many of the men who stayed home, had intended to get across the ocean but been prevented from doing so by his poor eyesight. He had pursued a career in law instead, and now taught at a small liberal arts university in town. Ten months after their wedding, they had welcomed their first son, followed by another a year later. The youngest slept in the corner of the room now, unbothered by the sonorous chimes of the grandfather clock that rang every hour, while her eldest napped in the other room.

"And you," Mae beams. "How are you?"

"I've been well," Rose says with sincerity, though she might not have meant it even a few weeks ago. The ocean air has revived her, as Jeanne promised. "Spending time with Jeanne and her little ones has been wonderful."

Mae turns to look at the baby in his cot. "They are a joy, aren't they?" She gazes at him for a moment before refocusing her attention. "And how are your father and Anna?"

Rose chews on her bottom lip. "Perhaps not so well."

Mae's cheerful demeanour falters. "It must be so challenging for her—for all of you."

"To be frank, I came to the coast for a bit of an escape."

Rose had also arranged her visit to Mae in New Brunswick to avoid Anna's planned arrival, still not feeling ready to face her, but much to Rose's relief, Anna had cancelled her visit, citing illness. "Has she said anything more to you?" Jeanne had asked when she had received the news. Rose had simply shaken her head, averting her eyes. "No," she said casually. "Not a word."

Mae reaches for her hand. "That's awful. I'm sorry to hear you're still struggling."

Rose grips her hand again and they smile weakly at each other. There is a beat, a moment for grief, and then things snap back in place, both eager in their conversation again.

"I thought perhaps you were visiting for different reasons," Mae says, puckering her lips to the lemonade gliding down her glass.

It is what Rose loves about Mae. Only in her presence had she ever experienced this shift, this quick pendulum swing from sorrow to joy. It was something which had become increasingly crucial as the war dragged on and they found little time to grapple with their reality.

Rose raises an eyebrow. "What do you mean?"

"Didn't Jeanne have a brother-in-law?"

"She does."

Mae nods, a smug smile on her lips. "You once sent him a care package. While we were in France."

Rose blinks. "I had forgotten about that."

"So, does that mean we can expect you to visit more often?"

Rose smiles and looks down at the rug beneath her feet. "Yes. I hope so."

Mae turns her head to listen more closely to the baby's coos. She proceeds to ask about Jeanne's children, then Margot, and the pendulum swings again.

"She stayed in France?"

"Yes," Rose says. "She married a doctor and stayed in the village where she was stationed. A true physician's wife, I hear."

"She never came home?"

"No. Though I suppose that's partly my fault." Rose hesitates, lips parted. "I wrote to her when Leo…I wrote to them all. But by the time she got the news, I had already buried him and left France. I don't think she ever truly forgave me."

Mae looks sympathetic. "But how could she blame you?"

Rose shrugs. The lemon slice bobs, and she places her cup on the table in front of her. "I suppose I was in a daze. Not thinking clearly."

Mae studies her for a moment. "It was different, wasn't it? Nursing on the Front. Even different from nursing on the coast."

"Yes. It was…" Rose searches for the right words, and a memory flashes: the clanging of metal instruments in the pail while she carried a gangrenous knee away after an operation. Dropping the bloodied instruments into a pot of boiling water and plunging her hand into the next pot to retrieve sterilized ones, the scalding heat barely registering. Captain Kerr had called her back to the theatre in a rush, and hours later, Rose had returned to the prep station, wondering who had brought mutton for lunch, only to realize it was the knee she had left on the counter earlier.

"It was quite impersonal," she tells Mae. "There was never any time for conversation, and the men were too broken to engage in any case. Everything was quick, bloody, and urgent. And then, when I learned about Leo, when I reached him…it became personal again. It wasn't about the war or my role in it. I wasn't a nurse. I was a sister, an aunt. He was gone. And for a moment, so was I."

Mae rises from her seat and joins Rose on the sofa, her arms already encircling her shoulders.

"I wish I could have been there for you," Mae says softly.

Tears well in Rose's eyes. "I know."

They hold each other for a moment longer, finding solace in the silence that stretches between them.

The baby emits soft sleeping noises from the corner, and Rose is suddenly fearful that this moment of vulnerability, of sincerity, will slip away. "How do you do it, Mae?" she asks, her voice barely a whisper.

"Do what?"

Rose hesitates, considering her question. "Do you ever think we took a part of France with us when we came back?"

"Of course, we did."

"How do you reconcile those two realities? What we saw, what we witnessed, and this? How can we simply…move forward?"

Mae takes a moment to consider the weight of the question. "All I wanted after seeing so much death was to experience life. It helped to have a husband who knew nothing of the true horrors of war. Whose life had gone uninterrupted. He had lost brothers and friends, but he never feared for his own life. So, it continued to move. And I became part of that forward momentum."

Rose finds she is unable to look at Mae, her thoughts tangled in the remnants of the past.

"And the children," Mae adds, the corners of her mouth lifting into a smile. "They are bright, and new, and have their whole life ahead of them. I'm only here to make sure it will be a good one." She glances affectionately at the corner of the room.

"But don't you sometimes feel like everyone has forgotten? Like we were never there?"

"What do you mean?"

"I mean—they are building memorials for those men we cared for. We came back to nothing."

This had never been her priority. Before this summer, Rose had hardly given it a thought. She had done her duty and done it well, and though at times she felt guilty for the part she had played in the war, she could not deny the sense of purpose it had given her. She was proud of her work—proud of her journals, of the countless hours spent tending to wounds that would never fully heal, of the role she had played in helping those men survive. But now, as she watched the war being reduced to stone monuments and polished speeches, it was clear that her role, and the roles of so many others, had been conveniently forgotten.

Since attending the unveiling of the cenotaph, since the meeting, Rose has considered petitioning for a memorial for nurses. Something to recognize their efforts. What they had gained. What they had lost. But then, what would Leo get?

Mae thinks about this for a moment.

"Perhaps because Alfred never served, he takes every opportunity to remind others that I did."

"That's considerate of him."

Mae shakes her head. "It is. But it usually elicits perplexed looks." She peers into Rose's eyes. "In their minds, nurses don't count."

"Doesn't that bother you? We were there. We did our part." Rose's voice is tinged with frustration.

"That's all that should matter. We did our part. We saved lives, Rose. The men whose lives we saved know that."

"You're right. I guess I look around and see dead men being hailed as heroes. But Leo will never be remembered that way. And neither will I."

"But who is holding remembrance?" Mae says. "It's the women, the mothers. Because that's all they can do. They need to tell themselves those stories—that their sons died valiantly, that they died for a cause—because otherwise, it was all for nothing."

Rose falls into a contemplative silence.

"We did what we could, Rose," Mae continues. "All of us did. Everyone played their part. And the difference between those men and us is that we came back. We have the chance to live our lives."

The boys awaken shortly after, bringing a burst of cheerfulness to the room. The eldest is shy, hiding behind his mother's legs as Rose crouches down to greet him.

"Joseph, darling, Rose is one of Mama's old friends," Mae says, trying to coax him from behind her. "Say hello."

The boy twists one of his legs behind him and peeks one eye, his tiny fingers still clutching his mother's skirts. Rose smiles warmly, but he hides again.

"I'm sorry, he's not usually like this," Mae laughs.

Rose rises to her feet. "It's perfectly fine."

Mae passes her the baby instead. "Here. Take Edwin."

The child is heavy and warm from sleep and settles comfortably into her arms. Rose studies him, instinctively swaying back and forth. Her hand gently rubs his small back, and she feels him move his head. She pulls back slightly as his small hands grasp at the neckline of her sweater. He looks up at her with large inquisitive eyes, as blue as his mother's.

"Hello there," Rose whispers softly, her breath brushing against his cheek. He blinks and extends his hand, reaching towards her lips. She purses them into a kiss.

Mae looks up and smiles. "Aunt Rose," she says in the singsong voice she uses with both of her children, and reaches for Edwin.

The loss of his weight in Rose's arms feels strangely heavy.

CHAPTER 21

Frederick had fallen ill in the summer of 1918. Spanish influenza had knocked most of them down, sweeping through the camp like wildfire even in the heat of midsummer. It is another aspect of camp life that he downplayed in his letters home, but the long absence of correspondence that summer brings into sharp clarity the fatigue, the dizziness that had struck him one morning as he worked on weeding the garden, the sun beating down on his neck. He had assumed it was sunstroke until he'd fainted out in the field.

When he woke, it was in his bunk in the stall. His head ached frightfully, the room spinning. All around him, the sound of coughing. He groaned, closing his eyes again.

"Frederick?"

He tried to turn at the sound of Ira's voice but found it impossible to focus on the figure seated at the table a few feet away.

"I left some aspirin for you on the edge of the bed," Ira said. "To your left."

Frederick grasped at the blankets under him. His skin felt hot, but he had the sudden urge to be under them, to have a mountain of quilts draped over him. His fingers found two small capsules. Normally, he would have swallowed them whole, but his throat felt swollen and thick. He sighed, closing his eyes.

"There's a glass of water on the chair by your bed if you're able to reach it."

Frederick raised a hand but found he could not lift his head to look over the side of the bed. He let his arm drop heavily.

"Here," Ira said. The voice moved closer.

Frederick opened his eyes and saw Ira standing over him, a glass of water in hand. The collar of his shirt had been pulled over his mouth and nose. He lifted the glass to Frederick's lips. The water felt like silk on his tongue. He had never been so thirsty in his life. He gulped the contents of the glass, nearly forgetting the aspirin, and almost immediately began shivering.

"Let me help you," Ira said.

Frederick closed his eyes again. The glass slipped from his grip, and he felt his limbs moving until a heavy blanket covered him.

"Thank you," he managed before sleep took hold of him once more.

For days he scarcely knew where he was. It was dark, then light. Someone continued to give him capsules (Ira, he assumed). The only sound that roused him was the agonizing coughing that resonated all around him. In the darkness, he longed for home, for the soft touch of his mother's hand on his forehead. He dreamt of Silas. He dreamt of his father. He dreamt of his mother crying over a corpse in Germany. His corpse. He dreamt of rats as large as horses occupying the stalls they had fit for themselves. He dreamt of Klara. He dreamt of her brandishing a wooden sword like those children he had seen in Berlin at the start of the war. He dreamt of waking up trapped inside a coffin in a cauldron of acorn coffee.

When he woke again, it was to the sight of the sun filtering through the filthy window. Frederick blinked, finding that he could see the room again. The dull headache continued, his limbs aching, but he managed to take stock of his surroundings. Ira was awake, writing a letter at the table. When he heard Frederick move, he glanced up.

"Good morning," he said cheerfully. "Are you feeling better?"

Frederick swallowed. His stomach grumbled, suddenly ravenous. "Yes, better. I think." Fog still clouded his mind and he frowned. "What happened?"

Ira's eyebrows shot up. "The 'flu arrived." The outbreak had swept the camp in a matter of days, he explained. Nearly half the men had fallen ill. Everything had shut down. The school, the sports, the plays, the debates.

Bolstered by his hunger, Frederick tried to get out of bed, but was immediately struck by dizziness.

"Lie down," Ira ordered. He brought him a piece of bread and poured tea from the pot on the table.

"How long was I out?" Frederick asked when he had managed a sip and a bite, the dry bread sticking to the roof of his mouth.

"Four days."

It was another two before Frederick felt strong enough to get out of bed and sit at the table. He tried to write a letter to his mother. *Only a mild headache and cough. I'm not certain I even had a fever. Ira was here to help me recover. Sadly, two men died in another barrack, but the low number really does speak to decent hygiene in the camp.* He did not say that in those hours he'd lain delirious with fever, he feared he might die in this place.

A few days later, the influenza had all but disappeared from the camp, leaving as quickly as it had arrived, but the same could not be said for the rest of Germany.

"It might not be so terrible to be isolated," Ira said over breakfast one morning, a German newspaper spread out on the table in front of him. Headlines screaming death.

And it was true that while things finally seemed to have improved in the camp, Germany was straining at the seams. It was difficult to parse out the truth, but even in their delusional optimism, newspapers made clear that the country was crumbling under the relentless weight of the war.

"It serves them right," Frederick said.

Ira gave him a strange look.

Early that fall, a man appeared before Frederick as he worked in the garden, pulling vegetables from the ground.

"Munro?"

Frederick uncovered another head of lettuce and tossed it in the crate. "Yes?"

"Someone is looking for you."

Frederick sat back on his muddied heels. He lifted a dirty hand to his face and tried to wipe the sweat from his eyes with his forearm. "Who is it?"

"You better follow me."

He saw the curve of her silhouette before he recognized her, standing behind the barbed wire fence. She turned, hand on her stomach, the rounded edge visible under the waistline of her dress. "Hello, Frederick," Klara said.

He eyed first her stomach, then the thin band glinting on the third finger of her left hand, before glancing at her face, her features sharper, thinner than he remembered. Words failed him entirely. What could he say after three long years? Years in which her life had evidently propelled forward while his had remained static?

"I'm glad to see you so well," she said.

The summer sun had given him some colour, his arms golden, his face freckled, but he did not need to look down at the patched pants and dusty, sweat-stained shirt he wore to know she was exaggerating. "You as well," he said, shifting his eyes to her hand and her stomach again, to make clear that he understood. "Congratulations."

She offered a tight smile. "Thank you." She seemed on the verge of saying more—I waited? I couldn't wait any longer?—but reconsidered the charade they had, years ago, kept up for far too long. "I came to ask for a favour." She took a step forward.

He had almost forgotten the barbed wire fence that separated them and became suddenly aware that a guard might see her. He looked up at one of the towers, which stood empty. Even the guards had grown bored of their duties in recent months. The spring had seen several successful escapes from the camp, and though the guards threatened punishment ("for not escaping," someone pointed out), they did very little to stop the inmates from trying. Frederick often thought about those who had escaped and managed to evade capture, wondering where they had gone. Where would he go? He did not think he would even make it to the border.

"I won't be long," Klara added. "But I need your help."

He nearly laughed. What kind of help could he offer her now? But he saw that the polite mask she had worn had fallen, revealing anxious eyes and a twitching mouth. "What is it?"

"I need food. My family needs food." She rubbed her stomach for emphasis. It was unusual for women to flaunt their predicament in public, but they were alone, and Frederick had once touched that same stomach with an intimacy that seemed impossible now.

She must have seen the hesitation in his eyes, for she rushed to add, "I know you get food here. I know you receive packages. You are being fed while we starve." She paused, dry lips parted. "Aren't we all prisoners of this war?"

Frederick wanted to point out the barbed wire separating them, point out the ease with which she could travel here, travel anywhere—how she spent those years he had lost getting married and starting a family. It was not the same. And yet, he knew there was a kind of truth to her claim. He had seen the way the guards eyed the packages entering the camp, knew that they stole vegetables from the garden when they thought no one was looking. The food situation in Germany was growing dire, civilian morale sinking from desperate hunger.

He looked at the slim hand on her stomach, and nodded. "Hide until I return."

Relief flooded her features for an instant before being replaced by mild confusion. "You were always so kind," she said in a tone that suggested she didn't understand.

Frederick returned a while later with a rucksack filled with vegetables from the garden, a loaf of bread, and two tins of meat. When she materialized again from behind a tree, he motioned for her to follow and walked the length of the fence until he found an opening, the dirt freshly turned. He slid the pack under the fence and began walking backwards quickly, afraid one of the guards might accuse him of trying to escape.

Klara bent forward uneasily, reaching for the sack. She rose, clutching it to her chest with more care than she had clutched at her stomach.

"Danke," she said, a look of surprise still on her slim face.

Frederick gave a curt nod. "Good luck," he said, because he did not know what else to say. Because he could not find the words for the absurdity of this war which had made prisoners more fortunate than citizens in a country that struggled to achieve the victory they had so confidently promised.

He had kept no letters from Klara. In those years before her visit to the camp, when all she had offered was cold silence, he had burned everything. And yet, his memory of her is just as clear, even years later.

Sitting in the living room, the trunk's contents scattered across the room, Frederick once more considers what he might do with them. Discarding them feels unthinkable, but these are not memories he wants to revisit often. He picks up a photograph, then another, sifting through the piles spread across the table, wishing more than anything that he had kept Ira's notes.

By the time Ira and Frederick had gathered enough information and experience to inform their writing, the tides of war were changing. There was a sense in the air that the war would soon end, though Frederick was still unsure which side would win. But it was different now than it had been during previous explosions of rumours. Everybody spoke of it. The guards, the prisoners, the newspapers—even the letters from home.

Still, they continued to prepare as they always did for the coming winter. The horticulture society cleaned debris from the garden, removing plants killed by the frost, and raking the leaves. Students at the camp school signed up for fall courses. The library continued to acquire new books. Sports, debates, and plays were as popular as ever.

And yet, behind the scenes, plans were being laid. An elected council of inmates prepared for the dissolution of the camp in the event that the guards deserted their posts. Ira told Frederick about the measures over tea late one evening in October. "We have to be ready for the possibility that we might need to seize arms and defend ourselves, should local residents become desperate enough to attack us."

"Whatever for?" Frederick had asked.

"Looting for food, or weapons."

Frederick glanced at their stores of food, some of their recent Red Cross parcels still unopened. That night, he dreamt of having to brandish a weapon at a hungry mother holding wailing children in her arms. His hands turned to clay against the cold metal of the gun and when he woke, he was relieved for the first time that he had spent the war without having to hold a gun.

It was through the barbed wire fence that the prisoners of Ruhleben witnessed the revolution that took hold of Berlin, the gate becoming something to keep others out rather than the prisoners in. Newspapers ceased to arrive in late October, plunging them back into the unknown of those early days of the camp. They knew nothing of what was happening other than the odd snippets that sometimes reached them. It was dizzying to know something momentous was occurring just beyond their reach.

"We must try to capture this," Ira said, his face enraptured.

There was still no sign of either side weakening in early November, but it was clear Berlin would revolt sooner or later. One morning, as the prisoners were marched onto the field for roll call, they were interrupted by the jubilant sounds of cheering coming from the train tracks passing Ruhleben for Berlin. One by one, they turned to watch the train crowded with workers rejoicing, some shouting from the roof.

"Is the war over?" someone asked.

Frederick looked to the gate, which stood firmly shut.

Rumours flooded the camp. The Kaiser had abdicated, and Berlin was now in socialist hands. But while things unravelled outside the camp, little changed inside the barbed wire fence. That same afternoon, Frederick attended an art exhibition, then participated in a football tournament.

"Is it true?" he asked when they returned to their stall that evening.

Ira nodded, his face grave, yet alive. "It appears to be." He cracked a smile at seeing Frederick's disbelief. But under the current of excitement was fear that liberty might not come as easily as opening a gate. Raids were likely. Men had already started hiding their valuables. Under the cover of dusk, Frederick and Ira hid a few tins of string beans and pork in the flower box outside their window, now bereft of flowers. Then, on his way back from the library one afternoon, Frederick saw the Prussian monarchical flag being lowered from its poll outside the Commandant's office.

"What's happening?" he asked one of the men standing by.

"The guards formed a soldiers' council and deposed the officers," the man said. "Stripped them of their swords and epaulettes."

Frederick watched as the flag was removed and a piece of red cloth was hoisted in its place.

"We made that," one of the other men told Frederick, standing proud. "Tablecloth and some dye in the workshop."

The socialist revolution had come to Ruhleben.

Then, impossibly, the armistice was announced and chaos erupted. The prisoners were advised to stay in the camp for their own safety, but they were now free men. Frederick felt an immediate pull towards the gate, towards Berlin, and yet feared what he would find there. For an entire day, he hesitated, pacing the camp, before finally deciding to leave.

When he reached the city, the Berlin he had once known was unrecognizable. He wandered the quieter streets, disoriented and overwhelmed. The bustle of former days had vanished, replaced by a heavy stillness. Many shops were shuttered, their windows dark or broken. Those that remained open displayed shelves that were pitifully bare, the faint odour of spoiled goods wafting through open doors. The people he passed, sallow, hollow-eyed, dressed in threadbare clothes, moved with a weariness that betrayed years of deprivation.

In the city squares, the energy shifted. Crowds gathered, their voices raised in furious chants, denouncing the men who had brought the nation to its knees. The air crackled with anger and desperation. Gunshots rang in the distance, but no one seemed to flinch. Lingering at the edge of a group, Frederick watched. For years, he had kept their faces close, sharp and unchanging in his mind. The sight of them jeering outside the police station, revelling in his ruin. In those moments he had needed someone to blame, someone to hold responsible for everything he had lost, their mocking expressions had been there, front of mind.

But now they only looked tired, worn down by the same forces that had laid waste to his life. The fury he remembered was gone.

They had all lost.

And for what?

They waited, and waited, for their passage home to be arranged.

"When will we get word?" Frederick asked.

Ira could only shrug.

They assisted in the dismantling of the library and took advantage of their newfound freedom to visit the corners of the camp that had been strictly Verboten. The rapidity with which everything they had built had fallen apart was staggering. For the first time in years, there were no lectures, no concerts, no meetings, and no sports. Only restless waiting. Frederick and Ira tried to write, but their project seemed too immense. There was no way they could capture everything that had happened here. It had been too absurd, too simple, all at once. At times it felt impossible that it had happened at all.

Lying awake at night, Frederick considered all the emotions whirling inside him. The relief, the excitement at the prospect of going home, of resuming a normal life—but also the anxiety. The fear, the grief at the thought of leaving behind the only world he had known these past few years and being thrust into one reshaped by war.

It took more than a week after armistice for them to learn that they would leave for England via Sassnitz and Copenhagen in two transfers. Frederick and Ira were included in the first transfer, which was scheduled to leave a few days later. They rushed to pack, surprised by how many items they had managed to accumulate over the course of four years. Frederick tried to find space between his clothes for his books, correspondence, journals, and food stores. He knew nothing in his possession would suit him outside the camp, and yet what was he to do with them? He had already lost everything he had left behind in his apartment during his arrest. He made a note to keep enough money to get a new suit made when he reached London. New shoes, too. Perhaps even a hat.

They toasted goodbye to the barrack and to each other, circulating their addresses like it was the last day of school. In the morning, without a wink of sleep, they dragged their luggage to the tracks and were slowly loaded onto the dilapidated fourth-class carriages.

Frederick held his breath as the engine hissed and the train started moving forward. He turned in his seat to wave at the others left behind, catching one last glimpse of Ruhleben. In that moment, all he felt was an intense and disorienting sense of loss.

The journey to Sassnitz, which would have normally taken five or six hours, lasted all night and well into the following morning. The train had no lighting or heat, the windows shattered. By the time they reached their destination, Frederick could no longer feel his fingers from the cold.

In Sassnitz, they were handed coffee, bread, and sausage before reaching port, where two Danish ships were waiting—as was, it seemed, half the German population. Starved faces stood on the docks scrambling for the food the men had brought with them from the camp. Reaching into his bag, Frederick handed a young mother and child two cans of corned beef, bread, and milk.

"Danke," she said, grasping at the offering. "Vielen dank." She clutched his hand as she took the food and hurried away. Frederick thought again of Klara and the child who must have arrived by now. He was glad that the steel slipping from his fingers contained food rather than gunpowder.

They docked in Copenhagen shortly before midnight and were transferred to a much larger boat, where they were treated to luxuries Frederick had started to doubt even existed. Hot food, a bed with sheets. He grabbed at the cotton that evening, falling into a deep sleep as the movements of the waves rocked him. It was morning by the time Frederick realized he had left Germany for the first time in five years.

They reached London early one morning. It was a different London than the one Frederick had seen years earlier—damaged by German bombs during the war, the streets lined with debris, buildings boarded up or in a state of disrepair—but London, nonetheless.

They remained a week, trying to arrange passage home. "We might not reach home before Christmas," Frederick said, studying the passenger ship schedule. He pulled at the collar of his stiff new shirt, feeling slightly suffocated by the tie.

"I was thinking," Ira said, hardly above a whisper. An ambulance rang nearby, drowning his words in the sounds of the city.

Had London always been so loud?

Frederick turned. "What is it?"

"I'm going to stay. In England, I mean."

Frederick looked him over. "Why?" The only thing he wanted, desperately, was to reach home. He had seen enough of the world for now. He only wanted home.

Ira laughed humourlessly. "It's my job to observe, to inform. It's all I've wanted to do since the moment I was arrested—precisely because I was doing my job. It'll be easier for me to do that from here, in the centre of things, than back home."

Frederick was quiet for a moment, then nodded. "You should stay."

Ira asked to keep the notes from their book, and Frederick agreed, though he wondered if anything would ever come of it. Perhaps it had only been something to keep them going, to distract them from the bleakness of internment.

Ira accompanied him to the port a week later.

"I'll write when I get home," Frederick said. "I hope we'll see each other again soon." He put out his hand.

Ira looked down at it, his lips curving into a smile. He opened his arms wide instead and took him in. "Please do," he said, tapping Frederick on the back.

They looked at each other for a moment longer, and then went their separate ways.

As the boat pulled out of the harbour, Frederick watched Ira wave his hat in the air from the docks until he was but a spot in the distance.

CHAPTER 22

Rose sends Frederick a note as soon as she returns from visiting Mae, eager to see him again. *You did promise me a visit to the museum,* she reminds him. But then, only silence. For days, nothing. She begins to wonder if he has left again, returned to Montreal. Even Silas seems unaware, though she senses his frustration at his brother's continued absences. "I thought this job would settle him," she overhears him tell Jeanne after dinner one night. "My father would not have tolerated this. But what am I to do?"

A week passes before she decides to pay him a visit, swallowing her pride. But when Rose arrives at the cottage, she finds it quiet. She knocks three times before venturing out back, peering into the shed, then climbing down the stairs leading to the ocean, but there is no sign of him. For a moment she thinks she spots him swimming in the distance, but cannot be sure. She hesitates on the stairs, wondering whether she should wait for him. She recalls the last time she waited for him on these steps, and her face grows hot. If he is this hard to find, perhaps he does not want to be found. Maybe he regrets their evening together. Maybe he thinks he owes her something now. She cannot bear the conversation that might follow, so she leaves.

Her days are mostly spent helping Jeanne entertain the children—taking them to the park, the beach, filling the hours with games of hide-and-seek around the house. But now Jeanne insists that Rose take some time for herself. "Why don't you go out? Explore a little bit."

"It's almost as if you're trying to get me out of the house," Rose says.

Jeanne smiles and shakes her head. "Of course not. But why not take advantage of it while you're here?"

There it is—the artful mention of Rose's indefinite departure. Rose has yet to set a date. She does not want to leave. But she understands that she cannot remain in this house indefinitely. Already, she has been here for close to two months. Even her father wrote to ask when she would be back, a letter Rose delayed answering until there seemed no point in replying at all.

Rose ventures into town. She stops by the same few businesses she usually frequents with Jeanne: the small bookstore nestled between the grocer and the barber, the flower shop, and the bakery, the aroma of freshly baked bread leading her all the way down the sidewalk. At the bakery, she finds a notice posted to the wall, announcing a new fossil exhibition at the museum. She checks the date, disappointed to see that the opening took place the previous afternoon. She turns to the baker's wife as she bags her scones. "Is the museum open today?"

"I believe so," she says. "Are you going to see the fossils?"

"Yes, I think I'd quite like to go. Can you point me in the right direction?"

Rose locates the address as instructed, finding a grand Edwardian house situated on the outskirts of Main Street. The stained-glass windows gleam with vibrant colours, casting fractured patterns of light that ripple across the wide stone steps leading to the door. She might have hesitated to approach had it not been for the small sign indicating it was the meeting place for the historical society. Another sign hangs behind the glass of the door. *Please come in.* She turns the brass knob and pushes the door open.

There is a guest book at the entrance, but no one to greet her. She waits a moment in the foyer, listening for any signs of activity.

"Hello?" Rose calls after a moment.

A small woman appears, peering out from behind a door at the end of the corridor. "Hello!" She says. "Welcome. Are you here to see the new exhibition?" She does not move to greet Rose, staying firmly planted behind the door, with only her head and upper body visible as she leans forward.

"Yes, I am."

"It's right through there on your left. Please feel free to look around."

"Thank you," Rose calls out, but the woman has already disappeared behind the door.

Rose steps cautiously into the room, the wooden floorboards creaking under the heel of her shoe. Bright sunlight streaming through the windows forms a glare on the glass cabinets throughout the room. She approaches one and peers inside. On the centre shelf she finds a large brown ammonite disk traced with intricate white lines leading to its centre. It is so large she can hardly believe anyone managed to dig this up from the earth and carry it here.

"May I help you?"

Rose jumps back with a start.

"Pardon me, I did not mean to frighten you." The man is standing behind her in a trim grey suit, hands clasped behind his back.

"Mr. Cameron!" Rose says in surprise.

He raises his eyebrows, then seems to recognize her. "Ah, Miss Avery. How lovely to see you here."

"What a funny coincidence."

Mr. Cameron offers a smile. "Well, perhaps not if you'd known I was the curator of this establishment. All three times you've seen me now, we've been looking at fossils."

"Yes, that's true." Rose says, straightening her back. "So, are all of these yours?" She takes a step towards a different display case, bringing her face as close to the glass as she can, trying to read the labels detailing the type of fossil and origin.

"Not all, but most of them were found by members of our historical society."

"Any by your son?" Rose looks up to see him give a faint smile.

"Yes, in fact, there are a few."

She had not been sure the boy was in fact his son. Mr. Cameron looks much older than she would have expected for the father of a boy that age. "Quite a young man you have there," she says.

Mr. Cameron seems almost to blush. "Oh, that I know."

He offers to give her a tour of the exhibition, and Rose gratefully accepts. He speaks, his voice animated yet serious, as though fossils were the most important thing in the world. She supposes for some they are. A record of the past, were they not? In the same way of some cherished family letters, or great works of art. Preservation required care, and it was clear great care had been taken to locate and extract these petrified remains from their original locations. What truly amazes Rose is that the earth had accomplished this on its own for thousands of years, unaided by anyone, before they were rediscovered.

"And here we have some of our smaller fossils," Mr. Cameron continues, gesturing to a case on their left.

Rose's gaze follows his hand, and her eyes alight upon the specimens on display.

"You will see there an ancient mollusk shell." Mr. Cameron points to a perfectly preserved spiral-shaped shell, its smooth contours hinting at the creature that once inhabited it. "And here," he says, drawing her attention to a small, spiky formation, "we have a remarkable sea urchin spine."

Rose nods appreciatively, her eyes roaming over objects, listening but not engaging, letting Mr. Cameron share his knowledge uninterrupted.

It is only when they reach the final display case, Mr. Cameron asking if she has any questions, that she finds herself saying, "Did you serve in the war, Mr. Cameron?"

She noticed a slight limp in his walk, a stiffness in his right leg. She had observed it on the beach as well, though at the time she assumed it was due to the uneven footing of the sunken sea floor. Seeing him move around the room now, she wonders if his leg had been amputated and replaced by a wooden prosthetic.

He stands motionless for a moment, then says, "Yes, I did. Like many others."

"As did I," she says, meeting his gaze. Daring him to react.

But he only nods. "As a nurse, I presume?"

"Yes. Canadian Army Medical Corps."

"I must say, I might not be standing here were it not for the nurses who cared for me in Belgium."

She attempts a weak smile. "I appreciate you acknowledging that."

"Of course. It is only the truth."

"Sometimes I get the sense that most people forgot about our contributions. Forgot the war, really. The brutality of it, at least."

"Sometimes it is best to forget."

Rose turns to look at the piece of ammonite resting on its white drape. "You said you served in Belgium?"

"Yes, at the Front."

"So, we saw the same things." She does not name them—the mud, the blood, the boys crying for their mothers, jaws blasted off.

But Mr. Cameron nods. "I presume we did."

Rose hesitates, eyes roaming the room. She does not know why she is so bold with him. Perhaps because he is a stranger. "Why do we pretend?" she asks. "Why do we all pretend like none of it happened?"

He is silent for a moment. "You mentioned my son," he finally says.

"Clyde, is it?"

"Yes." Mr. Cameron takes a deep breath. "He's young. Terribly young. And yet, during those long years, I often considered the possibility that this war might drag on long enough to swallow him whole. It seemed interminable at times. The fact that he was spared—silly as that might seem, given his age—is a constant relief. The fact that he will never know a war like this is all I need."

"Do you not fear that he will grow up thinking war is glorious?"

Mr. Cameron looks at her, then shakes his head. "No."

"Why not, when it seems to be all anyone ever talks about?"

Mr. Cameron purses his lips. "My wife—she's a nervous woman," he confides, his voice barely above a whisper. "Always has been, but it got worse after our son was born. The fear of something happening to him, to us, was relentless. She always had a justification for not taking risks. I tried to be her voice of reason, to help her see things from a different perspective. When the war came, she begged me not to go, and I promised I would stay. But as the years passed and I saw more and more of our young neighbours' names on the honour roll…" He sighs and scratches the top of his head. "Well, I couldn't help but wonder how I would feel if it was my son being sacrificed, instead of old men like me. I couldn't hold back any longer. I had to enlist. For Clyde." He shakes his head. "I thought I at least knew what I was signing up for. But of course, I did not."

He looks around himself, likely for a chair, but finds none. "I started receiving distressing letters from my wife almost as soon as I left," he continues. "She was distraught, detailing every imagined way I might get injured or die. I couldn't understand what compelled her to put those fears to paper, to send them all the way across the Atlantic, when I was the one in the trenches, praying not to be hit by flying bullets, praying not to fall before the rest when we charged. Then I realized." He looks up, and his gaze locks on Rose, unblinking. "She still needed me to be the voice of reason, to deny her fears, despite the undeniable reality—that her fears were entirely real. That they mirrored my own. So, I wrote her cheerful letters. Letters filled only with thoughts of the future. I never mentioned the war, not once, not even when all I wanted was for her to tell me that all would be well."

He takes a deep breath. "War was not glorious. None of it was brave or honourable. And yet isn't that precisely what we wanted them to think? To tell them otherwise now would mean telling them the truth. The whole truth."

Rose notices his hands begin to shake, but he quickly conceals them in his pockets.

"I don't want my wife or son to know what I witnessed over there," Mr. Cameron says, squaring his shoulders. "I would much rather shield them from the darkness that tried to consume our world."

In the heavy silence that follows, Rose thinks of Anna. Anna, who seemed so willfully oblivious to her suffering. And yet, had Rose not done the same? Tried to shield her sister from the truth?

"I'm sorry, Mr. Cameron. I suppose I had not considered that."

Mr. Cameron gives a shrug. "I can't speak for all veterans. I know many of them do claim a greatness I never saw on the battlefield. Perhaps it is simply easier for them to think of it as a grand adventure, to remember the camaraderie, the rare moments of joy amidst the horror. It's a way to cope, and I cannot fault them for it. We've all lost so much already. If this is what allows them to find peace, even if it is fictional—well, that may be the last thing we can give them."

Rose studies Mr. Cameron's resigned expression for a moment before averting her eyes. She wishes now that she had not brought the subject up, though she is glad for his insight. "Thank you," she says finally. "You might never know how much you helped me today."

When Rose leaves, the wind has picked up, leaves rustling in the trees. She turns over Mr. Cameron's words in her mind. She had tried to shield Anna from the pain of the truth, but at what cost? And what would it mean to tell her the truth after so much silence?

It happened in September 1918. Rose was wiping sweat from a Lung's brow, dampness pooling on her back. There seemed to be a pause in the attacks, resulting in an unusual lull at the clearing station. The stretcher bearers passed behind her, muttering apologies as they brushed her skirt. Rose glanced over her shoulder, catching only a glimpse of muddied boots.

When the incoming patient had been placed on one of the tables, Rose motioned for the orderlies to pick up the Lung and bring him to an empty bed in recovery. He was still too weak to move down the line and would need to stay here a few more days.

"Abdomen wound," she heard Captain Ogilvie say behind her. He sounded tired. He had been in the operating theatre for the last six hours, working on a particularly difficult Chest. A lull in the line meant fewer patients, but more time to give to the most severe cases, and the surgeons took every chance they had to save the lives that might have otherwise slipped between their fingers. Interludes were the only time they could dedicate hours of uninterrupted work to a single patient, and they endeavoured to do everything in their power to keep them alive.

The men talked in worried whispers as Rose gathered the rest of the instruments and stripped the table. The Lung had hemorrhaged, and the floor was littered with red-stained sheets and bandages.

"Sister Avery and I can take this one," Captain Kerr told Captain Ogilvie. He always requested Rose's assistance. For months, they had been working side by side in the operating theatre, developing a silent rhythm as they moved in unison. He addressed her next. "Please prepare a tray for the Abdomen. Blast wound. Exposed stomach and intestines."

The air smelled of copper and rot. Rose nodded and hurried to the sterilizing room, leaving the orderlies to gather the bloodied linen.

She looked down at her apron and slipped it off. She did not have another one with her, but it was much too stained to be of any help.

Captain Ogilvie thanked Captain Kerr in his tired voice and left. The operating theatre emptied. Rose prepared a tray and returned to where Captain Kerr stood over the patient. He was examining the wound, trying to determine how to put this man back together.

"How?" He muttered to himself. He rose and lifted the tag fixed to the soldier's lapel.

Sister Hume rushed into the tent. Frowning, Captain Kerr looked up, a protest forming on his lips.

"A note for Sister Avery," she said, brandishing a piece of paper.

Captain Kerr closed his mouth and returned his attention to the wound. Sister Hume approached Rose in a hurry and handed her a single leaf of paper. Rose looked at her with growing concern. She could tell from the expression on Sister Hume's face that the news was not good. She accepted the piece of paper and dropped her eyes to the fuzzy pencil script.

Leo at No. 7 Stationary in Camiers.

Her breath caught in her throat. She felt the urgent need to run, to go to Leo, but was frozen in place, panic gripping her chest.

"What is it?" Captain Kerr asked, his voice soft.

Rose opened her mouth, but no words came. Blood was pounding in her ears.

"My nephew..." she finally managed to say, and suddenly she understood why so many people mistook them for siblings. Because now that connection sounded too distant. My brother, she wanted to say. My son. My twin. My heart.

Captain Kerr looked to Sister Hume, who gave a slight nod. His eyes grew wide, and then his frown returned. "Go," he said.

It took a moment for Rose's limbs to move. She wanted to protest, to acknowledge that he needed her help with this case, knowing full well that she would be of no help in her current state.

"I'll assist with the operation," Sister Hume said.

Captain Kerr's hand was on her shoulder. "*Go*," he pressed.

And she was gone.

She hurried out of the tent trying to think of everything she should bring with her, but her ears rang loudly, *Leo, Leo, Leo*. In her tent, she quickly changed out of her sullied dress, wishing she could wear one of her own skirts, feel normal for once, but retrieved a clean blue dress and starched white veil instead. She packed a small bag of essentials and rushed out the door.

There were a few ambulances waiting near the entrance of the compound. She approached one of the drivers. "Where are you going?" She asked, ready to climb in the back.

The man shook his head, sliding a cigarette between his lips. "Not going far tonight. Unless you want to go to the Front." He took a long drag. "Try Parker." He motioned to his left with his chin.

Rose made her way to the next lorry. "Are you heading back towards Étaples?"

He gave the slightest shake of the head, but stopped, his eyes searching her face. Something in her expression must have alarmed him, for he pulled his sleeve back to look at his wristwatch. "Where to?"

"Camiers. No. 7 Stationary."

He hesitated for a moment, then nodded. "Hop in."

Her mind raced as they travelled towards the coast, thinking of all the terrible things that might have happened. Leo was dead. No, surely, they would have told her if he was dead. Injured, then. In need of amputation. Or lucid and asking for her? She did not even know who had sent her the note. Did she know anyone at No. 7? She vaguely recalled one of the nurses being sent there. Perhaps one of the orderlies from No. 1 CGH. She could not hear anything but her own tumbling thoughts over the loud humming of the motor.

The ambulance driver took her directly to the entrance of the field hospital. Rose did not know where to go from there, nor who to ask to see. She unfurled her fist to find the note crumpled in the pit of her damp hand. Her heart was still pounding, her limbs aching to move, to run, but not knowing where.

"Sister Avery?"

She turned to find Patrick Blake, the orderly from No. 1 CGH, slipping out from under the flap of a tent, running his hand through a bloodstained cloth. He seemed relieved to see her.

She moved in his direction. "Captain Blake." She'd heard he had returned to Canada to complete his medical studies.

"You received my note. I wasn't sure. Someone told me you were at No. 2, but I did not have time to confirm."

"Where is he? Where's Leo?"

The shadowy contours of his eyes seemed to grow darker. "Follow me."

He led her to a post-surgical ward at the rear of a hut. There were only three patients. Rose had assumed she would immediately know Leo, but she stood at the entrance moving her eyes from one bed to the next. Captain Blake peered down to see her confused expression.

"He's over there," he said, pointing to a bed on the right.

Rose approached cautiously, still not quite believing this was Leo, but when she reached the bed, she realized he looked more like himself than the last time she had seen him. He had been changed out of his uniform, the dirt washed from his face, neck, and hands, his head bandaged tightly in clean white gauze. She reached for it delicately, wishing she could pull it off to inspect the wound herself.

"What happened?" She kept her voice low even though she suspected Leo was heavily sedated. She could sense Captain Blake was behind her. She did not turn to look at him.

He was quiet for a moment. "Head wound. Bullet through the forehead."

She peered into her nephew's sallow face. "You removed it? The surgery was successful?"

"Yes, we were able to remove the bullet." Captain Blake's voice was low, his tone grave.

"And he'll survive?"

There was silence. She turned to see Captain Blake hesitating, his mouth open. "Yes," he finally said. "In all likelihood, he will survive the surgery."

A nurse entered the tent and, after a brief whispered exchange with Captain Blake, brought Rose a chair.

"Would you like anything? Some tea perhaps?" the nurse asked.

"Thank you. I'm fine."

The nurse nodded, a sympathetic smile on her face. "I'll be back later to check on him."

Rose stayed at his bedside all night, listening to the slow rhythm of his breath. For the first time since she had arrived in France more than three years earlier, she allowed herself to imagine both of them returning to Canada. Imagined Anna's reaction at having them safely home. The peculiar look of pride her father would wear, finding them so changed, so grown. In each of these visions, she never imagined Leo with a gaping hole in the centre of his forehead. He looked as pristine as the day he had first put on his uniform, freshly ironed.

Holding Leo's hand in hers, Rose wept silently for most of the night. She allowed herself this one night of relief, knowing that come morning, she would need to claw her way back into the depths of her delusions to return to work.

Sometime in the night she saw a ghostly arm rise from Leo's bed to pull at the bandage on his head. "Leo?" she asked, her voice low. "Leo, it's me. It's Rosie." She reached for the arm, trying to steer it away, but it continued to pull, to press, his face still closed. She tried his name again, drawing on his arm, but with one swift pull, he tore the gauze from his head.

She was shocked, as though he had torn at pieces of her heart. She knew it was an automatic reaction to the pain. The unconscious body trying to scratch the itch. His arm fell to the side, his hand still clutching the gauze. She reached for it, and it dropped from his hand. In the low light of the lamp, she examined the wound. Captain Blake had delayed suture, and the wound gaped, inflamed.

She addressed Leo soothingly. "Was the bandage bothering you?" She caressed his hair, her fingers twining in his curls. She moved to get more gauze and antiseptic. "I'll make you a fresh one," she said when she returned. She dipped the bottle over the cloth and bent forward to clean the wound. "We wouldn't want it to get infected, would we?"

She thought she saw him wince. She paused, keeping her eyes trained on his face for any sign of life, but finally convinced herself it must have been a trick of the light. She unravelled the gauze and lifted Leo's head from the pillow, careful not to wrap it too tightly as she stretched it over the wound.

Captain Blake entered the ward early the following morning and sat at the opposite side of Leo's bed. "How are you this morning?"

Rose looked up to see that he was addressing her. "Tired." She could not begin to express all the emotions whirling inside her.

He nodded and looked to Leo. "There's something we need to discuss."

She did not like his tone. His tranquility seemed charged. Cautious.

Captain Blake hesitated. "I have reason to suspect your nephew's wounds may be self-inflicted."

Rose stared at him. "What do you mean?"

He shifted uncomfortably in his chair. "It appears the bullet was fired at close range with a revolver, which suggests—"

"That's impossible," Rose said sharply.

His mouth hung open. His eyes glanced around the room. "Well," he started, his voice lower. "We can only presume—"

"Leo would never."

"We cannot explain the reasoning of men at war, Sister Avery."

"You don't know him." Rose felt the walls of the ward crumbling, fury simmering in her chest. She thought of all the times Blake had belittled her, all the times he had refused to listen to her, and yet here he was now, a man in charge. Fear suddenly gripped her heart. "What are you going to do?"

Captain Blake was quiet for a moment. "You know what I must do."

She shook her head. "We all receive hundreds of wounded men a day. We wipe the blood. We suture their skin. We examine attempts at *obliteration*." She paused on the last word. "You don't need to do this. They'll never know."

"I must report him, Sister Avery. You know I do."

"Why?" Her voice cracked, her vision blurred.

"It was written on his tag. Others already suspect."

"He'll be court-martialled. He'll be shot." She was crying now, clutching at Leo's hands.

Captain Blake shook his head, his hands gripping his knees. "I have no choice."

Her shoulders began to quake. Captain Blake reached into his pocket and pulled out a handkerchief. She accepted it, pressing it against her slick face. It smelled of antiseptic, like everything else in her life.

Captain Blake waited with her for a moment longer before rising to his feet. He paused at her side and placed a hand on her shoulder. "The men we knew before the war..." his voice was strained. "They died as soon as they stepped inside that labyrinthine coffin. They're not coming back, even if they step out of the trenches intact...you cannot understand what a man might do to escape this hell." He paused. "It goes deeper than physical wounds." He did not say it, but she could hear it in his tone. *You taught me that.*

She looked up at him. "Then why did you let him live?"

He seemed shocked by her question. "I had to."

"You took away his agency."

Wide-eyed, Captain Blake searched her face for a moment longer before leaving without another word.

Rose stayed with Leo all day. The nurse returned at intervals to check on him and change the dressing, while Rose stopped herself from saying she would do it herself.

"What's your name?" she asked eventually.

The nurse looked up with her same sympathetic smile. She must not have been doing this for long. "Sister Gallagher. Christina."

"I'm Rose."

"You look alike, you know."

Rose forced a smile.

Around noon, Sister Gallagher brought her tea and toast, and an apple before supper. "Would you like anything else? Some soup?"

Rose shook her head. She had barely touched the toast.

"The night nurse should be in shortly to look after him."

"Thank you."

Night returned. Rose had grown so used to hearing the guns nearby that the silence unnerved her. The night nurse came twice but did not speak.

When the ghostly hand lifted in the darkness of the night, Rose watched it closely. "Leo?"

No answer came. The arm tugged awkwardly at the gauze until it successful pulled it off. Instead of reaching for more, Rose bent forward and kissed Leo's cheek.

She sensed Death long before it showed itself, lurking like a shadow in the canvas folds of the tent. It was not the first time Rose had sensed it. It often visited when she sat by a patient's side long into the night. Usually, she resisted, her hands moving swiftly to fend off the inevitable. But tonight, she did not rise to meet it.

It hovered, hesitating, as if puzzled by her stillness, waiting for her to fuss, to resist. But she remained seated, allowing it to drift closer, until it settled over Leo with a terrible intimacy.

In that moment, Rose understood that this was her final gift to him not a fight, but a quiet acceptance, an acknowledgement of what may very well have been his final decision.

Rose had returned to No. 2 CCS the morning after the burial. Only then did she finally sit down to write a letter to Anna. She had avoided it, thinking words would fail her, but they ran from the tip of her nib effortlessly. The same words she had written innumerable times. The letters always said the same thing, regardless of the situation. That their husbands and sons had not suffered. That they had valiantly given their lives for their country. Most importantly for the mothers and wives, that they had not been alone at the end. She did not elaborate on the circumstances of Leo's death and vowed she never would. It would always be better for Anna to believe her son had died valiantly, to join the ranks of bereaved mothers rather than to face the shame that was likely to accompany the truth, even though the truth was far from simple.

Rose had seen men with self-inflicted wounds before. They were seen as cowards, undeserving of priority in care. But those had always been non-fatal. A shot through the leg or the hand. Something to send them home. It was clear Leo did not simply want to escape war. She had already pored over his letters, looking for any indication of his emotional state in recent months, but other than battle fatigue, she found nothing. Maybe that was enough. Maybe war had been plenty. She wished he had felt he could trust her with his thoughts. She wished she had pressed him, when he had turned silent. But she knew he had been brave, truly brave, until the end. Braver than most, perhaps.

The Medical Officer sent her on leave to England. This time, she did not refuse. When she was examined again by a physician in

London, her leave was extended. "You have suffered a terrible fate," he said, reading the note. "Go home to your family. Get some rest." He was old enough that she suspected he had come out of retirement for the war, the creases on his forehead compressing like valleys. Rose wondered how many sons he had lost to the war.

She had lied to Anna in that first letter, but now, after speaking with Mr. Cameron, Rose feels the weight of truth pressing down on her. It takes her several tries. She has not written to Anna since leaving Toronto, still nursing her anger over the argument that preceded her sudden departure. But now Rose sees that the tangled knot of her frustration is as much of her own making.

The letter is at once an apology and a confession, an olive branch that seems at times to more closely resemble a thorn. Rose writes about the war, finally freed from the constraints of censorship. It is easier to write than it ever would have been to speak, and yet she knows she should have written it long ago.

She tries to convey the depth of the destruction that words cannot capture—how so many were shattered beyond articulation, how their struggles remained locked away in silence. She tries to explain that, because of the circumstances surrounding his death, Leo will likely be excluded from the memorials being planned. She expresses her own disappointment, noting that she feels Leo has been doubly abandoned—once in life, and then in memory.

Rose reassures Anna again that Leo was not alone in the end. That she was there with him, though she regrets not arriving sooner, not recognizing the truth until it was too late.

She does not mention that Rufus knows as well. She will leave it to him to decide whether to tell Anna the truth, once she tells their father she knows.

The morning after her return home, Rose had slipped into his office at the break of first light, still carrying the scent of the train, of blood—still aching for the comfort of her uniform, though it reeked of sweat. She had found him reading by candlelight, flames flickering in his spectacles.

"It was by his own hand," she said, voice croaking.

Rufus looked up sharply. He was silent for a moment. "I know," he finally said. "I received a letter."

Rose stood there, stunned. She could only stare. For a moment, neither spoke a word, both of them taken aback by the weight of their shared knowledge. Then, quietly, Rufus had said, "Don't tell her." His eyes pleading, his tone weary.

Rose has to believe that her father will forgive her, in time.

She reads the letter over once more. It is a bridge of words—painful, revealing words, but ones she hopes will mend the fracture between her and her sister, even if it threatens to unravel the small piece of solace Anna has managed to hold onto since the death of her only son.

CHAPTER 23

Frederick spends days writing, the words tumbling from him like stones from a cliff. It is not an article. It is not a defence. It can only be a book. The book he and Ira had always intended to write.

The Monday following his dinner with Rose, he wires Silas, telling him he will be absent for a few days. He has already taken so much time away from work this summer, but it would feel absurd to meet with clients when this book feels so pressing. The memories in the trunk are helpful, yet they drain him. He takes care sifting through the records, trying to draw meaning from each, but even from a distance, some still manage to drag him down.

A knock interrupts his thoughts one afternoon. Reluctantly, Frederick rises from his desk to answer the door.

"Afternoon," Silas says.

"Hello," Frederick says, blinking against the bright sunlight. He has been holed up in the cottage all week, leaving only for his daily swim. There is a brief pause, a beat, before Frederick realizes Silas expects to come in, and he opens the door wider. "To what do I owe this visit?" he asks, leading the way to the living room.

"Well, you haven't been to work in more than a week. I thought I'd check on you, make sure you're still in one piece."

"I sent you a telegram," Frederick says.

"With precious little information, might I add."

Frederick looks around the room, at the records piled everywhere. He should explain, but he does not know where to start. He clears his throat. "I was just about to make coffee. Would you like some?"

"Yes, let's have coffee," Silas says, though there's a sharpness in his tone now, thick with sarcasm. "I'm glad to see you're still alive!"

"There was never any fear of that, was there?"

Frederick returns to find Silas at his desk, looking through the mess of postcards and photographs scattered across the top.

"What's all this?"

Frederick sets down the cups. "Only a few things I brought back from Ruhleben."

Silas peers at a photograph, the one of Frederick in his odd ensemble. "Is this you?"

"Yes."

He frowns in disbelief. "This was what you looked like? While you lived in the camp?"

"Yes." Frederick does not understand why he seems so surprised. "I suppose we all looked like that."

Silas shakes his head, then picks up another photograph. "Why have I never seen these?"

"You never asked," Frederick says before registering the wounded look on his brother's face. "I'm not sure I was ready to share them either," he adds. "Not yet."

"And now?" Silas asks, his eyes roaming across the desk to take it all in: the typed pages, the red-penciled notes.

"Now, it might be time."

Silas joins him in the living room, accepting a mug of coffee. "So you're all right?"

"I am."

"Good. But there is another reason for my visit."

Frederick takes a sip, the coffee scalding. "What is it?"

Silas leans back and looks him square in the face. "How are you finding the work at the company?"

Frederick blinks, surprised by the sudden shift in conversation. It seems an odd time for it, and he'd rather return to the book. "It's been fine."

"Be honest."

"You know I appreciate the opportunity. I know I've been away for a while. I just—I've had a lot of my mind."

Silas exhales, his expression softening as he leans forward. He sets his cup down on the table, in the small space between the letters and the issues of the camp magazine. "I have always meant it when I said you were welcome at the company. It is as much yours as it is mine. But I have begun to wonder if it's the right fit for you."

"What do you mean?" Frederick asks, furrowing his brow.

Silas studies him for a moment. "Well, for one thing, you don't seem to enjoy it—despite your very convincing protests."

Frederick had never really stopped to consider it. The stability, the routine, this had been enough when he had come home. "Do you not want me to work there anymore?"

Silas hesitates, choosing his words carefully. "Do you remember how Father would always whistle on Monday mornings? Throughout the house, getting ready for work, he would whistle," he says. "He enjoyed going to the office. He liked his work. And then on Fridays he came home early because he knew how important it was to spend time with his family. I feel the same way about my work. I enjoy running this company. I was trained for it. But we both know it was never your first choice."

Frederick runs his thumb against the side of his ceramic cup. "It wasn't," he agrees. "That's why Father left it to you." There is an edge in his tone that he did not expect.

Silas tilts his head. "He left it to both of us," he insists. "Is that the problem? That you felt pushed out?"

Frederick shakes his head. "No, of course not." Then, after a moment, "You always seemed so sure of yourself. Of your place in the world. And I thought I did too, once. But when I came back…it felt as though I had lost everything."

Silas is quiet for a moment. He reaches for one of the letters on the table. "It wasn't easy for us either, you know. Our parents never wanted to discuss you—the—Ruhleben." The word sounds foreign coming from Silas's mouth. "They talked about you often. About when you would come home. But Mother would wring her hands whenever I brought up things I had heard or read about the camp, and Father would smoke constantly as he read your letters. Puffing like a chimney."

Frederick falls into a quiet contemplation. "Why did you never tell me?"

"I didn't want you to feel worse than you already did, knowing how much it affected them."

This was not what his mother had said. She had only spoken of how they had tried to help, how they had tried to get him out. What else had he missed? "And Mother?"

Silas sighs. "When Father died…she became distraught. I think the shock of his sudden death was overwhelming. It might have been more than that. More than his death." He keeps his eyes fixed on his cup. "It was a bit of losing you, too," he finally admits, his voice quieter. "Like she thought she wouldn't see you again. She said this wasn't how it was supposed to go. That she wasn't supposed to lose you both at once."

Frederick listens uneasily to Silas's strained voice. They have never broached this topic before. Silas never mentioned what it was like for their family, waiting for him on the other side of the ocean.

"Father was sick. Maybe it was the stress. He drank more, smoked constantly, and when he died, I was surprised that it caught me off guard."

They are quiet for a moment. Then Frederick asks, "What about you?"

Silas turns to face him. He blinks a few times and looks away. "I don't resent you for being interned," he begins slowly. "I don't resent you at all, in fact. But I was left to hold the pieces together when everything fell apart here. I was left with the business, with our concerned, aging parents, with the house. Left to sort out a funeral and an estate. Some days, it felt like an anchor weighing me down to the bottom of the sea."

Frederick's gaze drops. "I'm sorry."

Silas shakes his head, waving it off. "It was never your fault. And it was worth it when you came back."

They share a brief smile. Silas gestures to the records. "Are you sure this is a good idea?"

"It might be the best idea I've had in a while."

"Good. I want you to be happy. Which is why I came here with a proposition."

"What is it?"

Silas observes him for a moment before speaking. "I would like to buy you out of the company," he says. "I'll give you half of what it's worth. I think it's only fair. I have enjoyed working with you these past few years, but frankly, you're doing more damage than good." He wrinkles his nose, then offers a smile, softening the blow. "That Fleming meeting? We nearly lost a client."

Frederick is stunned. He had not thought it had gone so poorly. "How?"

"You committed to an impossible timeline—two weeks faster than anything we could have ever accomplished on our own. I had to backtrack, take a hit at our own expense."

"I'm sorry…I suppose I still have a lot to learn."

Silas sighs. "You've been with us for almost three years. I understand the need to learn the ropes, but it's time for you to decide whether you want to accept more responsibility, or leave."

Frederick ponders this for a moment, the future suddenly too close, too uncertain.

"There's no shame in leaving, Frederick," Silas says softly. "Think of what you could do with the money. It would give you time to figure out your next step."

"I'm not even sure what I would do," Frederick admits.

"Teach?" Silas offers.

Frederick shakes his head, a bitter smile pulling at his lips. "I gave up on that a long time ago." He had loved it once, the way languages felt like worlds onto themselves. But it was a path that seemed to belong to another man now, one he no longer recognized.

"Well, whatever you want to do, you can. You have your freedom now. Use it."

Frederick nods slowly. "Only half?" he teases.

Silas laughs. "You're lucky to be getting that much after the Fleming disaster." He reaches over to pat Frederick's knee. "Think it over. I'll be here when you decide."

CHAPTER 24

Anna's reply arrives a few days later, and it is not what Rose expected. She had braced herself for accusations, a storm of anger. Instead, Anna asks her to come home. *I've lost so many of you already*, she writes. *I cannot lose you as well.*

It is easy to tell Jeanne, Rose having sensed for weeks that she has overstayed her welcome. Her sister feigns sadness, but there is a hint of relief in her tone. "You'll have to visit more often," she says.

It is harder to tell Émilie. Émilie, who has filled the void left by Anna, who encouraged Rose to speak her mind and treated her like one of her own. "I hope you always feel welcome here," she says. "My home is yours, whenever you need it."

"Thank you," Rose says, reaching out to her.

When Émilie pulls away, she is wearing an odd expression. "Have you told my son yet?"

"I'm visiting tomorrow," Rose says. "I'll tell him then."

"Be gentle."

Rose had finally received a response from Frederick after nearly two weeks. *I must assure you my silence has not been intentional*, he had said in his letter. *I have been busy with something I want to share with you, once the time comes. I wanted you to know that you have done nothing to upset me, but now I fear that is precisely what I have done to you. Please forgive my silence and absence.*

It felt genuine, but Rose had already made up her mind to go. She was glad at least that he had requested to see her, so that she could tell him in person.

She takes a cab but asks the driver to drop her off a few miles from the cottage so that she can walk the rest of the way. The day is cool and light, the breeze carrying a hint of autumn air. It is nearly September, and the flowers are resolved to go. Rose wants to savour every shade of the lush countryside before she returns to the hard edges of the city.

Rose had not known what she was seeking when she first arrived in Nova Scotia. She is not sure she has found it, or if it was only the courage to tell Anna the truth. Part of her hopes the tranquility she has found here will follow her home. But she is not certain it will. She is not certain of anything.

Rose reaches the cottage nestled behind pine trees and knocks at the door. There is no answer. Peering through the window, she checks her watch, then moves around the house, feeling the same drop of regret as during her last visit.

She finds Frederick in the backyard, crouched in front of a wooden bench beneath a willow tree, his shirt sleeves rolled up past his elbows, hair covered in sawdust. He straightens when he sees her, tucking a rag into his back pocket.

"Rose," he says.

"Hello."

"I didn't hear you arrive." He looks at his watch. "I'm sorry. Time seems to have gotten away from me."

"That's all right." She had planned to stay a while. To spend a few final hours with him before she had to say goodbye. But seeing him here, standing before her, she knows if she stays too long, she'll want to stay longer. Much longer.

"I'm leaving," she blurts out, the words tumbling from her before she can stop them. "I'm going back home. Tomorrow. I meant to tell you sooner, but I wanted to do it in person." She drops her gaze, unable to read his expression. "We both knew this was temporary. And I don't regret a moment of it. I think...I think we reconnected at a time we needed each other the most. I needed someone to listen, to understand, and I'm grateful you were here."

Frederick lets her speak, lets her get it all out, before he opens his mouth, then closes it again.

She sees him hesitate, and it feels like a tome on her chest. She wants him to say something, anything.

Then, he takes a step towards her, reaching into his breast pocket to retrieve a photograph. He holds it out to her. "I wanted you to have this," he says quietly.

Rose takes the photograph from his hand, her fingers brushing his for a moment. She examines it closely. It is a photograph of him—younger, but it is him. Hair cropped short, eyes hollow, standing in front of a brick wall in what she presumes is Ruhleben.

"That's me," he says. "That's the person I've been trying to reach. The one I've been trying to share with you. I haven't wanted to share that person. If anything I've spent the last few years trying to get back to the person I was before, when I first met you, before the war. But I'm not that person anymore. Neither of us are. And I think we were the only ones here who recognized that."

She looks from Frederick to the photograph, then back again. In both, she can see glimpses of the man she met so many years ago, the one who watched her from across the room at her sister's wedding. He seemed elsewhere then, caught far away, even when he was home. But now he is here. Grounded. Solid.

"I know you always intended to leave," Frederick continues. "And I won't presume that anything in the last few weeks will have changed your mind. I won't presume that you might have found a home here, too. But I hope this might be a step in that direction."

He moves to the side, revealing the small plaque he had been installing on the bench.

Rose approaches, her breath catching in her throat as she reads the inscription.

IN MEMORY OF LEONARD AVERY.

She takes in its surroundings: the willow branches sighing in the wind, the endless stretch of sea before her, its tides a direct connection to the distant place where Leo rests. It is more than she had ever hoped for, more than she could have imagined. It is the most fitting tribute. Rose looks at the plaque again, then at Frederick, his figure blurred at the edges, the details of him growing soft in the afternoon light.

In that moment, Rose knows, without any doubt, that no other place will ever truly feel like home.

EPILOGUE

Rose hears him pacing upstairs. She glances at the clock. They will be late if he does not hurry.

"Have you seen my shoes?" Frederick's voice echoes from above.

"Have you looked in the wardrobe?"

"No—I mean, yes. They're not there."

She moves closer to the stairs. "The black or the brown ones?"

"The brown ones."

"Look again."

The sound of a wardrobe door creaking open. "They're not there," Frederick says.

Rose places one foot on the landing.

"Never mind," he calls out, and she smiles. Eight months of marriage and already she wonders how he ever managed without her.

A moment later, Frederick comes bounding down the stairs, laces tied over shiny brown leather. "Are you ready?

"Yes. Let me fetch my hat." She picks up her purse and turns into the hallway. Frederick follows her, sneaking a kiss on the nape of her neck as she stands before the mirror pinning her hat in place. It matches the deep navy-blue frock she has picked for the occasion, a poppy red sash at her waist. She turns to look at him with a smile.

He reaches out to run his thumb against her cheek. "But are you ready?" he repeats, his tone more pressing.

She catches his meaning. "Yes. I am. Are you?"

"As ready as I'll ever be." He offers his arm and leads her outside.

Mr. Cameron is on the front porch when they arrive, dressed not in his usual grey or brown suits, but in his military uniform.

"Don't you look dashing," Rose says. "Will Mrs. Cameron be joining us today?"

Mr. Cameron smiles weakly. "Not today. Though I did bring some help."

Clyde comes running out of the museum, his short brown hair slicked back. "Mr. and Mrs. Munro!"

"Look at you," Frederick says, pretending to ruffle his hair.

Clyde jumps back. "This is an important day," he says with reproach.

"It is," Frederick agrees. "Are we all set?"

"A few more items arrived yesterday, and I was hoping you would help me move one of the cases," Mr. Cameron says.

"Of course." Frederick climbs the stone steps, and they disappear through the front door.

Clyde approaches Rose. "Is it too late to add something to the exhibition?"

"Not at all. What did you have in mind?"

Clyde digs into his pocket and fishes out a small plush bear, one ear reattached with red thread, its button eyes missing. "His name is Barry. I sent him to Belgium with Father when he left." He wiggles the bear's arms with his fingers. "Barry was meant to keep him safe. And he did. Father said I had to ask you before adding him to the case."

Rose places a hand on Clyde's shoulder. "That's a wonderful addition to the exhibition," she says. "Just the thing we were missing."

Clyde smiles proudly.

Inside, they find Frederick and Mr. Cameron red-faced and huffing, trying to push a heavy oak case against the wall. "I'm not certain it will fit," Frederick says, judging the space on either side.

"I'll help!" Clyde says, positioning himself between his father and Frederick.

Mr. Cameron directs them to pull the case an inch to the side, and with one final push, it slides neatly into place.

"There," Frederick says. "I guess we only needed another set of hands," he tells Clyde.

All the display cases save for this one are full, the dirt-encrusted fossils and mollusk shells replaced by photographs, letters, and an odd assortment of objects, all carefully curated by Rose, with help from Mr. Cameron.

Mr. Cameron points to the box on the chair by the door. "These are the last few items."

Rose turns to parse through it. Inside, she finds an ornamental locket that opens to two small photographs of young men in uniform, a handful of letters, and a red cross volunteer armband, embroidered with the initials *E. D. W.* Similar objects are already laid on the cloth-covered display cases around the room, but she will include them nonetheless. She knows each of these tell a different story. Deeper in the box, Rose finds a handknit sweater. She lifts the dark green wool by the shoulders.

"The woman came by yesterday," Mr. Cameron says, reappearing at her side. "Said she had been knitting this pullover for her husband when she received word that he had died. She never finished it. She learned about the exhibition through a friend, and asked if we might include it."

Rose examines the live stitches on the unfinished sleeve, still hanging from the thick ball of yarn. "How sad," she says, carefully placing it back in the box. She turns to look at the empty case. "Perhaps we could place it on the second shelf? I'll write the label."

Mr. Cameron nods, reaching for the desk set.

Rose pulls out a helmet, the final item in the box. She turns it over in her hands and is surprised to find a target painted on the front, the red, white, and blue hastily splattered on. She looks to Mr. Cameron.

He immediately reads the question in her expression and chuckles. "A young man brought that one in. Said it belonged to one of his pals. Apparently he got quite the reprimand for it, but he'd done it for a laugh. Was always trying to make the men laugh, his friend said. Especially in the trenches."

"Do you think it's appropriate?" Rose asks.

Mr. Cameron examines the helmet, a distant smile forming on his lips. "It might be the most honest representation we have."

Rose hands it over. "Then let's give it a prominent place, shall we? Highest shelf?"

Mr. Cameron nods. "Yes, Lieutenant."

Rose reaches for the labels and begins writing descriptions in the same neat script that adorns every card in the room. They have titled the exhibition *Remembering the Forgotten*. For months now, Rose had been canvassing the community, reaching out to various groups in order to collect evidence of how different people lived through the war: the mothers, fathers, wives, and children. The ones who served at home, and the ones who went abroad. Not only the soldiers, but the orderlies, the ambulance drivers, the radio operators, the messengers. CAMC as well as VAD nurses. Rose had even written to Margot, asking permission to include some of the news articles she had published in the *Toronto Star*, asking for donations for her patients. Margot's reply was warmer than any she had sent in years, saying she was glad her role was finally being acknowledged. It was another sentiment they seemed to have shared during the war but never voiced. Rose wrote back to tell her as much, and so much more.

Rose had also convinced Frederick to include a few photographs and letters from his time in Ruhleben. He'd allowed her, finally, to look through the trunk whose contents would soon be published in his book. Frederick had eventually agreed, but with the caveat that Rose must be the one to select which items told the most comprehensive story. "I would never be able to choose only a few, to untangle one aspect from another," he told her.

Frederick had reached out to Petro Koval to ask if he might like to participate. Koval had graciously declined but promised to pass the invitation along to others from the camp. None had reached out, but Frederick had managed to find the front page of a local newspaper from 1914 announcing the internment of enemy aliens in Canada. To provide context, he had transcribed a page from his manuscript, detailing the parallels between their experiences and his own, as well as the ways they diverged.

Clyde returns as Rose busies herself arranging the final case. "What about Barry?" he asks, holding out his bear.

"Of course." Rose studies the case for a moment, then nestles the bear next to the green knit pullover. "Do you want to do the honours?" she asks the boy, handing him a label.

Clyde leans on tiptoes against the nearest case to write the card. *MR BARRY, WHO KEPT MY FATHER SAFE.*

"Have you considered doing this yourself one day?" Rose asks once he is done.

"Do you mean build an exhibition?"

"Yes. Like your father."

The boy looks pensive for a moment. "Could it be for insects? I'm not sure these things interest me as much. No offence."

Rose laughs. "None taken. I suppose it could be about anything you find interesting."

"I find insects interesting."

"Then I look forward to seeing your entomology exhibition."

He smiles shyly.

Rose closes the case and steps back to look at her work. "There," she says. "Well done." She extends her hand towards Clyde and he shakes it.

"When are the people coming?"

Rose looks at her watch. "Any minute now."

Émilie and Anna are the first to arrive, Anna laughing softly at something Émilie said, her hand clasped at her elbow. Rose watches them walk up the drive. She remembers how easily Émilie had made her feel at home in this new place, and Rose is glad she has extended the same treatment to Anna, who arrived last week for her second visit this year. She has a room of her own at Silas and Jeanne's house, across the hall from the children, though she always makes a point of visiting Rose and Frederick at the cottage, arriving in the morning to walk along the shore with Rose while Frederick swims laps in the distance.

It is during those walks that Rose has shared the most about her time overseas, inspired by the work she was doing on the exhibition. Anna mostly listens, though she has shared some of her own experiences as well. What it was like for her to be left alone when all three of them left for France. The constant feeling of worry, the anxiety she felt whenever the postman came, hoping for a letter, dreading a telegram from the War Office.

She has said little about Leo, and has never asked for more details about his death. Rose suspects she feels some shame about it, though she has never admitted it. But perhaps it is best to say nothing at all. To let the world believe that Leo died valiantly like the rest of them. For now, his photograph sits among the others in the museum, a memorial as fitting as the bench Frederick made for her.

"Welcome," Rose says when Anna and Émilie reach her.

"This is all so wonderful," Émilie says, though she has yet to see the exhibition. Rose will give them a private tour, once the public has gone.

"Are Jeanne and Silas coming?" Rose asks.

"They were trying to rally the children when we left, so it might take a while. But they'll be here."

Rose smiles and leans in to kiss them both. She is perhaps most excited for the children to see the exhibition. *What did you do during the war?* Millicent might ask, and she will be able to point to her journals and say, *I helped the men heal.*

People begin to stream in at the appointed hour, and Rose takes her place amongst the display cases. Frederick winks at her from across the room. They have recruited a handful of volunteers to stand by the display for the duration of the event. In addition to the records and objects on display, Rose wants to encourage people to ask questions, and for her volunteers to have an opportunity to speak openly.

Mr. Cameron, she knows, will remain tight-lipped about his own experiences at the Front. But she is determined to answer any question that comes her way, as is Frederick and Mrs. O'Brien, the wife of a soldier who came home wounded, unable to recognize her. She has donated many of the letters he sent her during the war, the ones that included poetry he had written in the trenches. Rose was glad to include them, both for Mrs. O'Brien's sake and her own, knowing she would never have been able to display James's journal, not without his family's permission. Instead, the journal has been added to Frederick's trunk, alongside her own letters and photographs, her uniform and badges. All her memories of war are there, safely preserved, save for the few items she has brought out for the exhibition. Those, too, would return to the trunk once the exhibition closed in a month.

She has come to realize that there are many ways to remember, just as there are many ways to cope with the loss they all endured. Some people sought the unvarnished truth, others preferred a softer version, something easier to swallow, to carry forward. At least, by keeping her memories safe, Rose feels she is keeping the truth alive. The trunk, with its meticulously arranged contents, is her small attempt to ensure these stories endure. She hopes the exhibition will encourage a new kind of conversation about the war. But she knows it is temporary. Once the objects are returned to their owners, her role in their preservation will end. Unlike the stone cenotaphs rising across the country, her memorialization efforts are fleeting. Ephemeral. Still, she hopes that her efforts will plant a seed, so that when the world has nearly forgotten and becomes desperate to remember again, these stories will still be there, waiting.

Jeanne, Silas, and the children arrive in a flurry, waving from across the room. The museum is busy, and Millicent and Oliver have to cut through the crowd to find her.

"Hello," Rose says brightly, expecting, anticipating their questions.

It is Oliver who speaks rather than Millicent. "What is your necklace doing in there?" he asks, pointing at the case behind her.

She turns to look at the engraved rose locket gleaming under the glass. It rests beside the postcard photograph Leo had sent her when he shipped out.

There is so much Rose wants to say. She wants to tell him how Leo died. She wants to tell him what it was really like to be a soldier. What it was like for her, as well. But looking at his bright, young face, she thinks perhaps there is no harm in shielding him from the truth a while longer. She bends down to his level and directs his gaze to the photograph.

"This is your cousin Leo." Rose peers at Leo's sepia grin, glad to finally be able to look at it without pain. "He's the one who gave me the necklace. And I think it was, perhaps, what kept me safe during the war."

AUTHOR'S NOTE

The first spark of this novel came to me in the archives, as I was poring over the papers of a New Brunswick woman who had served as a Voluntary Aid Detachment (VAD) nurse in France during the First World War. Speaking with the archivist, I discovered that the woman's future husband had been a doctoral student in Germany at the start of the war and spent the next four years in a civilian internment camp. Immediately, I wondered: what had they shared with each other of those experiences? What had they kept to themselves? How did they move beyond those life-altering events to build a future together?

I remember only fragments of those early days of research: images of a young woman in uniform, smiling with fellow nurses and soldiers; the idyllic fields of France captured in her off-duty photographs; the postcards she sent home, describing the beautiful scenery while making only oblique references to the large numbers of wounded soldiers passing through her makeshift hospital, housed in a grand château. Then, in stark contrast, the photographs from Ruhleben: men playing baseball on barren, dusty fields; scientific instruments arranged on tables in dimly lit rooms; a horse stall converted into a library; issues of a satirical camp magazine, printed and bound as any other periodical of the time, with mentions of plays, debates, and concerts. None of these fit the images I had of internment camps or of the war itself. They stood apart from the visceral mud and blood of the literature and poetry I had read about the First World War, or the horrors of internment camps in the Second World War.

As my research expanded, I became increasingly interested by the idea of narrative. Whose stories of war do we remember? Whose stories are considered worth remembering? Whose experiences have been eclipsed, left out of memorialization efforts? Whose voices have been forgotten, or erased?

This novel is my attempt to explore those questions. Though inspired by real individuals, it is a work of fiction. Beyond a few surface details, Frederick and Rose are not direct representations of the people I first encountered in the archives but rather a synthesis of the many voices, experiences, and historical records that shaped this narrative.

The perspectives I ultimately wove into this book were influenced by the work of numerous scholars, historians, and individuals who lived through that era. I am deeply indebted to the following works, which helped frame my understanding of the war and its aftermath: *The Sleepwalkers: How Europe Went to War in 1914* (2012) by Christopher Clark; *Death So Noble: Memory, Meaning, and the First World War* (1997) by Jonathan F. Vance; *Remembering War: The Great War Between Memory and History in the Twentieth Century* (2006) by Jay Winter; *Paris 1919: Six Months that Changed the World* by Margaret MacMillan (2001); *Ruhleben, A Prison Camp Society* (1965) by J. Davidson Ketchum; *British Civilian Internees in Germany: The Ruhleben Camp, 1914-18* (2008) by Matthew Stibbe; *No Free Man: Canada, the Great War, and the Enemy Alien Experience* (2016) by Bohdan S. Kordan; *The Stories Were Not Told: Canada's First World War Internment Camps* (2019) by Sandra Semchuk; *War-Torn Exchanges: The Lives and Letters of Nursing Sisters Laura Holland and Mildred Forbes* (2016), edited by Andrea McKenzie; *Sister Soldiers of the Great War: The Nurses of the Canadian Army Medical Corps* (2016) by Cynthia Toman; *The War Diary of Clare Gass, 1915-1918* (2000), edited and introduced by Susan Mann. Records at the Mount Allison University Archives and the Lautarchiv of the Humboldt University in Berlin granted me an intimate look at the daily life of men in Ruhleben, and a small autograph album at the University of Waterloo Archives, where I completed part of my graduate work, inspired

Rose's own journal. I am also grateful to Israel Cohen, Nadja Durbach, Andrew Tait Jarboe, Joe Lunn, Jo Stanley, and Nicole M. Zehfuss, whose research illuminated the experiences of those often absent from mainstream war narratives—Indian soldiers, Black soldiers and civilian internees, Jewish internees, Ukrainian internees in Canada, and so many others whose stories have too often been overlooked.

I hope this book adds, in some small way, to the ongoing conversation about whose histories we preserve and whose we allow to fade. If the past is a story we tell ourselves, it is only by probing how it was shaped that we can begin to understand the world we've inherited.

ACKNOWLEDGEMENTS

There are many friends who have supported my writing in small but important ways: David, Pauline, Marcie, Melissa, Carolle, Anna, Erik, Corey, Jessica, Paula, and Isabelle. Thank you.

Sincere thanks to:
Kerry, for gently pushing me forward;
Stephanie, for helping me cut to the heart of this novel;
Whitney, for seeing its potential;
Bee, for creating a beautiful cover;
Aline, for nurturing my lifelong love of books;
Charles, for encouraging me to follow the things that bring me joy;
Rosie, for pinning me down in my chair through countless writing sessions;
and, last but not least, Keegan, for patiently answering all of my peculiar research questions. Thank you for sharing your brilliant mind—and your life—with me.

I am also grateful to ArtsNB and the Canada Council for the Arts for their financial support.

Renée Belliveau is the author of the novels *A Sense of Things Beyond* and *The Sound of Fire*, which was named a *Quill & Quire* book of the year and shortlisted for the ReLit Novel Award, as well as the memoir *Les étoiles à l'aube*. She draws inspiration from her work as an archivist, where she spends her days surrounded by records of the past. A proud acadienne from New Brunswick, she currently lives in Dartmouth, Nova Scotia (Punamu'kwati'jk), with her husband.